MARGERY ALLINGHAM

The Mind Readers

VINTAGE BOOKS
London

Published by Vintage 2008

4 6 8 10 9 7 5

First published in Great Britain in 1965 by
Chatto & Windus

Vintage
Random House, 20 Vauxhall Bridge Road,
London SW1V 2SA

www.vintage-books.co.uk

Addresses for companies within The Random House Group Limited
can be found at: www.randomhouse.co.uk/offices.htm

The Random House Group Limited Reg. No. 954009

A CIP catalogue record for this book
is available from the British Library

ISBN 9780099513278

The Random House Group Limited supports the Forest Stewardship
Council (FSC®), the leading international forest certification organisation.
Our books carrying the FSC label are printed on FSC® certified
paper. FSC is the only forest certification scheme endorsed by the
leading environmental organisations, including Greenpeace.
Our paper procurement policy can be found at
www.randomhouse.co.uk/environment

Printed and bound by CPI Group (UK) Ltd, Croydon, CR0 4YY

CONTENTS

To my technical advisers
in gratitude for their
astonishing new world
and in the hope
that I get this tale out
before they do.

I

The Breaking Ground

THE great city of London was once more her splendid self; mysterious as ever but bursting with new life.

In the tightly packed clusters of villages with the ancient names—Hackney, Holborn, Shoreditch, Putney, Paddington, Bow—new towers were rising into the yellow sky; the open spaces if fewer, were neater, the old houses were painted, the monuments clean.

Best news of all, the people were regrown. The same savagely cheerful race, fresh mixed with more new blood than ever in its history, jostled together in costumes inspired by every romantic fashion known to television. While round its knees in a luxuriant crop the educated children shot up like the towers, full of the future.

Early one Thursday evening, late in the year at one particular moment, just before the rush hour, when the lights were coming up and the shadows deepening, five apparently unrelated incidents in five ordinary, normal lives were taking place at points set far apart within the wide boundaries of the town. Five people, none of whom were particularly aware of the others, were taking the first casual steps in one of those mystic, curling patterns of human adventure which begin with imperceptible movement, like the infinitesimal commotion which surrounds a bud thrusting through the earth but which then sometimes develops and grows up swiftly into a huge and startling plume to alter the whole landscape of history.

The first of the five was no more than an idle thought. The D.D.I. of the Eastern Waterside Division of Metropolitan Police was sitting in his office kicking himself gently because he had forgotten to tell his old friend Detective Superintendent Charles Luke of the Central Office, who had just left after a routine visit, a little piece of nonsense which might have intrigued that great man. They had been so busy moralising over the effects of the latest threat of total world annihilation on the local suicide rate amongst teenagers that he had quite forgotten his own story about that well known city 'character', the End of the World Man, which had come into his mind and gone out again whilst Luke was talking.

It was an odd thing he had seen with his own eyes as he had travelled through the West End in a police car at the back end of the summer. As he had passed the corner of Wigmore Street and Orchard Street up by the Park, he had observed the familiar figure of the old fanatic in the dusty robes and hood carrying his banner proclaiming the worst, striding away from him among the shopping crowds on the pavement. Less than four minutes later by his own watch after a clear run, he had seen him again, head on this time, walking up the Haymarket from the direction of the Strand. So, as Luke might possibly have been entertained to hear, the man had either developed a power of miraculous transportation which seemed unlikely on form, or there were two of him dressed exactly alike and one of them at any rate taking great care to resemble the other. This was funny in view of what he and Luke had been saying about the increase of interest in these people's gloomy subject.

The second stirring in the hard ground, taking place at exactly the same time, was a conversation which occurred on the western side of the city where two people were talking in a Regency Rectory in a half forgotten backwater called St Peter's Gate Square.

They were in a book-filled study, the smaller of two down-stair reception rooms. Canon Avril had possessed the living so long that the tremendous changes which had dismembered the world outside had come very gently to his own household. Now in his old age, a widower for many years, his daughter married and away, he lived on the ground floor humbly but comfortably while William Talisman, his verger, made his home in the basement and Mrs Talisman kept an eye on them both.

Upstairs there was the Canon's daughter's suite, which was now let as a *pied à terre* to his nephew Mr Albert Campion and his wife when they visited London; and above that there was a cottage-like attic flat, at the moment also let to relatives. These were Helena Ferris and her brilliant young American husband, who fled to it whenever they could escape from the island research station on the East Coast where he was working.

The Canon was a big man with a great frame and untidy white hair. He had a fine face which, despite its intelligence, was almost disconcertingly serene. He had seen the neighbourhood decline from Edwardian affluence to near-slum conditions and now edge back again to moneyed elegance. Throughout all the changes his own income had remained the same and his present poverty could have been agonising, but he had few needs and no material worries whatever. He was certainly shabby and it was true that at the end of each week it was literally impossible to borrow so much as a shilling from him, but he remained not only happy but secure throughout the harrowing crises which so often sprang up around him. Nor was he a visionary. There was a practical element in his outlook, even if it was apt to appear slightly out of alignment to those who were unaware that he did not stand in the dead centre of his own universe.

One of his most sensible innovations was in the room with him at the moment, interrupting him almost unbearably with her well-meaning chatter.

Miss Dorothy Warburton was a maiden lady of certain everything—income, virtue and age; and she lived in one of the two cottages just past the Church next door. She managed the Canon's personal finances in exactly the same way as she managed the Church Fête. That is to say, firmly, openly and, of course, down to the last farthing. He had no privacy, nothing of his own. His charities were subject to her scrutiny and had to be justified and this kept him factual and informed about what things did or did not cost. However, apart from these, material considerations were not permitted to weigh

A*

upon him and he never forgot how blessed he was or how much he owed his dear Decimal Dot, as he called her.

On her side she respected him deeply, called him 'her Church Work' and bossed him as she would certainly have done a father. Mercifully she did not consider herself unduly religious, seeing her role as a Martha rather than a Mary, and it may have been something to do with the classic resentment which made her a little insensitive where he was concerned.

This was the hour which the Canon liked to set aside. It had become for him a period of professional activity for which few gave him credit. He never explained, being well aware of the pitfalls in that direction, but accepted interruptions meekly if he could not avoid them. On the other hand, he never permitted himself to be discouraged from what he felt was his chief duty. With the years he had become one of the more practised contemplative minds in a generation which neglected the art; simple people often thought him lovable but silly, and those who were not so simple, dangerous. Avril could not help that; he did what he had to do and looked after his parish, and every day he sat and thought about what he was doing and why and how he was doing it.

Miss Warburton could not make out what he was up to, wasting time and not even resting, and every so often when she had an excuse, she used to come in and prod him to find out.

Today she was full of news and chatter.

'House full tomorrow!' she said brightly. 'You *will* enjoy that! Albert and Amanda and their little nephew Edward, and Helena and Sam, all home for half term. That will be lovely for you and such a change!'

Avril knew it would be. After weeks of having the place empty he could hardly miss it. It was she who was most lonely, he feared, and he let her chatter on. 'Mrs Talisman is baking a cake in case they ask Superintendent Luke over. She thinks that because she can cook and lives in a basement it's the correct thing to do, since he's a policeman! I wonder she doesn't make it a rabbit pie and have done with it since we're all out to be Victorian. Poor Martin Ferris. He works far too hard on that dreadful electronics island.'

'Does he?'

'It sounds like it, if he can't be spared for a week-end up here with his family when the child comes home for half term, but must stay out on that freezing marsh researching. I never saw two young people so much in love when they started, but I warn you, Canon, that marriage could founder if they drive him like that. I suppose we're going to have another war.'

'I hope not!'

'So do I. Things are quite dear enough already. I only have to put my nose in the supermarket and I spend a pound. I saw Mrs Flooder by the way and heard a most extraordinary story. The poor wretched man could have died *and* burnt the house down.'

Avril did not rise to the bait but his eyes lost their intro-spection as a trickle of corrosive poison crept into his heart. She had reminded him of a silly incident and his own be-haviour in it which had been careless and not even like him. He would not have believed he could have been so stupid.

'She told me you saw her,' Miss Warburton continued in her instructive way. 'You ran right into her, I believe, just as she was coming out of the shop. She nearly dropped her parcels and you changed the subject by telling her that her sister's boy had put up the banns at last.'

The Canon bowed his venerable head. It had not happened like that at all. The bison of a woman, maddened with acquisitiveness and laden with loot, had almost knocked him over, sworn at him for being in the way and turned to syco-phantic mooing as she recognised her parish priest. It was then that the fatal statement had escaped him.

'Why, it's Mrs Flooder. I've just been hearing your nephew's good news. A grand wedding in the family, eh?'

Before the final word was out of his mouth he had recog-nised his mistake. He had broken rule number one in his book; he had made trouble.

The news had crept into Mrs Flooder's intelligence visibly like

11

a flame creeping up a fuse and the explosion was quite frightful.

'Cat! My sister Lily's a cat. Never told me one bloody word! Hoping I'll stay away. Just you wait until I get hold of her. Dirty little lying cat. I'll drop in as I go past!'

Avril had seen her rush off with his heart full of self-loathing. The tasteless blunder had bothered him out of all proportion and all today he had been irked by it. He slid a little lower in his chair.

'It was the first she'd heard of the marriage so she went straight to her sister's house,' continued Miss Warburton, relieved that she had interested him; at least he wasn't ill. 'She told me to tell you she would never have dreamed of dropping in if you hadn't mentioned the white wedding and the hired hall....'

'I said no such thing!'

'Never mind, it's a mercy if you did. Lily was out, you see, and Mrs Flooder found the poor man choking, smoke coming from under his door. It seems he'd fallen over and broken his hip—caught his foot in the cord of the electric bowl fire. He was too weak to shout by the time Mrs Flooder got there.'

Avril sat up in astonishment and concern.

'*Who* was this?'

'Lily's lodger—taken in to help pay for the wedding, I shouldn't be surprised. He could have burned to death if that woman Flooder hadn't broken in to look for her sister. She thought she was hiding up.'

'I'd never heard of him.'

'Nor had I. He moved in one evening and this happened the next morning. Mrs Flooder can't get over it. She said she'll always "take notice of a clergyman" because she'd "gone in to make a beastly row and before she knew it, there she was, a heroine!" There, I thought that would make you laugh so I'll leave you in peace. Have a little doze.'

As the door closed very softly behind her, presumably in case he had fallen asleep already, Avril tried to rearrange his mind so that the sense of insult which the story had aroused in him could be isolated and exorcised.

He was not in the least surprised by the coincidence. He spent his existence watching life's machinery and could hardly be expected to be astonished if he saw the slow wheels move, but he was startled by his grievance. What had so upset him was that it should be a weakness and not a strength of his own which had been graciously permitted to play its tiny part in assisting this unknown fellow-sojourner. He had caught himself thinking that surely he might have been allowed to make a kindly or constructive gesture instead of a vulgar breach of confidence. As the absurdity of his complaint crystallised he took himself in hand and his professional philosophy stirred itself to meet the tiny emergency.

At length he bent his head and folded his hands on his waistcoat; his eyes were bright and intelligent in the dusk. The question which had arisen so absurdly was, he saw, a vast one, beset with dangers. For the next half hour he proceeded through the spiritual minefield, his heart in his mouth. It was this, rather than the little coincidence which occasioned it, which was to be of such curious significance in the breakthrough.

The third of the five tiny incidents which seemed at first to be so slightly related to each other, was another private conversation which also concerned the vocation of the speakers, but this time of very different people.

While old Canon Avril was listening to Dot Warburton far across the Park, a black limousine with a custom-built body crept up the incline in Brick Street West, and stopped outside a small house whose windows were dark.

The shadow sitting in the back tossed a key to the chauffeur, who slid out of his seat to unlock the front door before returning to release his passenger who passed inside like a dark cloud. The chauffeur closed the street door behind him, faded back to the car and drove away, unaware that the visit was not quite the normal Thursday evening routine with the Boss in a black mood.

Within the house the vestibule was dimly lit and the grey walls and carpet gave no indication of the distinctive decor

13

of the one big room which took up most of the first floor.

The thin woman who waited in it was a little too old to be so palely blonde but was still extremely good-looking. As soon as she heard the car door slam she rose and stood waiting, a trace of deference by far the softest thing about her. The apartment surrounding her was remarkable and achieved the effect at which the designer had aimed, both reflecting and opposing the painting which was its centrepiece.

Miss Merle Rawlins had bought the picture at the fabulously successful Louis Celli's first post-surrealist exhibition. She had indicated where it should hang on the long wall directly opposite the door and had left the rest to a young Frenchman who was becoming almost equally well known. The result was that most people entering for the first time found themselves shocked without understanding why, although Miss Rawlins and Bertram Alexander, first Baron Ludor of Hollowhill in Surrey and Chairman of UCAI, who paid for it, had no difficulty whatever.

The painting was called *Gitto* and was a lifesize portrait of the fully-grown male gorilla of that name in the Wymondham Zoo. Celli's realism, which was always so much more than ruthlessly photographic, had here achieved a passionate quality and the great black primate, standing in a lime-green jungle with one paw on a tortured tree stump and the other scratching a thigh of truly terrible muscle, had captured the black-ice tragedy of the brute.

The portrait had caused a sensation when it was first shown, for the stony face was strong enough for nobility and probably sufficiently intelligent to recognise that it was without hope of evolution. It met one as one arrived, unutterably sad, but dangerous and certainly not for pity. Merle Rawlins had bought the work of art because she adored it and the Frenchman had hung the wall behind it with a formal Florentine flock paper of black on grey, flooded the floor with cherry pile, and shrouded all the window end of the room with lime-green glass fabric. He had then subdued the furnishing to one twelve-foot curved couch in black leather and simulated

14

monkey fur and the joke, such as it was, was over. Lord Ludor enjoyed it; he knew that whereas other people might snigger, if they were brave enough, at the likeness between himself and the portrait, Merle had certainly been crazy to get it and liked to live with it because it epitomised the terror and excitement he had always been able to kindle in her. She had been the finest secretary he had ever had and as a mistress she worked hard to please, studying him in all things, putting him first, soaking herself in his needs until, as on an evening like this, she came into her own and was irreplaceable. At his home in the Surrey town of Hollowhill Lady Ludor attended to the furnishings but here evidences of his own taste were everywhere. The only moving thing when he came in was the new toy which Merle had been given by the sales manager of a subsidiary in a more or less open attempt to capture Ludor's personal interest. It looked exactly like an orthodox television set, but showed film of a kind which even in these uninhibited days could not have been put out by any public broadcasting service in the world. She was running it without the sound because he expected her to be alone and might for a moment have mistaken the canned words for conversation and torn the house down. As it was, his heavy glance, which noted her and passed on without altering, came to rest on the screen and he stood for a second looking at its somewhat laborious salacity before he said: 'Turn that thing off.'

She obeyed him at once, but without hurry because he disliked jerky movement, and he came forward on to the rug before the synthetic log fire and stood where he usually did, under the picture.

Even when one saw the two together there was a definite likeness, and not only in spirit. Indeed, the sight would not be comic and bearable until he was much older and less powerful than he was now at sixty. Today he was still nine-tenths of the force he had been at forty-five when the huge electronics combine, the Universal Contacts empire, was being won.

Merle recognised his mood as any of his close associates would have done but she was probably less alarmed by it than

15

most. It was not that she knew how to dispel it, but because she understood that she would only be expected to do what she was told. Worry and decision and invention were not required of her; he would do all that.

He began at once. 'Did you lay on all the calls without trouble?'

'Not without trouble.'

'But you got all three arranged? Person to person?'

'Yes. They all want to speak to you so it was only technical delays. They are being put through for us at hourly intervals, starting at seven. No bother is expected except perhaps over Mr Kalek's, so I've made him last. He's at Lunea and there's no scrambler yet. Can you manage?'

'I shall have to, shan't I?' He never wasted energy on the unalterable. 'The Sheikh in clear would be more of a menace!'

'Oh, he's all right. He's at the Winter Palace with all the aids. I spoke to the Prince but the old man was in the room.'

'And Cornelius?'

'He's in Lausanne in the nursing home. Hetty is still in Johannesburg.'

'What about Daniels?'

'Mr Daniels is there with Mr Cornelius. He's being called the Secretary now.'

'I see.' He stood silent for a moment, hand on the back of one of the thin black chairs in unconscious imitation of the portrait, his face sombre.

'Oh well. Not bad.' It was great praise. She felt it almost more than she deserved although she had been at the telephone for sixteen hours and had performed miracles without any other priorities than those she could call her own. It was only on these very rare occasions when the business was most secret that he used her lines. She kept them, and sometimes used them, for social contacts so that the records could never conceivably show anything unusual.

'What's Kalek doing on that pimple in the Caribbean?'

'Resting. He likes to be with his ceramics. You've got an

island yourself, Bae.' It was not a pet name but the version of some of his initials used by those closest to him. He grunted:

'I don't try to live on it! Perhaps I should. This wouldn't have happened if I had. Nor do I need rest all the time. Damn Kalek. He's the youngest and the weakest of us all.'

'It's the world danger,' she said, edging to the door of the kitchen pantry because often, when he started to look about like this, he was hungry. 'He feels he wants to look at his pieces while he can. He's still frightened of the Bomb.'

Ludor laughed but his eyes did not change. 'He's old hat.' he said. 'He'll be more frightened by what I've got to tell him. This could hit him. Right in the gelt-bag.'

She stood waiting by the door of the pantry, knowing that it would be unwise either to question or to disappear. She had known Ludor intimately for something over fourteen years and he was still a mystery, and, as an intelligence herself, she found the fact irresistible. His sudden change of subject surprised her.

'Sanderton was buried today. You didn't send flowers, did you?'

'You said not.'

'Good. I don't want even a thought to go through any little mind in Fleet Street. He's got to be replaced by our new contact at once. His sudden flake-out took me by surprise; one never thinks of death at that age except on the road, and he was chauffeur-driven always. He ought to have told me about his blood pressure.'

Merle ventured a question which had been bothering her. She was a conventional soul and, in her own limited way, not unkind.

'I thought I might telephone Mrs Sanderton? Not write, just telephone and say I'm sorry. She adored him and they were up here such a lot.'

'I don't think I would. Not yet.' He was thinking about it, giving it the same consideration he afforded to every detail which could concern him or his great interests. 'Wait until we have our new man functioning. I've got old "Pa," Paling attending to it now. It's a little tricky because Lord Feste sees to it that they screen all their people so very carefully. He's nobody's fool and at this moment the old fox could surprise me any morning, which is damn dangerous! Leave it now and take the woman to lunch in a week or two and say you hadn't liked to intrude before. Then you need never see her again.'

She nodded but added: 'I quite liked her.'

'Did you? Predatory type. Nice line in dirt but fundamentally a clinger and a bore. Loyalish, I suppose.' He dismissed the subject and glanced at the clock face built into the ebony fitment which ran round half the room and was designed to contain the paraphernalia of modern living in much the same way as a Victorian work-box was arranged to hold crochet-hooks and bobbins.

'I've got twenty minutes,' he observed. 'What have you got in there that's hot?'

'The fridge is full. It wouldn't take me a minute to heat something.'

'Very well, smoked sprats; then I can have a scotch. Did you get any sprats?'

'After no end of bother. The last kiln in the South is at Tosey and even they're thinking of closing now. You'll have to buy it and run a campaign to popularise them. The fish are cheap enough.'

'Could do,' he said, and the proposition with all its pros and cons ran through his mind as visibly as if he had discussed it. He decided against and returned to immediate refreshment. 'One scotch now and one after I've spoken to Kalek. I shall need it. Do you want to know all about this or can you pick it up as I talk?'

'I expect I can get it,' she said from the pantry whose wide sliding-doorway brought it virtually into the room. 'It's the leak from Godley's island, I suppose? You didn't think it was going to be serious when you came in on Tuesday.'

'I don't now. It can be handled, of course. There is very little of this new element isolated and we're gathering in all there is as fast as we dare. However, more can always be obtained later and meanwhile we are investigating this crazy idea of Paggen Mayo's, so the big boys are entitled to ask what the hell I think I'm up to, letting some Commie spill the beans all over the foreign propaganda machine for any damned technician to read. I have to reassure them and yet point out that the danger of some success with the stuff must still persist. Then they can share my nightmares! I shall go down to the Island tomorrow and placate the Allied clients. They've been blowing off steam all day so I thought I'd have 'em all to lunch down there and let them see the personnel for themselves.'

'You'll be able to control the invention when it comes and, if necessary, stifle it,' she said placidly.

'Of course I shall, but only if I can keep it safe down there under my hand. That has been the intention from the beginning. It's such an amazing concept—what a secret weapon if it came off, eh? Everything is all right but the leak is a nuisance and I don't see how it happened—which is serious. Official security is completely useless. They've only just given us the all-clear after taking the place apart. It's some damned innocent. Some little head so full of wool it doesn't know it's bleating!'

His face had changed and she threw up her hands.

'Bae! You told me to tell you when you look like that. People *don't* understand. I'll just get your food. Could you help yourself to the drink?'

'Probably.' He was laughing at her admonition. He knew he made faces and thought it childlike and rather gay.

He went over to the ebony compendium and parted the panels to reveal a cut-glass glitter within which lit up as the shutter passed. He was relaxing visibly. His jungle fastness was warm and well stocked and very quiet, as he liked it best. When there was any noise at all he preferred it to be roaring, with himself the loudest of all, but now, in the very midst of the city, the sound-proofing was so thorough that they could have been in the depth of a forest.

His huge body was shaped like a grand piano on its tail, but his step was light and his hands sure and careful so that he took the glass from among the others without a sound. The telephone which would link him presently with the three other men, who with himself controlled directly or indirectly at least three parts of the whole of the world's communications, was an elegant crystal instrument. His sad eyes noted that it was to hand and that the extra-heavy table he liked to have beside him was waiting with a new pad on it for him to draw upon while he talked. He felt for his pen and found it ready and only then did he sigh and pour his pale drink, which was the exact colour of Merle's hair. This was, possibly, why he liked the tint and never let her change it although it no longer suited her as well as it once had done.

He sat down as she came in with the electric trolley, and looked almost domesticated waiting for his food, so that she ventured a flattery of the only kind he found amusing.

'I know why you like these damn sprats. Because you can bite them up whole!' she said.

As in the first, the fourth of the five stirrings heralding the main movement took place in one man's mind, and again closely concerned his own dedicated labours.

While the Waterside D.D.I. was regretting, Canon Avril meditating and Lord Ludor machinating, down in the centre of Fleet Street the office of Lord Feste's journal *The Daily Paper* had begun to stir. It was the youngest in spirit of all the 'mornings' and it had scooped the best publicity of its career on the day when it had first announced its impudent title to a string of established rivals. They had attempted to restrain it by due process of law but without avail, and it had never lost the initial lead. Just now its imposing building was beginning to vibrate as the staff came streaming back to whip up the nightly fit of excitement in which it was 'put to bed.'

As yet, the two editorial mezzanine floors were comparatively quiet and W. Pegg Braithwaite, working snugly in his sacred corner, was almost as peacefully comfortable as was decent in that bedlam of an office. If it had not been for the twitter from the John Aubrey Column cubicle which separated him from Features, he might have thought he was in his cubby-hole at home overlooking the river at Chiswick.

'Peggie' was one of the first journalists to popularise Science without insulting it and was by now a considerable figure in both fierce worlds. His other claim to rarity was that he was one of the very few men who had worked for Lord Feste continuously ever since they had both arrived in London in the same month many years before. The chief attribute they shared was an essential youthfulness, epitomised by that naïve and obstinate faith in the invincible might of the pen which is both the strength of Fleet Street and its Achilles' heel.

Compared with everybody else in the building Peggie was practically secure; he had a name and a following and a private reference library on his own subject kept safe from rivals in his own bald head. The chatter from next door came from two less happily placed people. The male voice, which belonged to the compiler of the column, was verging on the shrill as the nightly dilemma over the lead story became acute. The scout, a woman, was working hard. Her drawl, which Peggie had known when it was pure south London, was now very Mayfair and it jarred upon him most unreasonably; he himself became more Yorkshire the longer he stayed in the South.

'Journalists may be unimportant but Giles Sanderton was Business Editor. It really was quite a funeral,' she was saying.

'Who cares? We are playing the whole thing down. We can use your little bit about Edith Lady Trier being in black down to her pearls, but that will be all. There's to be a par in the news.'

'But why for Heaven's sake? Sanderton worked for Lord Feste, he held a very trusted and influential position on a leading newspaper, his death was tragically sudden and there were more names at his funeral than we tagged on to the Howard first night yesterday....'

'Dearest girl...' the man was talking through his teeth and old Peggie teetered softly to himself as he did when the nerves

21

of younger people showed through. 'Just take my word for it. *I do not want to irritate the Owner*. I can't and won't put it clearer.'

'Really?' She was on to it like a terrier. Peggie had to hand it to her. 'And he used to be the Old Man's white-headed boy! What was it? "The wrong associates", as they say?'

'I don't know and I don't want to know. Fortunately he's dead so nobody need know anything. Drop it. Now then, what else have we got? My God, this is thin!'

'There's the dress show and the wedding,' she said obediently. 'I shall have to fall back on my teashop.'

'Who? Oh, that old pansy teashop keeper you're always quoting. You eat there, don't you?'

'I have my coffee and croissant there in the mornings instead of breakfast, he's so near my flat. You can sneer at him if you like but it was my dear Mr Witty and his "pussums" who gave us the first whisper of the Coalhouse divorce.'

'Too clinical, my dear.' The other voice dropped easily into the revived twenties vernacular. 'Well, what had he got this morning?'

'Let me see, not a lot, but there might be something in it, if it was properly investigated. He was all on about a libel case pending between two masters—or a master and an examiner— in one of the public schools. The boys come home tomorrow for half term and he was going to hear more from one of the matrons and tell me. Shall we 'phone the School?'

'No. That's not *us*. That'll be a news story. We couldn't touch that.'

'Oh, it's nothing unpleasant. Neither Mr Witty nor his beautiful white cat would soil their claws with common dirt. You don't know Mr Witty. He calls his teashop the Milestone and he's always toying with the idea of changing his name to Whittington.... I think he sees himself as a principal boy! This is all about cheating in exams.'

'Is it? Well, there's nothing there for us. Give me that corny Talking Tiger story news turned in.'

Content in his corner, Peggie continued to doctor the article he was vetting for one of his young relatives who edited a technical journal round the corner at the 'Thousand and One Nights' Press.

The Braithwaites were a family of journalists as closely knit as any of the country's nuclei of born tradesmen; weavers, coachbuilders, masons or smiths. These were the families who had formed the Guilds and later inspired the birth of the trade unions. Powerful, obstinate, skilful men, they served their masters and earned their money but their greatest loyalty was always to the craft itself. Although Peggie was deep in his task he spared a secret grin at the inefficiency of the two next door. Gossip! They didn't recognise gossip when they heard it. The school they were talking about was St Josephus, the preparatory side of Totham, and whatever the facts of the pending libel action it was a twopenny-ha'penny tale compared with the real story which had involved that establishment earlier in the week when *Panda*, the propaganda journal of the Eastern Powers, had trotted out one of their periodic fairy tales. This one had been too wild even for the news boys and Peggie himself had been able to inform the Editor of *The Daily Paper*, that volatile demon Rafael, that there was nothing in it. They had both regretted it, despite their headshaking; but it really was no good; they had had to agree that even the incredible Ludor would hardly stand for that little item. Peggie just had to laugh whenever he thought of it. 'Guinea-pig public schoolboys'! The oriental propagandist was a performer on his own! Even Lord Feste himself, in the old days when his name had been Phil Jones, had not been quite in their class. Peggie dismissed the chatterers next door. They bored him and he closed his ears in the way he was trained to, finished his little job for the 'young 'un', and inserted a fresh sheet in his typewriter. Then he hitched his sleeves and settled down to the one utterly important task in his universe, the composition of his own authoritative Saturday Piece.

The fifth tremor round the rising bud was in its own way the most momentous of all and yet it was no more than a

23

reckless impulse in a young man who never appeared in the story again.

For him it was a moment which he remembered with horror all his life, the instant when he decided to take a risk without knowing the form.

While Peggie was in his corner, listening to the gossips, four floors above him young Peter Clew, who until the day before had been a very successful accountant and who was now the new Business Editor of *The Daily Paper* in the place of the late Mr Sanderton, stood regarding his new array of telephones. There were four of them and, scarcely aware of extending his neck, he made there and then a mental note to drop that celebrated 'fixer', 'Pa' Paling, forthwith.

The man had been most useful in putting him forward for this wonderful post which had been thrust into his hands like a gift from the gods, but Mr Clew felt in his sophisticated young bones that the fellow was not very *safe*.

He decided, therefore, that he would telephone him at home late on Saturday night and make an excuse to pass up the round of golf on the links at Hollowhill which had been so carefully arranged between them for Sunday morning. On the whole, he thought it would be better to meet Lord Ludor in some other way, at some other time. 'Pa' Paling might be a little sore but even so Peter Clew thought he could risk that. What was one enemy when one was as powerful as this oneself? A faint doubt assailed him but the sight of the telephones stiffened him; he sighed, and his mind closed with a snap.

Although he learned afterwards that at that moment he had flung his business career over a cliff, what he never knew was that he had also implemented one of those extraordinary little chances which have such disproportionate consequences in the history of mankind.

These five small indications appeared on the Thursday, and the pressure from below, at the centre, became evident on the Friday morning. Properly enough, it was most noticeable at Messrs. Godley's island research station.

2

Boffin Island

THE bedroom half of the converted Army hut had been done over at intervals, all the time they had been there, which was almost eighteen months, but it still looked very like the bedroom end of a converted Army hut. Helena Ferris, who was sitting at her dressing table touching her newly-tinted lips with a tissue, caught a fresh aspect of the irons in the roof through the looking glass.

'Martin. Suppose we hung a lot of cheap stage-jewellery, pearls and gold chains and coloured glass diamonds, from those things, do you think it would suggest a goldrush-town bar on the movies?' she enquired.

'No,' said her husband and added, not unreasonably, 'why the hell should it?'

'I don't know. I just thought it might.'

He sighed. 'Who wants to sleep in a goldrush-town bar on the movies, anyway? I just want to sleep with you, preferably anywhere else. I am several sorts of heel to make you stay on this godforsaken island. But not all research stations are like this. This is only Godley's and Lord Ludor's version. You haven't married a natural whelk.'

She laughed and turned back to the glass. 'Poor old Martin! You're not making me stay. I'm off for the whole half term week-end with my beloved Sam and the rest of my family. Why don't you play truant and come with me? Paggen Mayo can't kill you or even sack you, can he?'

He had been lying on the bed and now sat up and looked at her appraisingly, ignoring her question.

'Whacky!' he said. 'I'd almost forgotten you could look like that. Hell! That's a dangerous remark to make! Love you in slacks, too.'

She was beautiful, two years younger than himself, and she

looked now as he had always liked to see her, in a skirt and all dolled up for the city. She was very slender and naturally graceful, with deep gold hair brushed very carefully into a long bob. Her eyes were a true grey and she was clever and looked it without any of the arrogance or aloofness or, worse still, the over-shrewdness which so often goes with brains. He loved best her gaiety and an inbred elegance, a most attractive mixture of serenity and distinction which made him feel good whenever he looked at her. She was his and he adored her and his conviction was growing that this was a darn dangerous place to keep her.

He watched her slip the chunky amber bracelets on her narrow wrists and appreciated the inspiration which had made her wear them with the short golden wool jacket of her suit. Martin was an elegant young man himself by nature. He was from New England and was tall and very neatly made with long bones, a pale skin and dark hair and eyes, but just now he was uncomfortably aware of being at a disadvantage in the abominable slacks and oiled jersey which were almost a must with Paggen Mayo's team whilst working.

He moved over to the one window. All those in the front of the hut were shuttered against the ferocious north wind which roared over the saltings, but the back ones had a 'southern aspect' as the Ferrises took a derisive delight in reminding each other. At the moment the scene outside was a somewhat over-drawn picture of utter desolation. A thin autumn mist spread over the whole expanse of the East Coast estuary. The tide had been out for hours and the sea was no more than a bright trickle in the gutter of a clay channel. There was no sign of life whatever. Not a sail, not a shellfish gatherer. It was a scene of despair in a desolate world and was so completely dreary it made him laugh.

'I wish Paggen would hurry if he's coming,' he said over his shoulder. 'I did my best to stop him but he'd made up his mind. You know what he's like.'

Helena did not speak for a moment, then she said casually: 'He thinks Professor Tabard has insulted him, doesn't he?'

'Who told you that?' Martin was genuinely curious and rather surprised. 'I shouldn't have put it as fiercely as that. He was peeved because Tabard pretended not to understand him the other day—perhaps he couldn't. They're very different types of mind. It was nothing, though. Who told you?'

'His wife.'

'Oh.'

There was a long pause until she said. 'How long will he be? My train goes at Tudwick at eleven-fifteen and it's the last until three-thirty this afternoon so I mustn't miss it. Albert and Amanda can't get to London before lunch so I said I'd meet the children. Why does Paggen Mayo want to see us together. Do you know?'

He turned back from the window and came towards her and she rose so that he put his arms round her.

'I don't know,' he said awkwardly, his lips close to hers. 'He's got a sudden "thing" about security. I rather suspect that he has decided it would be safer to raise his ban on wives knowing about the work done here, than to have them speculate. It's an idea he's had some time and my bet is that he wants to come and talk about it.'

'But he can't!' She was staring at him in horror. 'He can't come out with all that *now*, not when I'm trying to catch a train!'

They both laughed but afterwards he stood looking at her helplessly. 'That's an attitude which isn't going to help, is it?' he demanded. 'Nor is it going to be a good idea to tell him that you've hardly been able to live here for eighteen months without getting a pretty clear idea of what your husband is up to. Nor that you can't see that there is anything to be very secret about. If he gets here before you go and he's in full flight, you'll just have to let him talk, I'm afraid, Sweetie.'

'Oh Martin!'

She did not pull back from him but turned her head so that her face was held away from his own. He recognised her mood gloomily.

'Sam will be O.K.' he said earnestly. 'He'll have Edward

27

with him who is twelve. They're not infants. They've got to St Peter's Gate Square on their own before.'

'Of course they have dear, but I want to be there. Sam is going to be heartbroken when he finds you're not going to get leave and he's sure to be worked up over this libel suit....'

'Worked up? He'll be tickled to death. I thought the solicitor was proving his evidence at the Rectory? The Examiner is being sued, isn't he?'

'Yes, but they want Sam's evidence for the defence. It's against his own form master, whom he likes. They think he may have seen the young man open the old boy's brief case and look at the exam papers. I don't know what the school thinks it's doing letting it happen at all! It's very upsetting to a small boy.'

She drew back from him and he thought how lovely she was and could not resist taking a little stab at her.

'Who sent Sam away? Who moved Heaven and earth to get him sent to boarding school at the earliest possible moment, despite the rules of this place against kids going back and forth?'

'I only did it because you and Paggen were experimenting with him....'

'Experimenting! For God's sake...!'

They were so near the old quarrel that its breath touched them and they both fell silent. Martin spoke first, miserably aware that he could only repeat a protestation made too often before.

'We only tried him out with a couple of E.S.P. tests, none as shattering as a game of noughts and crosses. He was very good at it but because we couldn't let you string along and play too, you suddenly rushed off to London and persuaded your influential relatives to get the security rule stretched so the kid could go to school ... thereby causing a lot of jealousy, let me tell you.'

'I know,' she said at last. 'I'm sorry. But I'm glad he went.'

There was another pause until she said. 'Melisande Mayo came and told me a long rigmarole about sending her girls to finishing school in the spring. Surely they're too old for that sort of thing now? The elder must be eighteen. Is Melisande all right, Martin?'

'All right?' He was lighting a cigarette and did not look at her. 'I'd say she's just bored like every other woman here. She's older than we are. I wouldn't take much notice of anything she said if I were you.'

'You're telling me! Paggen may be a genius but he must be hell to live with. Did you realise his name wasn't Paggen, by the way?'

'Isn't it?'

'No. He found it in the list of the first subscribers to the *Materia Medica*, and adopted it because it sounded exciting. I bet that woman wasn't christened Melisande, either! Mayo's real name is Paul, or it was when he was working in Canada in '59.'

'So what?' Martin was irritated. 'It's probably true. He has that kind of romantic streak. Those intensely practical people sometimes have. It makes him very human. Where did you get hold of the tale?'

Helena had the grace to look ashamed of herself. 'I ought not to have repeated it. I promised I wouldn't. I was gossiping with the staff. . . . Trying to ingratiate myself so that I was certain to get the car to the station this morning.' She caught her breath. 'Don't listen to me! I don't mean to be this sort of stinker.'

Her husband met her eyes and presently they both laughed, albeit a little regretfully.

'The whole set-up is crazy and a little degrading. I hand you that,' he agreed. 'Fred Arnold told you, I suppose? He knows most things. That's a strange guy, yet he's almost the only link this community has with normal everyday life. He'd be a good club factotum anywhere. He's a first-class barman and he manages that canteen as if it belonged to the Ritz; we're lucky to have him.'

'I don't think we would if Lord Ludor didn't use the place to entertain visiting firemen, do you? I don't make a habit of discussing the resident boffins with him but I just had to get that car reserved for me this morning. It's fantastic being this far from a railway station without a car ... how senior will you have to be before Paggen permits us to keep one? Oh blast! Forgive me! I don't mean to start on that one again. Truly I don't. I do know that if one person has one, everyone will want one, which isn't practical, they say—although Heaven knows why not, there's plenty of room. It just popped out. Now I'm ready. Oh, Martin, yes—I nearly forgot. Where did you put Sam's private bag?'

'The old brown Gladstone? I haven't touched it.'

'Then it's gone and he particularly wanted it.'

'How can it have gone?' He got up and wandered into the only other room. Here there were more evidences of their forlorn efforts to make a home.

Each of the prefabricated dwellings which had sprung up at intervals on the driveways to the marsh island's original mansion, now the headquarters of Messrs. Godley's research station, was provided with water, electricity and gas brought across the causeway from Tudwick. This estuary-side village had grown into a small town and possessed a railway station and a few shops, but the huts, although serviced, remained strictly utilitarian with varnished matchboarded walls and the kind of linoleum which was designed to last for ever and very dreadfully did. There were a few built-in lockers and Martin was searching these when Helena came after him.

'It's no good hunting anywhere there. I've turned out the entire place.'

'But I saw it the other day.'

'So did I. There was nothing in it but scribbles and cuttings and knives and the old cockyolly bird. I thought you might have thrown them out and used the bag for something...'

She regretted the words instantly. The face he turned to her was deeply hurt.

'I don't know what sort of animal you think I am. I've only let the boy go to school. I haven't taken a dislike to him! Where is his bag?'

'I can't imagine. No one comes in here, you see.'

'But that's crazy!' Surprise neutralised his anger like a chemical and his arm slid round her as they stood looking about them. 'The place is kept locked, isn't it? I do lock up automatically now, don't you? Whenever I go in or out.'

'Always. That Drummond business frightened me. I wish you didn't have to use subnormal people in your experiments....'

He jerked her more tightly to him. 'Don't talk like a Sunday newspaper. 'We do not experiment with anybody; we just try to find out who can help most!—I quote. To return to this elusive bag, I didn't steal it and nor did you, and our palatial home has been locked up like a hen-house so it can't be anywhere else but here. Change your mind and go by the later train and I'll guarantee to find it for you.'

'Darling, I can't! I've dressed, I've crossed Fred Arnold's palm with silver and got hold of a car and I must go this morning. I want to be on Liverpool Street Station to surprise Sam. Don't you see this is just Paggen playing up again? He's succeeded in spoiling your week-end and now he wants to ruin mine. He's only trying to show that he's the big boss; he always does. Oh, why couldn't he let us all be together just this one week-end?'

'Lay off him, will you?' Martin spoke mildly. 'He's a brilliant guy and my chief. You can say what you like about Godley's but old Paggen is a miracle worker.'

'You only say that because he's an electronics wizard and can construct. You're a physicist *and* a physician and fifty times as brilliant so that he has to rely on you even to communicate with his leader, but you're not an inventor.'

'Oh shut up!' His lips found her mouth and suddenly they each felt afresh all the warmth and tenderness of their affection for each other.

'We're all right,' he said making a question of it. 'Aren't we?'

'Of course we are. Listen. Is that the car?'

31

The tapping on the outside door was peculiar; a series of short jabs on the wood.

'That *is* Paggen.' Martin went over, unlocked the door and let in a blast of cold air followed by the visitor.

Paggen Mayo came in slowly, holding an umbrella like a sword, on the point of which was a ball of red, yellow and blue feathers.

'This is no way to treat a child's beloved toy,' he said with affected gravity. 'The infant Samuel would be rightly outraged. I've just removed it from your ventilator. I saw the gleam of feathers as I came by. Are the draughts really as bad as that?'

He was in early middle age but his wild hair was already grey and his thin red face deeply scored. He wore the oiled jersey and slacks which he had made the accepted dress of his department, but dignified his appearance with a pair of heavy chrome spectacles of original and rather eccentric design and certainly highly expensive workmanship. Anyone who gave the subject thought came to the conclusion that the aim was 'university don', but the strong element of neat-handed practical man belied that effect and the umbrella which he always carried looked like the affectation it was. At the moment he was in his 'social' mood, an exaggerated pseudo-eighteenth century performance which he kept for 'wives and VIPs'.

Martin took the toy from the spike and handed it to Helena. 'This is perfectly insane,' he said. 'We've been looking for this all over, haven't we, Helena?'

She nodded and turned the tousled bundle about tenderly. It had never been an elegant fowl but she had made it for Sam when he was little and first enchanted by the classic tale. Its success with him had been enormous and through the years it had become one of those treasures which remain secretly important long after all other baby toys are outgrown.

'I'm so glad it's come back,' she said.

'Well, there it was, sprouting out of the pantry ventilator. I came round that side because I walked along the sea wall. You haven't been by there this morning, Martin?'

'I haven't been round there for days. Was there anything else around? A very battered old brown bag, for instance?' He was about to step out to see for himself when Mayo barred his way with the umbrella.

'Later, young sir, if you don't mind,' he said. 'I have grave matters to impart, especially to you Ma'am ... you look very beautiful this morning.'

Martin was frowning. 'You see what it means, though,' he said, pointing to the bird. 'Someone must have gotten a key of this place.'

'Oh come.' Mayo had very bright blue eyes. 'That's no diagnosis, Doctor. What is the margin of human error?' It was one of his typical asininities. A piece of jargon in unconvincing imitation of people who, because of the odd nature of their joint enterprise, happened to be working with him. He was like a bad mimic who yet insists on attempting impressions of people to their faces. Helena looked embarrassed and Martin laughed with indulgent exasperation.

'What can we do for you, Paggen?'

Mayo pulled a chair towards him and sat down. 'May I?' he said to Helena. 'My dear lady. Circumstances have arisen which make it necessary for me to take you into my confidence. Do I make myself clear?'

'Not particularly,' Martin was leaning forward. 'As a matter of fact I did tell Helena that you were thinking of lifting the ban on wives knowing anything at all about the work here. That's it, isn't it? She has to go to London this morning by the way.'

'Too bad; you'll have to postpone it.' Mayo glanced at Helena and spoke with complete finality. He had dropped his manner and reverted to type. He hitched one arm over the back of his chair and stretched his legs, ignoring her rising colour. 'I've just had a long briefing from Lord Ludor's office. The VIP luncheon today is to be more important than we'd thought. An American Admiral is flying over, so is the man Martin knows of from Reykjavick. General Smythe-White will be there and so will someone from the Ministry. We shall need

B

you Helena, Martin and I, and that's why I'm going to give you my lecture right away.'

'I'm so sorry, Paggen we ...'

'Be quiet, dear.' He was much more of a force now that he had given up presenting himself. 'I shan't tell you any more than I think is good for you but if you're going to be any use at all you must understand enough to know what not to talk about. I'm only trusting you because I've got to. The first thing to remember is this: although every important country in the world is having a stab at what we're trying to do the whole subject is still considered pretty absurd by all but the initiated. *That is how we want it.*'

Helena looked at her watch openly and Martin shook his head at her but Mayo went on as if he had not noticed.

'Extra Sensory Perception, Thought-reading, Telepathy, they are all the same thing to the uninformed: mumbo jumbo. Splendid! Keep it that way as long as you can. Do you follow me?' She nodded politely, her ears strained for the sound of a car on the track outside.

'Well now,' he said. 'As you know, modern communications in almost every form are all in our orbit here at Godley's and there aren't many gaps, but a little while ago it became necessary to explore every other conceivable means of one man getting in touch with another ... I shan't be more specific than that and don't let it worry you; just take it from me that in America and the Soviet Union, in West Germany, Holland, Sweden, France and here in Britain some very intelligent people started thinking around merely because no one could afford not to, and no possibility, however wild and unlikely, was neglected.' He had a slightly nasal intonation and a very penetrating voice but he knew what he was talking about and it was difficult not to be impressed. 'From now on,' he said, pointing the umbrella at her, 'I'm only interested in scientific actuality and so are our clients. Get that straight. If your lady mother in Suffolk started to worry in the night that you were in distress and suffocating and got on the telephone and woke you from a nightmare in which you were being strangled and you both came and told me about it I might be entertained but I shouldn't be very interested. My subject is electronics. I'm an engineer. Before I'm convinced a message has passed I want something which *someone else*, someone other than the two people originally concerned, can see, hear or taste. I want a light or a bell or I might conceivably accept a stink. I don't know. Do you understand me?'

'Yes,' she said. 'But...'

'If you're going to be a good girl and not a blasted nuisance to me and your brilliant young husband, you'll have to listen and understand this,' he said. 'The people who started us off on our particular line of enquiry were the Navy. That has surprised you, hasn't it? I thought so. You imagined that we were mainly commercial. No. It was the Navy who discovered the Drummond brothers and that discovery set the ball rolling.' His explosive laugh echoed round the boarded walls. 'The Army's only real contribution is General Smythe-White but he's an asset in his own right. He's that rare type which knows exactly what it wants even if it happens to be the Earth. The picture which he has in his mind's eye is of some splendid young guardsman in uniform sitting in some place inaccessible to radio and utterly unconnected with the rest of the world by any known means of communication. The only equipment he is to possess are two bulbs (sticking out of his ears, I imagine) green on the left, red on the right, and a mirror. Meanwhile, sitting at attention in an Army lecture room miles away is his opposite number, working a buzzer or a flasher, and connected by telephone to Command. One flash from number two at home intensifies the red bulb in the ear of number one: two flashes and the green one glows. No flash and there's no change. Three signals which an ordinary digital computor can translate into any message Smythe-White can imagine wanting to send. That's all he's asking for and it was a pipe dream until along came the Navy with the Drummond brothers.'

Helena was looking at him, captured at last, and he risked a glance at Martin.

'I know you can give her much more about the Drummonds

than I can but I'd rather do it my way. I hope you don't object. I'm taking the responsibility and I'm only telling as much as I think I need to. The Drummond brothers were non-identical twins, Helena. They came from an industrial slum in the North where they were both considered gormless. That is "slow" and "not very bright". Len was the stronger character and the better specimen and he wasn't a fool but Willie was definitely "sub", or I thought so. Martin here and Tabard had a name for him. Anyway, Willie only got into the service because Len saw that he did. The extraordinary link between these two men was first noticed on board ship. A Medical Officer who observed it had the sense to report it and fortunately the two were passed on up the line until they finished where they ought to have been from their babyhood, in the hands of our Professor Tabard who was then in Cambridge.' He paused and Martin ventured to intervene.

'They broke entirely new ground, Helena. No one had recorded anything quite like them before.'

'They provided the missing ingredient,' Mayo agreed. 'In them, Nature had taken the one vital step forward and had provided us with the concrete physical phenomenon which made their communication capable of test. Willie had two birth-marks. It sounds damn silly but there they were. They were pale pink patches, one inside his left wrist and one beside his left eye. In the normal way there was nothing unusual about them and they weren't very noticeable, but when Len Drummond sent his brother a message of warning—when he released an unfriendly impulse towards him—the birth marks changed colour and became deep livid bruises. Anyone could see them and they could be recorded. So you see it did not matter what Willie *thought*, or received by way of thought transference, because we had something more definite to go on. Distance did not appear to have much effect on the phenomenon and nor did one or two other more important location factors. As long as Len was in good health and was permitted to think about his brother (to see his photograph or hear his recorded voice—that sort of thing) then the thought was transferred. One could prove it and see it.' He shook his head. 'The positive signal was not so satisfactory. When Len sent an approving or affirmative impulse towards Willie—he used to send these messages *on command* you understand—it was quite fantastic: Willie used to giggle in an idiot way and his eyes watered. This could be made to happen whatever he was thinking or doing at the time. It was perfectly distinctive and we never found anything else to make him behave in that particular fashion but Smythe-White didn't like it. I think he expects us to improve on it. But it was good enough for us. The Drummonds were the beginning of the whole thing. They responded to every test made and Professor Tabard was cock-a-hoop because his theory, which he'd had for a very long time, looked like being proved. Naturally he wanted to get down to a full investigation of the two men, which would have taken quite a few years. However, fortunately for us, there were developments elsewhere and time was seen to be pretty damn short. So the Ministry became interested and took over. They came to Godley's and offered them Tabard, myself and Martin, plus a research grant. What they hope to get for their money is a fund of two-way, man-controlled, one-hundred-per-cent-efficient pairs of Drummonds, live or mechanical, whenever and wherever they may need them. It won't work out quite like that of course. But, because of those brothers and the work we did on them, it's by no means the ridiculous assignment it may sound to the ignorant.'

Helena's intelligent eyes met his own. 'I thought it was someone called Drummond who broke into the huts here late last spring and went mad and committed suicide,' she said slowly.

'That was Willie.' Mayo was scowling. 'It wasn't suicide. The coroner was only trying to get a little notoriety. If petty officials get their noses into an outfit like this they always look for drama. The drowning was a complete accident. Professor Tabard was trying to interrupt the link between the brothers. He thought Len was the active factor and he wanted to see if he could teach him to establish the same contact with a third person. He had some success using hypnotism but meanwhile no one realised what was happening to Willie until he went berserk. He broke into nearly every building on the island looking for his brother and finished up in the mud just as the tide came in. That frightened everybody including you, I'm afraid. I'm sorry for that but it left us all in a rather difficult position, as you can guess.'

'You couldn't continue the work without him?'

'Good God, of course we could!' He was irritated with her for making him even consider such a disaster. 'If there had been something phoney about the Drummonds, we couldn't. If their communication had been some sort of trick or a fantastic series of coincidences then we'd have been umpered, but Tabard had been working on the men for over three years and he'd satisfied first himself and then all the rest of us that there really was a genuine impulse carried by some sort of wave. Identification of each of these proceeds just as fast as we can.'

He leaned back in the chair.

'Lecture ends. Now I tell you what you can do. You can see we've had progress held up for some months and it's only now that we're able to get a glimmer of a way to manufacture something faintly comparable. But meanwhile we've lost our party piece which kept the clients happy. The General particularly misses the performance. It used to give him a tremendous thrill and he thought out several little trick tests himself, some of them excellent. But now he's getting restless. He wants to be sure that we're coming up with something just as good and at the moment we just haven't got it. I have something up my sleeve which will be useful if it comes off but I will not ruin the idea by attempting to talk about it too soon. So you, Helena, will attend this blessed luncheon today and you'll sit by old Smythe-White and take his mind off any other form of entertainment. I'm certain that's how he sees it. We don't want him prodding Lord Ludor into demanding to 'see something'. It isn't ready. They must go on hoping for a while yet and then we'll show them.'

'You sound as if there was a flap on,' Martin was eyeing him curiously. 'What is it?'

'I don't know.' Mayo gave him a deliberately blank stare. 'The message I got was that his Lordship would see me in the library or snug or whatever that plush room is called, just as soon as it pleased him to get here. I translated that as a request for some sort of display which we cannot give so I put my intention to take your wife into the hallowed circle a few days forward. I'm sorry if your week-end is curtailed, Helena, but there are other considerations.'

Helena got up. She avoided looking at Martin but met the visitor squarely.

'I'm so sorry,' she said. 'But you see it's all arranged. I'm meeting the child. I've only just got time to get to the station. The car must be waiting.'

Paggen let her get to the door before he spoke over his shoulder. 'All transport was commandeered an hour ago. You won't get to any station this morning, dear. This is a research establishment, not a creche.'

Helena jerked the door open and looked up and down the track. It was completely deserted. The railway station was five miles away and the time was seven minutes past eleven.

3

Half Term

THE main line approach to London from the east country
has not changed in half a century. Just before one o'clock,
as the party of boys travelling up from St Josephus, the preparatory school for Totham College, approached Liverpool Street
Station the carriages were dark as in a winter's evening and
outside the windows the soot-covered arches were as black and
mysterious as the entrance to a thousand little tombs. The
smell of the city, unbearably exciting and nostalgic to young
Londoners, was already pervading the train, stinging eyes and
noses and forcing itself into mouths sick and tired of fresh air
and plain food.

The games-master who was in charge of the party, a square
young man called Mason, not very long out of university, was
smoking in the corridor where he could keep an eye on three
compartments. Two of these were full, for the London con-
tingent was strong this year, but in the third there were only
two boys. He had thought it best to keep little Sam Ferris and
his cousin apart from the rest. There had been too much
chatter about the libel suit already and he did not want the
child ragged. He was a sensitive little beast and there was no
telling how seriously he was concerned by the whole infuriat-
ing business. The cousin, Edward Longfox, was a different
type entirely. He was older of course, but young Mr Mason
very much wondered if he had ever been very different even in
his perambulator. He could see him now sitting in the corner
closest to the corridor, his small shoulders hunched, his curiously wizened face expressionless and his flaming red hair
burning in the gloom. The hair really was remarkable. Some
children would have found it an intolerable affliction but
young Longfox bore it as stoically as he did his name. They
were both marks of distinction, of course, in their way.

Richard Longfox the father had had a brilliant career as a scientist, and had made a reputation for himself before he met his untimely death on the Antarctic 507 expedition. In the opinion of the Head the boy had inherited his brains. The hair on the other hand, had come from his mother's family. She was Sophia, daughter of the Earl of Pontisbright, whose title had been revived so romantically in the nineteen thirties and whose family colouring was a legend. At the moment she was in South America with her father, and Edward was to spend the short holiday with another member of the clan, the Lady Amanda of Alandel Aeroplanes fame. She, of course, was married to that very odd character Albert Campion. It occurred to Mason that Edward would fit in with that family very well; the child looked like some sort of eccentric already.

He walked down the corridor and glanced in at Sam. The small boy was sitting opposite his cousin, a comic paper folded on his knee and his pink and white face as inscrutable as only children's are. Kids were like eggs at that age Mason reflected. God alone knew how each was going to hatch out later on.

At the moment Helena Ferris's son was angel-faced, with straw-coloured hair and eyes as grey as her own. He was sitting up straight on the edge of the seat, one sandalled foot stretched to touch the floor to ensure his balance as the train lurched over the points. He seemed as lost in thought as his cousin. Whereas the children in the other two compartments were swarming over the windows like caged puppies in a pet shop, these two were behaving like little old men engrossed by inner cares. The master was reminded again of the libel suit, and his irritation increased. He did not belong to that section of the Common Room which felt that Philip Allenbury was not justified in sueing 'Tabloid' Pellett, the examiner, whatever the stupid old idiot had written to the Headmaster about him, but it seemed a pity that he could not vindicate himself without dragging the children into the quarrel. He was still thinking about the whole extraordinary business and wondering what on earth *had* happened, since, however one looked at them, the circumstances were pretty fishy, when the train lurched into the station and he was surrounded by a milling crowd.

The coach reserved for St Josephus was in the front of the train and came to rest under the footbridge so that the platform there was very narrow and darker even than the rest of the station. The train was full and the little crowd of relatives waiting for the boys was constantly broken up by the stream of travellers from the back. There was considerable confusion and the schoolmaster solved the problem by keeping his charges in the corridor and only letting each one out as an escort appeared for him. He was half way through the task when he came to the turn of a hatless young woman in decorated spectacles and a dark coat who spoke to him earnestly for a few seconds. The children in the train could not hear her but a trickle of anxiety ran through the throng and the message was passed back hastily. 'Ferris and Longfox, Ferris and Longfox. Hurry. Come on. Buck up.'

Mason looked up from the platform as the two appeared. Although he was over eleven, Edward was no taller than his eight and a half year old cousin and they made a rather pathetic picture, their startled faces unnaturally solemn in the gloom, as they hung for a moment at the top of the steps looking at the woman who was clearly a stranger to them.

Mason lifted the younger boy down and beckoned to the other and they all stood for a moment beside the girl who was smiling encouragingly at the children.

The young man cleared his throat awkwardly, as anxious as the boys. 'Look Ferris,' he said very gently. 'This is Miss...?'

'Lewis,' she supplied quickly. 'From the hospital.'

'Yes, yes I see.' He tried to silence her. 'But you told me it was not serious?'

'No, it's not but she would like to see him. He should come with me now.' She put out a hand and took Sam's own. He submitted very meekly and said nothing at all but glanced sharply at his cousin who pressed forward.

'We wondered if Mrs Ferris was going to meet us?' Edward said, revealing a husky voice unexpectedly precise from such a small person.

'She's been detained.' Mason spoke before Miss Lewis could explain. 'There has been a slight accident but it is not serious. His mother would like to see Sam and so he's going straight to her. You can manage on your own, can you Longfox?'

'Or perhaps his cousin would come too?' Miss Lewis spoke briskly. It was evident that she was worried and anxious to get back. 'It would be nice for the young one to have a friend with him.'

Mason hesitated. The situation sounded more serious than he had thought but before he could intervene Miss Lewis had smiled at Edward, who somewhat unexpectedly took her other hand and they all three hurried off down the platform to the ticket barrier.

Mason was claimed at once by the mother of one of the other boys and had no time to consider the incident although in the back of his mind he was uneasy. He wondered if he should have made the woman wait so that he could go with the boys himself, but meanwhile he was very fully occupied and Miss Lewis had certainly seemed in a hurry. He hoped nothing really frightful had happened to young Ferris's mum.

The hatless girl with the floating coat and the two boys, each of whom carried a small suitcase in his free hand, sped across the concrete in silence. The children made no attempt to speak and the woman seemed too worried, but once the barrier was passed and they climbed the footbridge and came down into the wide glass hall of the main departure platform she relaxed a little.

'We have a nice big car waiting for us out in the street,' she said. 'Do you know your way about here? We only have to go through the main booking hall and up the ramp and there it will be. You will see your mother very soon.'

Sam nodded. He was very white and had begun to tremble but he kept up with her, running a little when he had to as did Edward on her other side. There was nothing extraordinary in the picture they made. The whole station seemed to be dotted with striding women leading running children home for half term but since it was not crowded they got on very quickly.

43

The booking office, which is also the main entrance to the station, has two sets of large double doors leading to the covered way where the taxicabs wait, and beside the first set of these there stands as a rule a City of London police constable. The City police are taller than most and, as some say, even handsomer and more splendid.

P.C. Godfrey Hawkins, who was on duty on this occasion, was six foot four in his socks, in the prime of life and looking bored and magnificent as he stared idly over the heads of the stream of outgoing passengers, his helmet and silver buttons worthy emblems of authority.

A husky voice somewhere about his waist startled him suddenly and the astonishing statement it conveyed took him so completely by surprise that he reacted slowly.

'Officer!' said the voice, young but unmistakable in background and temper. 'I wish to give this lady in charge. She is attempting to kidnap me and my cousin.'

There was a flurry before him and Godfrey looked down to see a flash of red hair, two struggling children, a black coat whipping round someone wearing spectacles and then the second child broke free. He flung himself at the policeman's solid blue legs and hung on to one of them as if it had been a tree.

'Look out!' The voice was high and shrill. 'Look out. She's a spy!'

Everything which, as a policeman, he had ever learned about the irrepressible idiocy of the human boy leapt into the constable's mind and he was in the act of scooping young Sam to his feet with a few well chosen words about the inadvisability of behaving like a goat whilst dealing with the Law, when the incredible thing happened.

Miss Lewis took to her heels and fled up the hill towards the busy street, her coat flying out behind her and her shoes clattering on the pavement.

At the same moment a man who had been loitering in the shadow of the ticket bureau swept past the astounded little group and pressed on up the drive after her.

4

Sanctuary

'OH Darlings! I'm so sorry!' Helena was trying to stop shivering. Despite the careful make-up and the golden wool suit, she looked dishevelled. She had been in an odd mood when she came in, and the news of the boys' adventure which had greeted her on arrival at the Rectory had shaken her self-control. 'Please forgive me, Uncle Hubert, and you too, Amanda. It's really only because I'm so glad to get here. You don't know what Heaven this room is after the Island!'

She shot a watery smile at them across the table with its red chenille cloth, its square of crochet and the tea-tray bearing china strewn with flowers and a battered but glowing silver pot.

It was nearly six and the parlour was much as everyone present had always remembered it, homely and cosy and apparently for ever.

Canon Avril was sitting by the fire in his high-backed best chair. He was enormously interested and very happy indeed to see them. Opposite him in the window alcove sat the Lady Amanda, sister to the Earl of Pontisbright and to Lady Mary who was Helena's mother. She was a remarkable person who had made a career for herself in the late nineteen thirties and forties as one of the principal designers of Alandel Aeroplanes. Now she was still a slender woman with a heart-shaped face and clear light brown eyes. The blazing Pontisbright hair tends to grow darker with the years but there was still a glint of its smouldering fire in the sleek bob which hugged her round head. One of her chief charms was her voice which had remained as young as her enthusiasm, and now when she spoke it could have belonged to a girl.

'Any shock is a tear-jerker,' she said. 'We were so full of our story we just shot it at you as you appeared. Albert dashed down to Liverpool Street when the call came in from the Stationmaster, and he'd just telephoned back to say they were going on to Scotland Yard to look at the records when you arrived. Uncle Hubert and I were trying to work out how the boys could have been so clever.'

'Just suppose they had gone with her!'

'But they didn't,' said Avril, 'they waited until they were in front of a policeman and acted together. Edward accused her and Sam backed his cousin up.'

'What did he say?'

'We don't know yet,' Amanda put in. 'All we heard was that a woman tried to collect them and they saw through her. They'll be a bit above themselves if they've found her in the "Rogues Gallery". I suppose she was hoping to demand ransom.'

Helena shuddered. 'It could be something quite different. I wish they were home. Albert wouldn't keep them out, would he?'

Amanda grinned. 'They wouldn't all go to the pictures, if that's what you mean. But as they're going to be in the building they might look up Charley Luke. That could take hours, especially if they wanted to talk too.'

The Canon glanced at the skeleton clock on the mantelshelf. 'Albert will be here at any moment now,' he said. 'A solicitor is calling to see Sam. Albert told me so himself. Why in the world does that child need a lawyer?'

'It's the libel case, Uncle. Didn't they explain?'

'No. I'm afraid we didn't. We'd only just arrived when the call from the station came in.' Amanda was apologetic. 'I've said nothing since because it seems so mad. I should have thought both the school and the prep would have frowned at members of the common Room dragging each other into court.'

'They do.' Helena seized on the new subject. 'Sam's young form master at St Josephus, whose name is Philip Allenbury, has been forced to sue a retired English Master from Totham who was acting as a special examiner. It all happened last term—Sam's first. Sam is going to be asked to say that he saw Mr Allenbury open a briefcase which had been left on his desk and look at the examination paper prepared for one of the boys laid up in the sicker with a broken leg. It mattered terribly to the child because it meant he either did get into Totham or failed utterly. The examiner is old and a stinker and he made the accusation on paper to the Head. He also wrote to all the Governors.'

'Oh dear, how awfully thorough.' Amanda was laughing in spite of herself. 'Yes, of course, the young man would have to clear himself. What does Sam say?'

'He's so quiet. I don't understand it. He was the only witness. He was alone in the classroom where it happened, kept in, writing an exercise. Both sides went to talk to him and the Head thought it would be better if the lawyers saw him at home.'

'Is there any other evidence?'

'Rather a lot. The boy with the leg—he's a friend of Edward's—had lost six weeks' work and couldn't prepare all the set English books. English is his one bad subject. There were six of these books, all the usual ones: *A Midsummer Night's Dream, The Fortunes of Nigel, Treasure Island, The Lays of Ancient Rome* and a couple more I can't remember. The boy had only worked on the Shakespeare seriously. The examiner—his name is Pellett and they call him Tabloid— arrived at St Josephus on the evening before the exam and went in to see Mr Allenbury, who was making all the arrangements. Allenbury was alone, except for Sam sitting at the back of the room. The two men chatted normally until Allenbury said something about the injured boy's beastly bad luck and mentioned that he'd only had time to do the one book. Sam says Pellett went black in the face at once and said: "That was a singularly ill-advised remark, Allenbury!" and stamped out leaving the briefcase on the desk.'

'He thought he was being got at.' Avril seemed inclined to sympathise. 'Then what?'

'Then Mr Pellett came back, snatched up his property with a scowl and rushed off again.'

'Had Allenbury looked in the case?' Amanda demanded.

'I don't know. The solicitor may be able to get it out of Sam, I couldn't.' Helena's grey eyes met hers briefly. 'Unfortunately, later on that evening Allenbury went over to see the boy in hospital and, according to him, the child asked him suddenly for a copy of *The Lays* which he'd not even taken over there. Allenbury came back to the school and got one for him and the boy spent the night swotting it up. In the morning when Pellett produced the paper, all the English Lit. questions *were* on *The Lays*.'

'Oh dear.'

'I know. To make things worse, all the St Josephus masters were certain they wouldn't be chosen. Macaulay is out of fashion and Pellett was known to dislike them because the thumpity bump of the verse is so easy to learn.'

'Unhappy man!' said Avril. 'Oh hello, Mrs Talisman, what is it?'

'A gentleman, sir.' She was a little excited. 'A Mr Anderton to see Sam.'

Helena got up. 'That's Mr Pellett's solicitor. He's early. Shall I take him into your study, Uncle Hubert?'

'No, I don't think so. Ask him to step this way, Mrs Talisman.' Avril's authority was of the old-fashioned kind. 'We don't want any interviews to be too private, do we? That was the Headmaster's feeling. I agree. We'll see if we can help him.'

The two women had no opportunity to object. Mr Anderton came lightly into the room, his expression changing as he saw the unexpected group. He was a slim, youngish person, not quite the glossy type of modern legal business man, but shrewd enough, with a smooth approach and an unexpected leaven of humour in his outlook. At the moment his chief concern appeared to be curiosity. It came into the room with him like an odour.

He recognised Avril's authority and made his explanation to him with only a sidelong deference to Helena.

'I came a little early because I thought I might perhaps have a word with the boy's father,' he said, looking about him, his glance taking in the old furniture, the silver, the worn Persian rugs. 'I didn't realise he didn't live here ... ?'

He left the question in the air and Helena answered it obligingly.

'My husband had to stay at the Research Station,' she said. 'He's a scientist you see....'

'Research station?' He was both so surprised and so enlightened that he repeated the words. 'Really? Oh, I do beg your pardon. I didn't understand that at all! You must forgive me. I thought... I mean I assumed that he had some sort of Diplomatic...' He took himself firmly in hand. 'You must forgive me,' he repeated, starting again. 'I shouldn't have bothered you. I should have telephoned but the appointment was made and I was, as it were, on my way home and so I took the liberty of dropping in.'

'So you don't want to see Sam after all? Splendid!' Old Avril appeared to have followed the newcomer without difficulty. 'Excellent! It might have proved a very grown-up problem for a very young person. May I enquire why you have decided not to worry him?'

'Mr Pellett has withdrawn the accusation and is apologising, and Mr Allenbury is withdrawing the action.' Mr Anderton was startled into simplicity. 'I only heard half an hour before I came out.'

'You seem to find that very surprising?' The Canon was interested as he always was in anybody's news. 'Didn't you think Mr Pellett would give way?'

'I could have sworn he wouldn't!' The reaction was explosive. 'Mr Pellett is a very determined man indeed. Frankly, I'm amazed by this development. However, he told me himself or I shouldn't have believed it. I gathered that some pressure had been put on both sides and, rightly or wrongly, I understood that it had emanated from *here*, from the child's family? I'm probably quite wrong?'

'I think you must be. I don't know of anything of the sort.'

49

'I see. Then perhaps the pressure was put upon the two schools by something very authoritative? Your husband's . . . ah . . . place of work, for instance, Mrs Ferris?' His eyes were knowing but she met them blankly and the shadow in her face was noticeable.

'If that were true, it really would be the last thing any of us here would know about,' she said coldly, and added, to soften the snub, 'Can we offer you some tea?'

He refused politely and set about taking his leave with as much grace as possible. 'What a view that is!' he remarked, nodding at the window. 'From outside one hasn't a clue it exists.'

The change of the subject was successful and for a moment everybody paused to look out at one of those London scenes which make the city one of the best loved and most unexpected in the world.

On the far side of the little square there was a wall with a pierced decorative border in brickwork. Behind it, quite ten feet below the level of the pavement, a short wide road ran down to the brightly lit shopping centre of Portminster Row where the scarlet buses teetered among the traffic and the hurrying crowds streamed homeward. The architect who had designed the Rectory must have envisaged the picture, the silhouettes of the trees in the square and the lace-like insertion in the wall showing up against the lights in the road; while above them, like a drop-cloth, the deep blue of London's evening shadow blotted out the towers and chimney-pots of the remoter reaches of the town. It was a nightly vision at the Rectory but, even so, the worn red velvet curtains were never drawn until the sapphire had faded and the lights had turned from yellow to white.

This evening, as they looked, a car turned in from the square's only entrance and Amanda got up. 'There they are!' she said with relief.

Mr Anderton fled, passing two boys and two men in the hallway. They did not speak to him, merely stepping aside briefly in their descent upon the open parlour doorway.

It was not until the front door had closed behind him and the others were all in the room that he was mentioned at all

By then Sam was swinging on his mother's arm, Edward was shaking hands gravely with Amanda, and Superintendent Charles Luke was being welcomed affectionately by the Canon, with whom he was a favourite. Albert Campion, who had been the last to come in, put the question as he closed the door behind him.

'Who was that running away?' His light affable voice only just penetrated the din but the enquiry was authoritative and the reply came back spontaneously, without thought, from the youngest mouth in the room.

'That was only the silly old lawyer,' said Sam from Helena's arms. 'He doesn't want to see me now, thank goodness.'

5

Long fox's I.G.

FOR some moments there was an astonished silence. Sam had become very red and was staring intently at his shoes, while keeping very close to his mother who was sitting at the table with her arm round him.

The two adult newcomers were startled. Mr Albert Campion, a thin man with pale hair and eyes and a misleadingly blank expression, shot a thoughtful glance at the youngster through his horn-rimmed spectacles and Superintendent Luke permitted himself a bewildered smile. He was about to speak when Helena forestalled him by turning not on Sam but on Edward with actual ferocity.

'How did Sam know that?'

The boy did not reply at once. He had crossed the room and was standing with his shoulders hunched and his hands in the pockets of his raincoat. His long school muffler, blue with horizontal stripes, was wound twice round his neck and he appeared embarrassed, like some shy elderly person overtaken by an awkward social situation.

'Oh, I think he guessed, you know,' he murmured at last. 'It wasn't awfully difficult, was it?'

'How could you know the case had been dropped?'

'*I* didn't, Aunt Helena.' He revealed a charming deference towards her which transformed his peaky face. 'But Sam might have worked it out. After all, the solicitor hadn't waited to see him, had he?'

She turned her back on him with unreasonable exasperation. 'Oh Edward—please let Sam speak for himself!'

'Don't worry so,' the younger boy whispered, putting his ear against her cheek. 'Edward and I are pretty tired. We got rid of a fearful woman at the station. We both did it. We thought of it together. Since then we've been looking at photographs trying to spot her.'

'They're making an identikit portrait.' Edward's natural interest made everybody feel much more comfortable. 'It may go on television,' he added with a sidelong glance at Amanda.

'We'll go downstairs and look,' she promised. 'How about some food now?'

'We had some.' Sam was relaxing. 'We went to the Canteen. Sergeant Ferguson took us. He's wonderful. He's got thousands of pictures of peculiar sorts of villains. All different kinds. Jolly interesting. We had beans and listened to him until Superintendent Luke was ready for us. He was ready before Uncle Albert. That's why we're so late.'

'I got a message from an old friend and drifted over the road to see him,' Mr Campion said, making it an apology. 'He showed me his new office and we forgot the time. We were talking.'

'About who the spies are and how to catch them.' Sam uttered the words gaily. He was laughing and very happy. The room grew quite quiet. Mr Campion's expression froze and Luke, whose natural reaction was of the opposite kind, took a brisk step forward.

'That's done it, young 'un. What do you know?'

'Perhaps not, don't you think?' The thin man intervened swiftly. 'Tell us about the exam paper and Mr Pellett, Sam. Don't get upset, old man. Who's been talking to you? You're on to something exciting, aren't you?'

'Oh don't, Albert! Don't you see? It's not Sam at all. It's the other one!' Helena's outburst was more disconcerting than her son's disclosure. 'I know what it is; and it's frightful! They're like the Drummond Brothers, the twins who used to be on the Island until one of them was driven to death. I've only just heard the full story. I must get hold of Martin at once; he'll know what to do.' She was holding her son so tightly that he wriggled. 'Martin loves Sam. He didn't mean anything like this to happen and he won't let it, even if

53

Paggen tries to force it. Sam and Edward are cousins, that's the point, and Edward is older and more clever and...'

'You're quite wrong, you know.' Edward had scarcely moved. He made a very dignified pygmy, wrapped up in his raincoat and muffler, and his aloof intelligence reproved her and kept her at a distance. 'You are being a little thick, Auntie, but it's only because—forgive me—you're far too old. Sam is better at something than I am and it's because he is younger, or I think so.'

Amanda sat up and her most valuable characteristic, which was an inspired vein of common sense, flowed smoothly across the tingling room.

'If you two are trying to make yourselves interesting you've done it as far as I'm concerned,' she said briskly. 'This is when you produce the goods jolly quickly or get sent to bed.'

Edward sighed and he turned to Sam. 'I think you ought to tell them about the exam paper,' he said. 'Don't forget we thought you might have to explain to the solicitor.' He broke off abruptly and looked towards Helena as if she had spoken. 'I'm not "dominating" him! If I were, would I let him keep dribbling it all out like this?'

Sam crowed. He had a delightful chuckle, mischievous and utterly normal. 'It was *me*!' he declared proudly. 'I told Edward what Mr Pellett had put in the exam paper. I mean I described the book, but he guessed which it was and that made it fair to tell old Woodie in the sicker.'

'Most dishonest. How did you know?' Amanda appeared to have decided to conduct the inquisition. 'Was it you who looked in the briefcase?'

'Oh no, Auntie, I wouldn't do that. Honestly I wouldn't.' Sam had ceased to be interestingly 'fey' and had become a very ordinary small boy defending himself. 'I got it from Mr Pellett when he ticked off Allie.'

'*Mister* Allenbury. Did Mr Pellett say it to him?'

'No.' Once again he grew crimson.

'Under his breath, then?'

He shook his head.

'Oh come *on*, Sam. Don't be wet!' Edward was irritable. 'If you're going to say it, say it.'

'Well, Mr Pellett was in a bate and he thought: *'Sucks to you, Allie. It's not what you think!* Then he thought of what it really was and I received the flash bright and clear.'

'Of course!' The Canon exclaimed easily. 'That's what we used to call telepathy. Some people do have the gift to a marked degree at various times in their lives. I don't think you should cultivate it, Sam. It's not very healthy and you can easily begin to fancy you're not quite like anybody else. You must feed him on suet pudding, Helena. That'll cure him.' It occurred to him that he was being a little harsh and he smiled at the child who was eyeing him with a very odd expression. 'Tell me this,' he said. 'Did you get your "flash" from Mr Pellett in words or pictures?'

'The 'sucks to you Allie! was a "feel" of course.' Sam had been questioned like this before. 'And the description of the book was a picture—Romans pretending to fight on a bridge.'

'*"The good sword stood a hand's breadth out behind the Tuscan's head"*' The Canon was astonished. 'I should hardly call that pretending!'

'I didn't know.' The little boy was embarrassed. 'I'm not old enough to go into that form yet. I've not read that book. Mr Pellett believed they were pretending.'

'Mr Pellett sounds as if he might not envisage that sort of fighting very clearly, don't you think?' Mr Campion ventured. 'That's extraordinarily interesting, Sam, and it goes a long way to explain the mystery. You told Edward about the Romans on the Bridge I suppose, and he recognised *The Lays*? I see.'

Charley Luke, who was fidgeting, stepped back into the circle.

'What about you?' he enquired, looking down at Edward. 'Can you pick up thought messages like this, too? It was you who realised there was an attempted kidnapping this morning, and you appealed to the bobbie. How do you do it? Train yourselves?'

Edward considered him anxiously.

55

'It takes training,' he agreed at last. 'I'm not very good at it.'

'Who's teaching you? A master, perhaps?' The disapproving gleam was already alight in the black eyes.

'Good Heavens, no!' Edward was contemptuous. 'Masters would be useless!'

'Too old?'

'Well, I should think so!'

The Superintendent had a new idea.

'What am I thinking now?' he demanded and composed his features as he concentrated.

'I don't know. It doesn't work like that. The last message I got from you was when you asked me if we trained. You felt angry. You thought I was lying.'

'He thought the whole thing was lying,' Sam chimed in.

A wave of dusky colour rose up over the Superintendent's face and both children spoke together.

'That's too much feel. Now there's no flash at all.'

'What *is* all this? I don't like it.' Old Avril was frowning. 'What have you children got hold of? Edward, come here. Now my boy, just the truth, if you please! Explain. Make it quite clear to us all.'

Edward capitulated wearily. 'Very well, Uncle Hubert,' he said, 'but I should think it might be very dangerous to show it to you, considering the people who seem to be after it.' He was pulling off his muffler as he spoke and they stared at him as his skinny neck became revealed. His shirt was open and a piece of woollen undervest appeared across the bird ribs high on his chest. At the side of his throat there was a piece of elasticised plaster. He prised it off cautiously and when the unattractive scrap of sticky fabric lay in his hand he held it out to them. In its centre, embedded in the white adhesive, was a small silvery cylinder, about half an inch long.

Amanda bent over it. 'What on earth is it? It looks like some peculiar kind of transistor valve.'

'Yes,' said Edward and added casually, 'Sam can wear his under his arm where there's not so much danger of it being seen but I can't make mine work unless it's on the jugular itself, and so I have to wear my scarf.' He glanced up at the Canon reproachfully. 'You didn't really think we were being witchy, did you? We do come of scientific families. We don't go in for magic!'

'What is it? What do you call it?' Luke was inclined to splutter.

'The kids call it an "iggy-tube",' Edward could not keep the pride out of his voice. 'That's because of the initials. When it gets going properly I should like to call it *"Longfox's Instant Gen"* if nobody minds, in memory of my father; but of course much of the credit is Sam's. He did some of the worst of the research and now, while he's young, no one can operate it better.'

6

Interested Persons

'I'D much rather leave the boys to the Canon. I certainly don't want to upset Helena.' Luke spoke fervently as he followed Mr Campion into the deserted study.

He was still young, a tall swarthy man, very much the classic cockney, with a dark, shrewd face and narrow eyes whose brows were peaked like gothic gables. A fine policeman, naturally even-tempered, his courage not merely physical and his brains as good as they came. His rise to authority had been swift but was almost unbegrudged and the most extraordinary thing about him was the tremendous nervous force which emanated from him, making him many friends and just a few jumpy enemies.

The untidy room was warm and homely, the neatest thing in it, the evening paper still folded, lying where Mrs Talisman had put it on the edge of the desk.

From force of habit Luke bent over to glance at the Stop Press where there was an announcement about a famous murderer's appeal.

'No reprieve for Toller,' he said softly. 'I can't say I'm surprised. I don't like the idea of him loose again.'

Mr Campion nodded absently. 'How's your Sergeant?'

'He'll live but he'll never walk. The watchman died, so did the constable; only twenty-three. Toller is an evil chap. He hates me too, he'll go to his grave cursing me because I caught him.'

He straightened his back and looked across the room at his friend. He had dismissed the subject and returned to the new and breath-taking problem.

'Well?' he enquired.

'I simply don't believe it,' said the thin man slowly. 'It can't be true.'

'Couldn't it?' There was a streak of naïveté in Luke. It did not appear in the ordinary way but when utterly out of his depth he was, occasionally, prepared to see wonders.

'I can't credit it,' Mr Campion insisted. 'Why hasn't it happened before? People have been trying to do this since civilisation began.'

The Superintendent was not impressed. 'They said that about wireless,' he objected. ' "They'll be catching crooks with it next!" That's what my father said when he first heard of Radio. This is a top secret I grant you. There's no doubt about that.' He paused and his sharp eyes were inquisitive. 'I thought that might have been what Security told you when they sent for you this afternoon?'

The thin man did not answer directly. Instead he said slowly, 'If it's genuine it's sensational. What is that thing exactly and where did the children get not only one but two?'

'We'll soon know.' Luke was amused by him. 'They'll come across. Sam must have pinched it from his father's lab, or workshop or whatever they have down there at Godleys. . . .'

'And nobody missed it? It's not possible. They've had it for months.'

'You never know what the co-operation is like in that sort of a place,' Luke said darkly. 'By all I hear, these backroom boffins can be very human for all their brains. . . .'

'I know, but this is working. It could be demonstrated.'

'Wait a minute.' The Superintendent put up his hand. 'Wait. Is it working? What did Edward keep saying about people being too old to understand it? How old is he, nine?'

'Over eleven.'

'Is he? He's very small. He thinks he's past it. I wonder if . . . ?'

He was silenced by the arrival of the old Canon who came in slowly, carrying a saucer. He put it down on the desk and looked at them questioningly.

'I carried these in like this because I don't think they ought to be dropped. But on the other hand I really don't think the boys should have them, do you? I know there are many remarkable machines in these days but these seem to me to be so *unsuitable*—bad manners, if nothing worse.'

The two grubby cylinders, each in its bed of sticky tape, lay on the flowered porcelain looking unattractive. The younger man regarded them dubiously and the Canon sat down in the visitor's chair.

'I couldn't persuade the boys to tell me where they got them,' he said cheerfully. 'I don't think little Sam knew and Edward was very tense and quite obstinate. The only thing he insisted was that they were not stolen. "They are truly ours" he said and I believed him. I don't think they could have made them, do you?'

Luke, who was investigating the plain silver tubes, looked up. 'Not in a million years!'

'I thought not. So someone has given them to them. I didn't press them. I brought these in here for safety and sent them up to help the girls with the rooms. We shall get on much better in the morning when they've all settled. I wondered if Edward could be under some sort of an allegiance.'

'Who to?' Luke was horrified, his mind leaping to security.

'Oh, some friend, don't you know. Bound by some boyish oath.' It was evident that Avril saw nothing very amazing in the whole business. A great many remarkable devices had appeared in his lifetime. 'He was very reluctant to trust me with these,' he went on. 'I think he feels they are beyond me and fears I might break them or give them to someone unsuitable. They don't look very serviceable, do they? I've agreed to keep them under lock and key.'

'So you shall, sir. In ten minutes.' Luke was taking off his jacket and tie. 'On the jugular, Campion, if you please. Just about *there*, I should say.' He exposed a splendid sinewy throat and sat down at the desk.

The Canon settled down to watch and Mr Campion held out the saucer. 'It's merciful they decided on strapping and not insertion,' he remarked, looking at the mighty vein. 'Any preference?'

'I'll have Sam's; he's the best they said. Now; I'll have a minute by the clock. I'll concentrate like hell. You time me,

Campion, and send me a message. Something unlikely. Right? Off we go.'

He took up one of the patches and slapped it into place and then, closing his eyes, sat back stiff and frowning. It seemed a very long wait. Luke remained perfectly still but he was certainly trying; the room vibrated with his effort. Finally Mr Campion touched him on the shoulder and he relaxed.

'Not a whisper!' His eyes flickered open and he was laughing. 'I'm afraid...' The words faded on his lips and an expression of amazement appeared in his widening eyes. The next few seconds were never forgotten by the men who watched him. He had an expressive face and they were able to see some of the agony which went on behind it. His initial surprise was followed by bewilderment, giving place to anger and then to fear as one emotion after another passed over his mask like the shadows of driving leaves flying across the sky. They saw him struggle to get hold of himself. The sweat came out on his forehead and, as his effort increased and his knuckles grew white on the arm of the chair, it ran down the flanks of his cheeks and on to his neck. Gradually his great strength of character emerged and suddenly, after less than thirty seconds, he put up his hand and tore the plaster away.

'Strewth!' he said.

'What happened?' Mr Campion was looking at him in alarm and the old Canon bent forward anxiously.

The Superintendent shook his head as if he had been under water.

'How long?' he demanded huskily. 'Half an hour? I fainted in the end, did I?'

'The whole thing took less than half a minute.' Mr Campion was too surprised to be tactful.

'Getaway!' Luke was silent for a moment and then got up and stretched himself cautiously. 'I thought I was having a stroke,' he said seriously. 'I'd made up my mind there was nothing there you see, and I relaxed and it got me....'

'*What* did?'

'I don't know, quite.' He mopped his face and neck. 'It was

61

like going barmy, I suppose. I was thinking at tremendous speed, one thought chasing out the next before it had begun. Nothing was related. I was feeling everything very strongly but not for long. Then I got the wind up because I thought I was dying and I tried to get out of the chaos—*It was a brain storm*!' The idea seemed to comfort him. 'That's about it. What do you know! I've had a blessed brain storm!'

'Which cleared up miraculously the moment you pulled this bit of filth off your neck?' Mr Campion bent to retrieve the scrap of plaster where it lay on the carpet.

Luke turned away from it. 'Put it back with the other,' he said firmly. 'The—er—the negative stuff I got was quite incredible. Not at all suitable here.' He looked at Avril apologetically. 'I'd have sworn I hadn't got it in me!' His glance fell on the newspaper before him. 'It was more in *his* class,' he added, nodding at it. 'That's about the quality. If Toller had suddenly got into my skin...?' He broke off and his brows rose. 'Strewth!' he said again. 'He's only just heard his bad news. He could well be thinking of me! But it wasn't only him. There was yards of stuff, hundreds of people. What about you, Campion? Were you trying to send me something? I was aware of you. You were terribly embarrassed about Prune.'

Mr Campion gaped at him, a touch of colour appearing in his thin cheeks. Luke's love affair and the short-lived marriage which had left him a widower with a small daughter was the one and only subject upon which the two friends had never achieved complete understanding. Today, at the beginning of the experiment Mr Campion had first concentrated upon a village inn they both knew, and had then remembered that at the time when the Superintendent had known it best, he had been courting the girl whom all his friends had thought to be the most unsuitable woman in the world for him. A wave of irritation at himself for choosing such an unfortunate subject had passed over Campion. Now, it seemed, this was the only part of his thought which had reached the other man.

He realised that he must make a clean breast of it, if only in the interest of science.

'I was trying to remind you of the pub where they served peacock,' he said unhappily. 'Then it came into my mind that I was a clot for choosing it. I didn't send embarrassment. I felt it.'

Luke sat blinking. 'If emotions come through from outside as well as the thought, it would account for a lot,' he said presently. 'I thought they were all mine and it scared me stiff.'

'Sam said that Mr Pellett's "sucks to you!" was what he called a "feel",' Avril remarked. 'Emotion is a force. It could be the propelling one.'

Luke was still trying himself out, moving his head about and stretching his fingers.

'It's a horror,' he said. 'I couldn't have isolated anything. It was total chaos, confusion.'

'So is an untuned radio set,' murmured Mr Campion.

'This was much worse than that. I wouldn't try it again and I wouldn't let you, not without a doctor. One could be driven stark staring bonkers by this. It's *awful*.'

'Yet you weren't aware of anything at all until you relaxed.'

'That's right!' He was surprised. 'While I was trying to receive I didn't get a thing. As soon as I gave up, it all leapt on me like a pack of wolves. If those children can sort out one person and one thought from that lot they're geniuses ... or perhaps they've got another gadget. What about that?'

'That is it!' said the Canon suddenly. 'That explains why it suits the children and no one else. Their gadget will be built in. The younger you are the fewer people you know, the fewer emotions you arouse and the fewer facts of which you are aware. Children don't receive as much as you do. One can't recognise what one doesn't know.'

Luke was watching him curiously.

'The kids only receive what they know? Getaway! What about all the rest of it? That's enough to frighten anyone out of his wits if he recognises it or not! Toller alone...'

'I don't think so.' Avril was gently adamant. 'The less you know the less you are afraid of the unknown. An infant can listen for his mother's voice in a babel and never miss it; it's the only one which makes any sense, the only one he hears.'

Luke digested the announcement. Then he laughed.

'I'm too old for it,' he said. 'Thank God!' And added after a pause. 'What are we going to do about it?'

Mr Campion met his eyes. 'I was thinking. How do you feel?'

'It'll have to *be* reported.' Luke said at last. ' "Can be worn by young children for long stretches but terrified Detective Superintendent into a coma in less than one half minute." That'll look well in triplicate!'

The matter was still unresolved when Helena came in to tell them that the children were in bed and there was cold food in the parlour. But later still, when the meal was over and was being cleared away, Mr Campion went after Luke who had gone to take a call on the main house telephone from which each floor had an extension. It was housed unexpectedly in the cloakroom, a need overlooked by the original builders and constructed at a later date partly from a cupboard under the hall stairs and partly from a butler's pantry half a floor below. Its design, though practical, was unusual and Campion sat on the short flight of stairs which was one of its features and listened to Luke, who was washing in an alcove under the window.

'That was from my office,' the Superintendent said. He was a little aggrieved. 'Your pals at Security have asked if we'll drop the whole matter of the attempted kidnapping this afternoon. Drop it flat. Just like that. Exactly as they must have called off the school libel suit. No explanation. Hardly a "please".'

'I'm not surprised.'

'Aren't you? Then they know who the woman was?'

'My dear chap, I had to wait until you were officially informed but a report did come in when I was in their office.'

'Did it! And who was she?

'A not very beautiful spy, or so I was given to understand.'

'So Sam was right?'

'It seems so. She is very small-time but is classed as an agent. A car belonging to an Embassy was waiting at the top of the ramp. When she appeared without the children but with someone after her it drove off.'

'Security must have had someone tailing her. He chased her up into the street and lost her.'

'He wasn't tailing *her*. He'd been called off his assignment, which was watching the school. He'd been on the train and had seen the whole incident. He recognised the woman. She's British-with-a-chip and works at one of the bookshops.'

'Why was there a security watch on the school? Or mustn't I ask? Upon my soul, you chaps get my goat. You must spend pounds.'

Mr Campion shrugged his shoulders. 'It was a routine business. Back in the summer a young man whose name was on the American list of doubtfuls applied for and got a job as junior science master at St Josephus. It seemed quite pointless until someone noticed that among the new boys there was a child from a Research Station, Sam. It still seemed rather ridiculous but the Head was tipped off and the young man left.'

'Why was the watch kept on?'

Mr Campion scratched his ear. 'I don't know. The boy was still there, I suppose.'

Luke laughed. 'Money to burn, your lot!' he said. 'You knew all about these things the kids have got, then?'

'I didn't.' Mr Campion spoke fervently. 'What is more I don't, and I shall be amazed if anybody else in our line of country has any ideas.'

'It seems as if the other side has had an inkling.' Luke was peering through a towel, his crisp black curls bristling. 'It's a Godley baby, of course?'

'It must be, I suppose.' Mr Campion sounded very uncertain. 'I know Paggen Mayo is thought to have some sort of electronic device up his sleeve to take the place of something else they had which seems to have petered out—I don't know what it was. But the latest reports are that it's a long way from completion. If this is it, he's succeeded far beyond anyone's wildest hopes and to keep so quiet about it is out of character

C

both in him and Lord Ludor. That's why I'm against you reporting it.'

'I don't see how I can help it.'

'You can, you know. The kidnapping enquiry has been called off. This has nothing to do with you. Look, Charles, if you turn those things in, what will happen to them? They'll go to the Special Branch who will contact us and we shall then have to send them straight to Godley's through open—or at least orthodox—channels. That's so, isn't it?'

'I suppose so.'

'Well, is it wise? I think you may be right about the possibility of inter-team rivalry down there. We may have stumbled on Catherine Wheels within Catherine Wheels and that can so easily lead to rockets all round, if I make myself plain. Let me try and handle it.'

Luke did not reply immediately. Finally he shook his head.

'Someone other than Godley's knows something,' he said, 'or the attempt to get hold of the kids couldn't have been made. What makes you so certain they're safe now?'

'My information is that this particular Interested Party never sticks its neck out through the same bullet hole twice.'

Luke grunted. 'You do know each other, don't you! You all sit and play Happy Families together, no doubt.' He was peering through the curtain out at the square and spoke over his shoulder. 'No one very obvious about out here. There's a white cat. Oh yes, and an enthusiastic courting couple. If they're in your employ you're paying them too much. They're enjoying themselves!'

Mr Campion yawned. 'More likely the Enemy . . . one watching the other.'

'That's right.' Luke had cheered. 'Now I see them more clearly, he's got a pig-tail and she's stamping snow off her boots. Hello!' He craned forward with great interest but a moment later dropped back into the room and let the curtains close. 'It was only the old End of the World man going home. I couldn't think what the hell he *was*, for a moment. He's taking a short cut. He lives somewhere round the back here.'

'Is that the sinister figure in the insanitary cowl who slips up the stairs beside the Church at dusk?' Mr Campion was interested. 'I often see him. He carries his banner face downward; is the work done elsewhere?'

'In the shopping centre as a rule. Oxford Street, Wigmore Street. Round there. Sometimes the real West End.' Luke spoke almost fondly. London characters fascinated him. '"*Death to You All and Good Luck—You'll Need It!*" That's his message or something very like it. His name is Deeds, always called "Good" Deeds of course. We're forever pulling him in to give him a cupper and see how his poor chest is and if he's been to the Assistance Board lately. He doesn't beg, he's got a tiny war wound pension and one of the Nut Societies employs him from time to time to give away pamphlets....'

'Albert?' Helena was calling from the hall. 'Uncle Hubert has tried one of those things and...'

'Oh *no*!' Luke sprang to the doorway. 'It could kill him. The *silly* old boy!'

Mr Campion followed with less anxiety. He had no illusions about Uncle Hubert's nervous stamina and was not surprised to see him sitting behind his desk with Amanda at his side, his face only slightly flushed and that, apparently, with guilt.

'I agree. I should have told someone first,' he was saying. 'It was very stupid of me but you were quite right, a most remarkable experience. It was five past ten when I awoke. I slept in the end.'

The mild answer had had its effect and Luke sat down deflated. 'I think you'll find you passed out,' he said.

'No, Charles. It was sleep. I dreamed. Besides, I was being most careful. Don't forget I'd seen your reaction which was most alarming, but I noticed that it was only when you ceased to concentrate that the impressions began to bombard you.'

'Bombard is right!'

'I know. I saw. So I concentrated in the only way I am able, keeping my mind on words I know well, and I edged my mind out, so to speak, to meet the impact. It was like sharpening a chisel. Did you feel that? The mind touched the grating wheel

67

and the sparks flew for a second or so and then, as I concentrated on the words again, I escaped. This went on, backwards and forwards, until I slept. Concentration is very exhausting and when one is old one drops off to sleep at any provocation, I find. I woke with a tremendous start—you know how one does sometimes? And I found I was thinking of Martin and feeling dismay at something long expected. Some dreadful thing he feared seemed to have happened at last. Then the cacophony—I can't call it anything else—flooded over me again and I just had the sense to pull the thing away. The impression has remained, though. Martin and a sort of surprised dismay that something dreaded had really occurred.'

'Uncle Hubert wants us to telephone the island,' Helena explained nervously. 'But I don't know. It might make a lot of trouble. All calls are monitored and I haven't even spoken to Martin yet about the children's adventure....'

This rather extraordinary fact which had escaped the Superintendent made him turn to look at her. Now that her first terror was allayed, and she no longer saw Sam and Edward as some fearful potential version of the Drummond twins, her natural intelligence had reasserted itself. She looked magnificent, a splendid blonde animal with plenty of courage and commonsense.

'There is a flap on down there at the moment. It began to show at a VIP luncheon they had this morning. I've just been telling Uncle Hubert. I think I must have been deliberately prevented from meeting the children and that does look as if there's someone there in league with the woman who tried to get hold of them.'

'Or the people who sent her,' Luke agreed. 'When you say "a flap on" do you mean that some sort of directive was sent round?'

Helena hesitated. 'It's not quite that sort of place,' she said awkwardly. 'It's more like a fashion house behind the scenes or a theatrical company. All very small and whispery and knives in the back.'

'Jealousy,' Avril observed without censoriousness. 'It's the occupational disease of creation, I'm afraid. Even Jehovah you know.'

'People at the luncheon seemed jumpy, did they?' Luke ignored the interruption. Avril often shocked him a little.

'They did. Paggen had been sent for by Lord Ludor before it began. He was expecting to be asked if he hadn't something to show and he was prepared to stick his toes in, but when we saw him again it was obvious that it hadn't been anything so simple as that.

'All the VIPs were rattled. Lord Ludor was making faces. The American admiral was looking down his nose, the English general seemed explosive and everybody else was fidgety. Martin didn't tell me much because he thinks we ought to obey the rules, and so he never does. But the way he spoke, when he sent me off to the station at last, made it pretty clear that there was going to be trouble and he was glad that Sam and I would be out of it. That's why I don't want to telephone. I don't want to call attention to us.'

'Helena. Do you think Sam is something to do with the excitement down there?' Amanda, who had been unnaturally withdrawn throughout the proceedings, now put the question directly. 'Do you think he has somehow got hold of something he shouldn't, and has given it—or lost it—to someone outside?'

The younger woman regarded her squarely.

'Sam said something odd when I was putting him to bed. He was pretending that he didn't care if his "iggy-tube" was taken away, because he said one of them had been confiscated before but its use hadn't been understood and it had been re-turned——'

'Did he say that was done by a young science master who didn't stay long?' Luke enquired without looking at Campion.

'No. But he did get very excited about his old Gladstone bag which he's been asking for and which seems to have got lost out of our hut. I had to tell him I could only think it might have been stolen and that did terrify him, but it was *Edward* he didn't want to find out about it, no one else.'

'Was there anything valuable in the bag?'

'Nothing at all. Only small-boy junk. No stolen grown-up notebooks or anything like that. We do know about Security down there.'

'What sort of island is it? Is there a road-bridge?' Luke appeared fascinated by the set-up.

'One. It was built by the Romans originally and is still called the Strada. It goes right across the mud and there's a military guard half way across it.'

'Military?' Luke enquired, surprised.

'There's a lot of experimental Government work going on down there,' Mr Campion murmured. 'E.S.P. occupies only one very small section.'

'Oh, I see. In that case . . .'

The telephone interrupted him. There was an extension to the study and the receiver stood on the cluttered desk. Amanda picked it up and her expression changed as she handed it to Helena.

'Yours,' she said. 'Paggen Mayo.'

Helena listened to the insistent voice, which was not quite loud enough for them to hear, with her eyes wide and the colour draining out of her face.

'I see,' she said at last, stiffness in her voice. 'How long will you be?'

Again there was a rush of urgent words and she nodded.

'Very well. No, I'm not frightened. Yes, I think we can get one. In ten minutes then.' She hung up and turned to them, her expression wooden with incredulity rather than alarm.

'It's Martin. He's all right now, but Paggen says they've dragged him out of a gas-filled room and are bringing him here *so that I can see he doesn't do it again*! He had the nerve to ask me if we can find a doctor we can trust! That really is ridiculous. Whatever has happened to Martin, he'd never commit suicide!'

Old Avril looked up. 'Oh no,' he said with complete conviction. 'That is a mistake.'

7

Brains at Work

'PERHAPS Paggen Mayo is hysterical.' Amanda's practical solution of what had appeared to be an insoluble mystery descended on the family group like a balm. 'How long are they going to be?'

'They're in London now.' Helena was bewildered. 'Paggen said he didn't want to ring from the Island and waited to stop at a call box when they got up here. He's leading the way and Fred Arnold is bringing Martin in the little van they use to fetch supplies. Paggen said they had to smuggle him past the guard on the Strada because he's hoping to keep the whole thing absolutely quiet.'

'That's not hysteria, it's lunacy,' said Luke abruptly. 'Unless he's trying to publicise it! Who is Fred Arnold?'

'The barman, the manager of the canteen, and when the big house is being used for VIPs he's the butler. He buys all the stores and he's almost the only ordinary normal person in the place.'

Luke ducked his chin into his neck. 'In that case he's almost certain to be part of the security squad so bang goes any hope of keeping the incident a secret from the authorities. On the other hand it's good news because it means Martin is more or less all right. If Arnold is that type he'd be far too wide to touch him if he wasn't.' He had moved to the window while he was talking and had parted the heavy curtains.

'I thought so. That call came from somewhere very close. Here they are now. A white Jag; and a little green van.'

Helena was in the hall before he had finished speaking and they all followed her and were on the doorstep when the white car, which had been creeping round the square as the driver read the house numbers, pulled up at the kerb.

Paggen Mayo climbed out in a great hurry. He was so full of

himself that he did not see the group in the doorway until he had reached the bottom of the flight of stone steps which ran up to it.

'Mrs Ferris?' He began speaking to Avril as if he thought he was some unlikely butler. 'Oh, there you are, Helena. Good girl! He's in the back of the van. Just conscious I think. Be very tactful dear, won't you?'

It occurred to Mr Campion, as they all trooped down into the street, that the man who instructs a woman how to talk to her husband even in times of stress is either out of touch with reality or up to something, and he wondered which it was in this case.

The van had already arrived and as it pulled up, to everybody's surprise not one but two people got out of the front seats. The driver, a sturdy figure in a Navy-surplus raincoat, climbed out and stood stamping on the pavement looking sheepish, while from the other side, a woman emerged and came swaggering towards them, clearly visible in the light of the street lamps.

She was in her early forties, still good-looking but tight-lipped. She wore a red tweed suit, carried her gloves as if they were a riding crop and came striding into the picture bringing with her an entirely new note of tension.

'Melisande!' Paggen Mayo's exclamation was appalled. 'What are you doing here?'

'I thought you might need help.'

It was not intended to be a serious explanation and he ignored it and turned on the driver, who kept his chin down.

'Mrs Mayo told me you expected her, sir,' he said, his voice smooth, his accent cosily off-white and his manner familiar. 'She rode in the back until she was sure Mr Ferris was all right and then she changed over and came in front.'

'When was this?'

'On the by-pass. She tapped on the side and I stopped and took her in with me.'

'I didn't see her when I looked back.'

'It was dark and you were moving. You wouldn't.'

'But I didn't see her when I stopped to telephone. You were less than a dozen yards behind me in a lighted street....'

'I think she bobbed down, sir.'

It was one of those ridiculous conversations which only take place when both parties are thoroughly rattled. The rest of the gathering got the back of the van open and left them to it.

Martin lay on a heap of cushions; he was snoring and the air in the van was thick with a curious pungent smell.

Luke glanced sharply at Campion and they were lifting the young man out when Mayo came pushing through the group.

'Just a minute, sir,' The Superintendent appeared to flick him aside without using his arms. 'We'll just get him into the air. You get the van closed. I'll take him in.' He lifted Martin bodily over his shoulder and carried him off, Helena at his heels. Mr Campion passed Mayo and his wife over to the Canon and Amanda, and concentrated on the driver whom he led into the house.

Luke had made for the spare bedroom which, with the Canon's own room, was situated at the back of the house a few steps down from the hall, and the Canon and Amanda were shepherding the angry Mayo and his disconcertingly triumphant wife into the parlour.

Mr Campion took Fred Arnold into the study. Luke's sharp enquiring glance when they had first got the van open had not been lost upon him. The symptoms of coal gas poisoning, which are dramatic, were well known to them both and there had been no sign of them on Martin's somewhat pallid face. On the other hand the smell of chloral hydrate, that oldest and most reliable of all the hypnotics, is unmistakable and its pungent reek had rushed towards them as the doors had swung open. Martin had not been in any very great trouble Campion could see and so, knowing the Superintendent, he thought it best to leave the patient to the expert and concentrate on finding a witness.

At first sight the man before him seemed to be an almost perfect example of that most distinctive product of the age, the communal manservant. It is a peculiar type, not particu-

c*

larly happy, as if the hero's friend and knave of classic story had been translated by a multiplicity of masters into the loneliest of dogs, unattached and in business on his own.

He sat on the edge of the visitor's chair looking wary but self possessed and he was wax faced with a shiny skin, a very wide mouth and small bald-looking eyes. His coat collar still stood up round his cropped head and he sat with his fresh pink hands folded and talked with the ease of the expert who is always being asked for advice or information.

'Oh yes, sir. Tonight Mr Ferris behaved just as he always did,' he said firmly. 'For a young man he's got almost un-naturally regular habits. He came in the bar at six and had a drink with Mr Mayo—as he seems to be expected to do—and then he went back to his place to have a wash and a change and a read as usual until seven-thirty, when he always comes up to the canteen for a meal.'

'Does he always eat at the canteen?'

'Always when the boy's at school, unless they're entertain-ing. There's a little of that among the ladies on the island. They try to pretend they're having a life. Mrs Helena had come to London today, though. I knew that.'

'But tonight Mr Ferris didn't come back?'

'That's right. Mr Mayo came in first and told me he was expecting him but that he was late. I keep an eye on the dining room and I issue the drinks for it. After about fifteen minutes Mr Mayo gave up waiting and ordered. You're not giving him much grace I thought to myself, but then Mrs Mayo turned up. . . .'

'Don't they eat together?'

'The Mayos? Hardly ever.' His eyes met Mr Campion's own. 'Well, she's got her daughters and she leads the social set such as it is round the mud huts!' He laughed with his mouth open showing a double row of inturned teeth.

'When did Mr Mayo become actually alarmed about Mr Ferris?'

'Very soon.' There was no mistaking his emphasis. 'He kept fidgeting and then he said he'd telephone, which he did from the bar, and when there was no reply he flew into a panic and nothing would suit him but he must go down at once and see if he was all right. Mrs M. said she'd go with him but he wouldn't have her. It was to be me or nobody, so I went. She came pattering after us. I could hear her.' He threw up his chin. 'We're a funny lot down there, I can tell you!' he said. 'More brains than "common"! But I shouldn't have thought it of Mr Ferris, I really shouldn't. If Mr Mayo hadn't pointed out to me that there was newspaper in the ventilators I should have been absolutely certain it was an accident.'

Mr Campion's brows rose. '*Stuffed* with newspaper?'

'Yes sir, and the gas escaping inside. There he was, sitting at the table with the reading light on and a book in front of him, dead to the wide. He'd got his back to the gas fire; it was half turned on and it wasn't lit.'

'What was the concentration like?'

'Not too bad. All the inner doors were open and it's a high roof in those places.'

'Did you have any trouble yourselves with the gas, getting him out?'

Charley Luke put the question from the doorway. He had come in so quietly that Campion had not heard him but the barman answered as smoothly as if he had been present throughout.

'None at all, sir. You could smell it and it wasn't healthy but we could get in and move him all right. How is he? Not too bad?'

'He'll be O.K. He isn't talking yet but it won't be long.' Luke glanced at Campion and nodded meaningly. 'You carry on,' he said. 'I'll go back to Helena in a minute; she's staying with him.'

'Where was Mrs Mayo all this time?' The thin man asked the barman with the object of putting Luke in the picture. 'I thought you said she was following you and Mayo at a discreet distance?'

'Oh she showed up as soon as we brought him out but when she saw something was up she stopped pretending she wasn't

75

with us. Mr Mayo sent her round the house to unstop the ventilators.'

'You mentioned ventilators before,' Mr Campion said curiously. 'Is the cavity on the outside? That's very unusual, isn't it?'

'No sir. These are sectional buildings with a minimum amount of brickwork but the ventilators, which are compulsory under the bye-laws, come in the solid parts. They're only perforated single bricks themselves, and to keep the wind from blowing through them, strong plastic hoods have been fixed above so the air has to go up and in. Tonight, these hoods were full of crumpled newspaper.'

'Did you notice it first or did Mr Mayo?'

'He did. He called my attention to it.'

'Why was Mrs Mayo told to collect the newspapers?' Luke spoke artlessly and the barman's underlying amusement was intensified although he spoke most respectfully.

'Because she was there, sir. I was working on Mr Ferris, and Mr Mayo was thinking what to do for the best, no doubt. "This could make a bit of scandal and we don't want that. That's vital." he said to me. "He's a very brilliant young man".'

'Those were his exact words, I suppose?'

'They were, sir.' Fred Arnold's eyes remained bold and entertained. 'Mr Mayo has his team to think of. Talk can be very harmful in their kind of world, so he told me. I understood that and it was why I agreed to help by making a run up to the early Covent Garden market. I'd have had to come up some time this week anyway, because the luncheon today ate us out of house and home. So I had an excuse.'

Luke's smile widened as the neatness of the manoeuvre emerged.

'Mr Mayo signed the work ticket for the van, I suppose?'

'He did.'

'Because he wanted Mr Ferris taken past the guards in secret while he was still unconscious?'

'I wouldn't care to put it like that myself, sir, but yes, he did want him off the Island and safe in his wife's hands. So he couldn't do it again, he said.'

'Is that the explanation he gave you?'

'Yes, sir.'

'And you,' murmured Mr Campion. 'You took the very sensible precaution of letting him go on ahead and then persuading Mrs Mayo to ride with you?'

'She didn't take much persuading! She begged and prayed me to take her.' It was the first openly negative sign towards the Mayos he had shown.

'Ah, she likes Ferris, does she?' Luke was sharp and the small eyes, laughing again now, met his own.

'She sees very little of him, sir. It's Mr Mayo she keeps her eye on.'

The piece of information was adroitly delivered and Luke explored another angle.

'When you found Mr Ferris in his hut, had he a glass by him?'

'No. He never takes more than two singles before dinner and he had those at the bar. He bought a round and Mr Mayo bought one.'

'Do you remember what they were?'

'Mr Mayo drank whisky, Mr Ferris pink gin.'

'At the bar?'

'No, they sit at a table near the wall. Always the same one. Mr Ferris fetched the first round, Mr Mayo the second. There's quite a crowd round the bar.'

'Did Mr Ferris happen to tell you you'd overdone the bitters tonight?'

'No sir, he didn't, but I did wonder afterwards. When I was trying to bring him round, I smelled something. I expect you did. It was strong in the van.'

Luke regarded him steadily. 'Are you sure you had nothing to do with that?'

'Absolutely sure, sir. There'd be no point in it, would there?'

'I suppose not. And you didn't see anything?'

'No sir. If I had I should have stopped it. It might redound on me.'

'As it has.'

'I hope not. Frankly, that's why I'm talking to you both, sir. Will you be wanting me to wait?'

Mr Campion, who was in the desk chair between them, put the question that was worrying him.

'How does household gas get on this island?'

'They make it at Tudwick and pipe it over the Strada, sir.'

'And it's ordinary gas?'

'Yes, sir. Tudwick was thought to be going to be a big place at the coming of the railway. The gentleman who lived in our big house at the time was very go-ahead and had everything up-to-date. Then the nineteen fourteen show put paid to all that and the place sank back to nothing until our company took over the whole island estate. The gas and water installation was there so they made use of it. It's cheaper than carting solid fuel.'

'Is it laid on to all these new bungalows?'

'That's right. They're built along the old drive and the gas main runs along it. It's just like a town. Each house has it's own main supply-pipe coming from the big one.'

Luke stood with his hands deep in his trousers pocket, the skirts of his jacket bunching out behind him.

'Are there outside inspection chambers? Little iron traps you'd hardly notice in the flower beds?'

Again the over-intelligent stare met his own.

'It's all rough salt grass round the prefabs. I believe I have seen some of the manhole covers you mean amongst it but I couldn't tell you off-hand which service they belonged to.'

'You see what I'm getting at?'

'I can see the obvious, sir. If the gas supply was turned off for a minute once the fire had been lit, and was then turned on again, it could be very dangerous if a person sitting in the room didn't notice.'

'Or was not in a condition to notice?'

'Exactly, sir. But who's to say?'

The story was perfectly clear and the comment summed up the position with disconcerting accuracy.

The ensuing silence had lasted a fraction too long when the door opened abruptly and Helena came into the room like a whirlwind. She was white-faced and appeared unaware of anybody except the man she had come to find.

'Can you come at once,' she said to Luke. 'He's awake but something's happened. He won't say he didn't do it!'

8

Expert Opinion

'I'M sorry, you fellows. No comment.'

Martin sat on the edge of the bed, his elbows on his knees, his head in his hands. His voice was thick and drunken and his thoughts muddled, but although they had been working on him for some time he had remained adamant. 'Forgive me, Campion,' he said with an attempt at a smile, 'but do take this friendly cop away. I can't tell him anything. If he thinks I was committing suicide, right, I was committing suicide.'

'Martin! You can't behave like this!' Helena had dropped on her knees beside him. 'You're muzzy and you don't see all the inferences.'

'Inferences? There are no inferences. Everybody scram, there's dear good people. If you want to help, get hold of the Island and tell Paggen I'm okay.'

As Mr Campion turned away, he came face to face with Fred Arnold, who was standing directly behind him. The man was taken off guard and open alarm showed for a moment in his small eyes. It faded at once but the query remained. Why the discovery that Martin Ferris was not going to defend himself should frighten a man who had spent the last half hour hinting that the youngster had been framed was more than Mr Campion could fathom.

Meanwhile Luke was having a last shot:

'Did you take the chloral hydrate intentionally, sir?' It was a shock tactic and got results. A flicker of astonishment appeared on the pallid face.

'I don't remember,' he said with exasperating finality. 'I don't remember a thing.'

'Martin!' Helena was frantic. 'You don't see what's happening. Charley Luke only happens to be here because there was an attempt to kidnap Sam.'

'Sam?' He sat looking at her dully. 'Why?'

'Don't you know? Don't you know about this thing that Sam has got hold of?' She was terrified of saying too much but her anxiety overcame her caution. 'It's the device,' she whispered. 'Don't you really know about it?'

Martin closed his eyes with sheer weariness.

'I think you're all crazy. If I don't lie down I'll drop dead at your feet. Goodnight Helena . . .'

'Did you know that Paggen Mayo brought you here and is in the house now?' Campion put the question and at his familiar voice the drugged eyes fluttered open once more.

'You mean *Mrs* Mayo,' the young man murmured. 'You should learn to dif'rentiate between them. They're not particularly alike.' He heeled over on the bed and began to snore.

Luke took Campion by the arm and led him out in the passage while Fred Arnold returned to Helena. 'I'll give you a hand,' he said and was at once respectful and familiar and comforting like a family retainer of legend.

The Superintendent paused at the foot of the flight of stairs leading up into the hall and replied to Mr Campion's murmured question.

'No, I don't think we need a doctor. I'm afraid I don't altogether believe in the sacred discretion of the dear old G.P. any more. If we really want this little dust-up dragged out into the open before we know what the hell has happened, that's the way to get it done. He's all right. You know it as well as I do. He's only had the old original Micky Finn, which is safe, dirty and utterly reliable. There was no real attempt to gas him. It was to look like it, that was all.'

'You're assuming it was a put-up job between him and Paggen Mayo?'

Luke's very white teeth gleamed in the half light.

'I'm blowed if I know. He seems to think *Mrs* Mayo brought him, which is just what he would if he wasn't in any picture himself and merely woke up in the van and found her there.

These clever people take a bit of handling! ... I suppose she's clever too?'

'It doesn't follow,' said Mr Campion. 'Wait! Did you hear that?'

The noise had come from the study. The door was closed but the shout was unmistakable and both men ran up the staircase and across the hall.

The moment they entered the room the situation was apparent.

Canon Avril was sitting in the visitor's chair, his fine face alight with interest and good humour, while in front of him, his shirt collar undone, his hair wilder than usual and black fury on his deeply scored face, was Paggen Mayo. The top drawer of the desk was open and the flowered saucer stood on the blotter. One piece of plaster, complete with tube, lay where Mayo had just thrown it on a pile of sermon paper. Neither took any notice of the newcomers but Mayo leant over the desk and pointed an angry two fingers at the Canon.

'All right!' he said, his voice shaking as he struggled to stop it rising again. 'All right. I don't like hypnotism but I don't deny its existence. I don't have to be made the subject of a demonstration, do I?'

'Sit down, my dear sir.' Old Avril indicated the chair behind the desk and glanced at the newcomers.

'I was telling Mr Mayo about the children's little machines,' he explained without a tremor. 'He said he'd like to see them and I brought him in here to show him how they work. He seems to be as astonished as we were.'

Luke and Campion did not dare to look at each other. The notion that Avril might do anything so uncharacteristically tactless and unwise as to talk about the secrets with which he had been entrusted, and that to the first visitor to arrive and in the first ten minutes, had not occurred to either of them.

Luke held himself to blame for not guessing that the old man might not take any man-made wonder very seriously, but Mr Campion was more disturbed. Ever since he had first encountered Longfox's Instant Gen he had been aware of a sense of inevitability concerning it and he found himself wondering if this most unlikely intervention was part of the pattern of the phenomenon.

Mayo was dressing himself; all his movements were short and angry. He had changed since the morning and now wore a blue suit with a chalk stripe a little too young for him. His pullover was buff and his tie spotted, and he had a matching handkerchief in his breast pocket. All of which had become very noticeable because he himself was almost out of his mind with indecision and bewilderment.

The Canon appeared to understand him completely.

'Don't worry,' he said placidly. 'When one can't credit one's senses it's the most natural thing in the world to feel that someone else is tampering with them. These are such extraordinary little devices though, aren't they? Of no use at all, you see, but interesting if you care for that sort of thing.'

Mayo pulled himself together, turned from the Canon whom he seemed to find frightening, and looked fiercely at the others. 'Who are you?' he demanded.

Luke explained. Listening to him, Mr Campion decided that the Superintendent was assuming, as indeed he did himself, that the devices had sprung from Mayo's own workshop. However, he was being careful not to admit that he thought so; he told the whole story factually and simply and gave his own name and rank before introducing Mr Campion as Edward's guardian. It was a successful move: the expert simmered down and began to think again. That much was evident; they were aware of his intelligence as a swift, hardworking machine starting up again after a particularly bad stall.

He picked up the little bandage and took it under the reading lamp where he stood studying it, his forehead wrinkled.

The Canon, apparently still sublimely unaware of the drama of the situation went on talking.

'As soon as the machine ceases to be a wonder it will cease to be frightening, I know,' he said. 'But at the moment I find it most disturbing, especially when children get hold of it. I feel

83

so strongly that they should learn to think for themselves. There are plenty of ways for them to gather stale ideas as it is. You'll have to harness it, of course, you clever people.'

Mayo took out his wallet and tucked the device into an old envelope. Then he put out his hand for the saucer holding the second one. It was obvious that, whatever he knew about the construction of the exhibit or its place of origin, he had made up his mind about the steps to be taken forthwith. As soon as he had stowed them away in his inside pocket, he drew a sheet of paper towards him and felt for a pencil which he seemed to expect to find under his display handkerchief. As it was not there he took up a ball-point pen from the desk and, with a nod of apology to Avril, turned to Luke.

'I'll give you a receipt for these, Superintendent,' he said. 'That'll cover us both if there's an enquiry. Will that suit you?'

'I'll certainly have to have one, sir,' Luke showed his relief and glanced at Campion. 'Is that all right with you?'

'Why shouldn't it be?' Mayo turned on the thin man suspiciously. 'What have you got to do with this?'

Mr Campion did not answer and the Expert hesitated: 'I was going to add that in my belief everybody in this room is entirely innocent,' he said abruptly. 'I hope so.'

'Then it is "truly yours", is it? My dear fellow, I can't tell you how relieved I am!' The Canon's declaration startled everybody. His sincerity was beyond question and Mayo's colour deepened.

'It's certainly Government property and should never have got into outside hands,' he said mendaciously. 'There'll be a row about it, naturally. However, I shall do what I can for everybody concerned. The only warning I can give you now is to hold your tongues. If this gets out, the consequences could be grim.' He paused, and they had time to assess him. He was keyed up, still very angry.

'Keep those kids quiet,' he said. 'Don't let them out of your sight until you've trained them to put all they know about this clean out of their minds, and just remember that, at this stage, anybody at all can be damn dangerous. Not all spies work for foreign powers. There you are, Super: *"Received: two experimental E.S.P. Tr. Amp. Suspected N.400 type"*. That should cover us both. Now, the sooner I get to work on these the better.'

'Don't you want to see the children?' Luke seemed nervous. 'They're the only ones who know where they got them.'

Mayo put his head on one side. 'Are they, indeed?' he said derisively. The inference that Martin alone could be the source of supply was obvious and Luke appeared almost to agree with him. Mr Campion managed to look innocently affable.

'I think I should just see Ferris before you go,' he suggested. 'I hate to say it but a thumping mistake at this juncture might be a considerable embarrassment for all concerned, don't you think?'

'Embarrassment!' Mayo was shaking and it occurred to them all that it was the Canon's "occupational disease of creators" which was consuming him so agonisingly before their eyes. 'I'm afraid you really must let me handle this as best I can, and in my own way. You don't understand. You can't realise that you've been monkeying with something revolutionary. The whole world's communications industry could be affected by this, not merely one country's defence system!' He was becoming more and more furious as the position crystallised in his mind. 'There are certain people,' he went on, biting off each word, 'who are so damned brilliant, such ruddy geniuses, that they think that everybody else's work is child's play, and it doesn't matter destroying it, pinching it, or giving it away! There are famous Professors whose feet don't touch the ground at any given point, and pathetic young men who are dazzled by their academic glory and bloody snobbishness generally and are liable to go off their cocky young heads. They see a chance to make a splash and they forget their elementary loyalties. They destroy their own interests and get themselves,—and the poor hard-working so-and-sos who are supposed to lead the teams they're paid to work for—into the father and mother of a mess. We're living in the damndest crazy world. I can tell you that.'

Avril cleared his throat.

'How are you going to square me with Edward?' he said. It was a most unexpected remark and Mayo's response to it was even more so.

'Oh yes,' he said. 'You told me he trusted you with them. Exactly. Well now, I think you'd better give him this.'

He took out his wallet again and produced a card.

'What's his name? Longfox? Right. "*Admit Edward Long-fox*." See? I've written that on the back. You give it to him and tell him I'll be very happy to see him any time. How's that?'

It was a curious little incident and both Luke and Campion were uneasily aware of a quality in the man which neither had suspected. The old Canon took the card. He seemed very satisfied.

'Thank you. You'll find him very intelligent. He was telling us that young Sam can use this machine so much better than he can. The younger boy is as yet so inexperienced and recognises so little that what he is able to receive doesn't swamp him.'

It was an elementary observation to them all now, but they saw it hit the target like a starshell, and for the first time they caught a glimpse of what it means to tackle a problem which only a combination of several very different types of mind can solve.

Mayo stood looking at the old man. 'The human unit has built-in valves then?'

'Possibly,' said Avril who was not at all clear on the subject. 'Can we get you a cup of tea?'

It appeared to be the end of the incident. Mayo was anxious to leave and like so many enthusiasts seemed liable to turn a social escape into a jail break if anything threatened to hinder him.

'I shall slip away at once, alone, if you don't mind,' he said hastily. 'My wife can go back in the van with Arnold.'

'Oh no, she can't, my dear!' The voice from the doorway was triumphant and Mrs Mayo, a little brighter than life, came into the room followed by a depressed Amanda. 'I told you,' she went on, looking back at her hostess. 'I was absolutely certain of it. I've been expecting it. That was why I came.' Her glance rested on her husband with open hostility, and she laughed. 'Lord Ludor may still trust him. I'm afraid I can't.'

She was neither drunk nor drugged, and indeed looked remarkably healthy and most unlikely to be the victim of some toxic condition, but everybody in the room recognised her typical symptoms with the same sense of dismay.

The breaking middle-class wife, driven by one of twenty possible short-comings of her own or her husband's, strained by a speed of living for which she was not designed, and permitted by the absence of any cast-iron code of manners to destroy them both by public attack, was a figure of the second post-war period. Melisande Mayo was a casualty as familiar and distinctive to the group in the Rectory as any gang of mods and rockers out for a bash and the fact did not make her any easier to have about the house.

She stood just inside the room, forcing Amanda to step round her. She was obviously desperately unhappy but was enjoying a change of torment and revelling in the general unease.

Mayo looked at her as though she had not said anything at all.

'I'm taking the Jag,' he said. 'I want to hurry.'

'I'm driving,' she persisted, the silly, obstinate smile still on her good-looking face. 'I'm your chauffeur-secretary, I believe? The accountant thinks so!'

'No.' In his own way he was as out of touch with reality as she was. 'I want to go alone.'

'Of course you do! It's tonight you're going, isn't it? I knew it as soon as I saw you putting something in Martin's gin....'

As he started and swung round on her in fury a little excited laugh escaped her.

'I did. I came into the bar and I saw you. That's why I came up with him.' She smiled round at the company, apparently inviting applause. 'I thought the poor boy should have someone to look after him.'

The remark fell flat. Nobody spoke. Mayo behaved like everybody else. He looked embarrassed but not any more than Luke; each man was inclined to stare woodenly in front of him.

Melisande Mayo was still carrying her tortured gloves and now she went so far as to slap the back of a chair with them.

'You don't consider what it will be like for me and the girls,' she said accusingly. 'We shall be pariahs. I suppose you are counting on us staying put until you care to send for us. You're making a great mistake. I shan't follow you through any iron curtain, my lad.'

She knew at once that she had gone too far and her laugh was for the first time nervous rather than delighted. 'Well, I shan't,' she said, but the fire had gone out of her and he began to walk towards her.

'You're raving,' he said mildly and the accusation was so reasonable in the circumstances that they could hardly help agreeing with him. 'I must go. I've got a lot of work to do tonight.'

'I shall drive you then.' She was still standing between him and the door, daring him to move her by force in their presence, and he took the wind out of her sails by capitulating.

'Very well, you drive me,' he said. 'But one of these days you'll get me shot. You're living in cloud-cuckoo land.' There was no anger in his attitude towards her. He was resigned, and on the whole patient, like a man with a very old illness. 'I must have a word with Arnold. Then we'll go.'

He stepped past her and called the barman's name down the hall. The response was suspiciously immediate and they went off together at once and stood at the top of the front steps just out of earshot.

Left with her unwilling audience Melisande Mayo regained her terrifying self possession. She gave them a sick little smile but the glitter of uncertainty still flickered over her.

'I'd better go after him before he cooks up something else with that poor little man,' she said. 'He doesn't care in the least if he gets him sacked. It's absolutely nothing to Paggen who gets hurt so long as his work is appreciated. That's the trouble between him and Martin. Professor Tabard understands Martin and appreciates him, but he can't be bothered with Paggen and Paggen simply can't make himself clear to the old man. He has to rely on Martin now. That's what makes the poor man so insanely jealous. Martin doesn't even notice it. It's pathetic, isn't it? Well, goodbye. It's been awfully nice to meet you, Lady Amanda.' The final remark was accompanied by the shy ghost of a pleasant smile, and Amanda seized the moment of blessed formality and offered her hand.

'Goodbye, Mrs Mayo. I'll see you to the car.'

Luke moved over to the window and watched them go.

'There she is, in the driving seat,' he said. 'She's got her own way. What a performance! She's going to make him notice her if she kills him.'

'She will, if she's going to say really dangerous things like that about him before every stranger.' Mr Campion was still shaken. 'I suppose he *is* all right, Charles? He hadn't seen those things before, had he? I mean, I take it we haven't just taken part in the greatest clanger of our joint careers?'

'Oh no, my boy. That was just her mischief.' The Canon was confident. 'Martin was telling me about him last time he came up to see me. Mayo is a most distinguished man and I was so glad to meet him. He's just the person to deal with those dreadful little machines. I really felt he was Heaven-sent. Martin has an enormous admiration for Paggen Mayo and he said he would trust him with his life.'

'Which he appears to have done tonight unless he's stalling,' muttered Luke, glancing at Campion with sudden misgiving. 'No,' he went on presently, answering himself, 'the Canon is right. He's a Government Number One, and he'll have been vetted by Security pretty well once a month as routine. Besides, as you said yourself, we'd only got to be good boys and

turn those things in and he'd get them anyway. I think the
lady is probably right about his jealousy of Martin. That
could account for all this, you know. It's mad but they live
mad lives.'

Mr Campion considered the suggestion.

'It went through my mind that the whole thing might be an
attempt to undermine Martin's prestige,' he admitted. 'It was
the only thing that made any sense—"attempted suicide: not
suitable for responsibility: only valuable if in a subordinate
position under Mayo". That sort of thing.'

'Martin believes that man has a very difficult time,' Avril
observed, ignoring the last part of the conversation. 'Obviously
he has a most uncomfortable marriage. When one is as clever
as that I suppose one has no time to live. He certainly has
none for her, poor woman.'

He noticed the card which was still in his hand and put it
on the shelf. The sight of it waiting there appeared to turn
over a fresh page in his mind and he stood looking at the
pasteboard with dawning misgiving.

'Of course, I could have insisted that we woke Edward and
that the boy gave his treasures to Mr Mayo himself,' he said at
last. 'How extraordinary of me not to do that.' He turned to his
nephew. 'What am I to say to the child?'

'Say you acted for the best, sir.' Luke was trying to be comforting and was surprised by the sudden startled look in the
intelligent old eyes.

'My goodness, I hope so!' said Avril. 'But there's no guarantee, you know. And no escape from the consequences even if I
did.'

9

The Promenading Cat

IT was after midnight when Mr Campion let himself out of the rectory and stepped into a well-lit but deserted city whose polished streets shone like skating rinks and whose tall, stucco houses were quiet and dark.

He noticed the white cat as he approached the steep drive leading down out of the square and recollected that Luke had mentioned it earlier. It was the kind of cat he liked because of its long front legs and high cheekbones, but he noticed the single smudge of tabby on the end of its tail which belied its air of breeding. It eyed him contemptuously as he came up with it and jumped up on to the balustrade as he passed. He gave it no great thought.

He was about to attend to his own homework. At the moment his link with Security was personal rather than professional. Once upon a time he had done a great deal of work for that curious Alice-in-Wonderland body which is purely civilian and contrives to have no specific master, no powers, and no means of defending itself save by adroit evasion, but which exists to protect the Realm within the Realm for just those precise periods when it can be shown to be in danger and for not one instant longer.

Mr Campion knew L. C. Corkran, the Director of the day, rather better than a brother since they had spent a war together, and that morning, after the incident at the railway station, he had been taken back on the strength in a temporary, unpaid and senior capacity. As he strode through the deserted streets he regretted his lost illusions. He was truly sorry he was not seeking some colourful contact lurking, perhaps, in a cabman's shelter, or, better still, conducting some unlikely bureau in a cupboard half-way down the emergency staircase of an underground station. As it was, he was merely looking for that safest of all telephone lines, the one belonging to a public call box one has never used before and never intends using again.

All the evening he had been trying not to think too much about the possible consequences of the extraordinary development the children had brought in. The one conclusion he had permitted himself was that so far as one could see, it was now only a discovery and hardly a working invention, but, as he had tried to suggest to Luke, the inventions would certainly come later. All that had been proved so far was that thought could be transferred from one mind to another sometimes, and that the process could be mechanically assisted, at least as far as reception was concerned. The transmitting end was still very dark. In the wrong hands...? He was off again, the thoughts racing. Which were the right hands, which the wrong hands? Scientific hands? Business hands? Government hands? Foreign hands? Kind but stupid hands?

He took a deep breath, dismissed the question from his mind and hurried on. Meantime he was glad to feel ordinary precautions were still important.

He crossed Portminster Row and walked out of one postal district into the next. It took him a little time but presently he found what he wanted. This was a single kiosk in a cul-de-sac at the back of a department store. It was well lit and there was only one approach to it.

He rang a Hampstead number which he had memorised that morning and was answered immediately by a rather prissy woman's voice, a little severe but very intelligent.

'Who is that?'

'It's me, Dearest.' It was not his favourite form of address but he had no choice in the matter.

'Who? No, don't tell me, let me guess!' Incredible! he thought. A voice like that made nonsense of the whole romantic subterfuge.

'All right,' he said dutifully. 'But I'm hurt.'

'Hurt?' That was the operative word. Now she should have identified him.

'Hurt as hell!' he assented.

'Mephy! Don't be such a rude boy!' She was so supremely arch that he wondered if the script was of her own devising. 'Aren't you late! I'm in bed, you know.'

'Lucky you! I haven't had a moment till now. Listen to my excuse.' Identification being complete he settled down to the message. If she were good at it, and he thought she might be, this was far and away the safest and most flexible of all telephone codes, but until one knew one's colleague one could not be too subtle. He started in clear.

'We had unexpected visitors; three from the seaside.'

'I know you did!' Apparently she was determined to sound like a teasing headmistress. 'You'll never guess who rang Elsie just now and told us all the gossip. Fred did. But perhaps you don't know him?'

So Corkran was "Elsie" still, he noted.

'Of course I know Fred!' he said and tried her out. 'But I knew old Matthew better.'

'His brother?' She was on the ball at once. 'I remember him. He used to write poetry.' Matthew Arnold—Fred Arnold. No cross-word expert could have been neater. 'Our news about Fred is that he's suddenly got attached to Elsie,' she went on. 'He used to have all his time monopolised by his firm, they thought so highly of him. But this morning he heard he's got a bit of a holiday at last and he's told Elsie he's all for *her*! She's very pleased. She likes him but he's not a regular boy friend yet. He'll make a spare, she says.'

'Third grade?'

'Fifth more likely!' she said, laughing.

'Congratulations!' He meant it. She was very careful and remarkably clear. He forgave her for her voice. He had now been told that Fred Arnold, the barman, was a minor colleague of his own, beginning operations only that morning, and accepted on the recommendation of the firm of Godley who had been employing him as a 'personal observer' for some time. Security was following its usual procedure and trusting the man as little as possible to begin with, but they thought he might prove useful. He had already reported on his trip to London this evening, telephoning presumably on his way to the market immediately after leaving the rectory.

'Well now,' Campion said, giving her time to get over the compliment. 'Did you hear about our clever young man who was taken ill and brought to London?'

'The American? Poor boy! It wasn't serious though, was it?'

'No, but it was unexpected and not what we thought at first, so of course we were worried. I shall satisfy myself and see he's all right.'

'Elsie said she thought you would. Of course, she didn't mention you to Fred.'

'Well, she wouldn't, would she? Did she know the old sinner brought a certain married lady up with him?'

'My dear man! Fred couldn't stop talking about her, she'd frightened him absolutely stiff. Elsie needed all her sense of humour!'

'Wonderful sense of humour Elsie's got!' he said drily. 'The lady is a great talker, you know.'

'You're telling me!' The voice could produce an off-white accent but could not lose its essential severity. 'Elsie always says she's mental. Her husband is such a good worker but if she doesn't stop talking balderdash they'll lose their "council house" down there.'

'But Elsie doesn't believe all the lady's fairy stories, does she?'

'Good Heavens no!' She was genuinely amused. 'The woman is always expecting her husband to leave her and the family. Talking of families, Fred said you'd found some wonderful new children's toys for Christmas. Very up-to-date I gather. When do we get some?'

'Damn! I was hoping to surprise you!' He was startled and covered it. 'How did Fred know about them?'

'Don't be so jealous! Fred overheard that young mother talking to her American husband when he was ill. She was telling him the new toys weren't quite right yet but that the children were trying to get them to work. Fred didn't hear any more, he said.'

'He's right. I've seen them. They're not much good as they are. We gave them to the top electrical expert to see what he could do with them. He wanted to take them home so we let him.'

'You couldn't do anything else. They'd be bound to go to him to be mended in the end.'

'That's what we thought. He was fascinated by them. He hadn't seen them before, you see. I was surprised, I thought his present firm had made them.'

He realised that he had shaken her. The interval before she spoke was appreciable and that was against the rules of the game, only complete evenness of exchange kept the conversation dull and quiet.

'Fancy!' she said at last, and added almost immediately. 'You're wrong, you know. They must have originated there.'

'I don't think so.'

'I do. They are the only people who do that sort of work. On the mechanical side, I mean.'

'I wondered if these novelties were imported.'

'Oh, I really shouldn't think so. I haven't heard of anyone manufacturing anything of the sort anywhere else. After all, we've been trying to get something on these lines for our little nephews for quite a time now. We'd have been told.'

'Never mind,' he said. 'We live and learn!' The cliché was a recognised rest sign and having delivered his message he changed the subject.

'You know there was a spot of legal bother? It's been settled out of court. I heard this evening. Did Elsie put her oar in?'

'Well, she doesn't like tales out of school, if that's what you mean.'

It was and he laughed to tell her so.

'I must say goodnight,' he said. 'Things are very quiet. If you hear of anything coming my way, let me know.'

'Oh, I will. There's been a rumour that there were some people who had your outfit in mind and it's been confirmed at

95

last, so you may be approached any time now. The name is Fungi.'

'I'll remember. Are they those contractors who collect pairs of little things at railway stations?'

'Oh, no, I don't think they'd ever do that. These people are not very big and they're British—I'm trying to get you their address. No luck so far.'

'Well, if I should hear anything interesting I'll let you know. Will you be home tomorrow night if I ring?'

'No. I shall be at my other sister's, the one at Welbeck. Goodnight, Mephy.'

'Goodnight, Dearest.'

As he hung up he reflected on her last piece of information. The existence of an espionage organisation in touch with the work being done at Godley's had been confirmed. They were nothing directly to do with the people who had inspired the attempt on the children, but were thought to be one of the small networks which had become so common of late in large cities. The nickname Fungi had been given to these because they resembled patches of dry rot, their ever-growing tentacles streaming out very quickly from a parent eye. These rings came and went and were often used for a specific job and then disbanded, so that they were very difficult to seek out and destroy. Any agent who showed special aptitude remained on the books and could be pounced on at any given moment to form the nucleus of a new ring.

It was a filthy business, as chill and stinking as dry rot itself. Individuals were usually bound to the parent stem by blackmailing holds but only the few who were natural traitors, the instinctive children of decay, became the spores from whom each little patch of disruption sprang.

Campion came out of the kiosk very satisfied with Dearest. As soon as her tape was typed out, the information, both given and received, would be there perfectly clear for her to put into formal language for the record. Meantime, no one who had picked up an isolated sentence or so of their spoken conversation would have been tempted to listen. There had been no identifying names, no intimacies and nothing in the least entertaining. The non sequiturs would not have been discernible unless one had listened carefully, by which time the main thread, if ever noticed, must have been lost forever. The secret lay in the pace. When conducted properly the stream flowed on steadily and soporifically in a flood of commonplaces like the droning of a couple of bees.

He walked down towards the main street which ran across the mouth of the cul-de-sac, his mind busy with the practical side of the position. The children were said to be safe now that the attempt had failed so openly. He thought they probably were, at least for the moment.

Much more worrying was the question of the mind behind their experiments with the devices. Who was the puppet master? Until Mayo's convincing disclaimer he had assumed that it must be Martin working with Mayo, which indeed was why he had been so anxious to avoid questioning the youngsters himself until he was sure. Now, presumably, it was Martin plus someone unknown.

As he reached the wide thoroughfare which, in the daytime, was a steady mass of crawling traffic, Mr Campion was thinking how remarkably few unknowns had appeared in the story so far. Fred Arnold was almost the only stranger and he had been explained almost as soon as he had appeared. It had just occurred to him that the horizon was almost suspiciously empty when he saw the white cat. It was the same cat. He had no doubt of it for he saw the disfiguring tail tip, as distinctive as a label. It came bounding across the glassy roadway, paused to look up at him, arched its beautiful back and leapt away again.

He assumed it had followed him, coming for a walk as cats do, not at heel like a dog but keeping at discreet distances on either side. He was surprised he had not noticed it before. If it was like any other cat he had ever known it ought to have crossed his own path a dozen times whilst working out its own erratic but roughly parallel routes. He was about to call to it when it rushed on down the path away from him and as he turned to look after it he saw something that startled him.

The cat was not his own escort; it had a master. In the distance, walking quickly in the direction of the West End, was a single figure. All he could see of him was that it was a man, tall, thin and well muffled. The harsh sodium light had taken every shred of colour out of his clothes and smoothed out every crease and contour. Campion stood watching until he disappeared. It was nothing, just an odd incident. Yet someone had been in the square for most of the evening and someone had walked behind him to the cul-de-sac and someone was now going home at a considerable pace. The white cat was going with him.

10

Husbands and Wives

MR Campion slept later than usual and awoke to find Amanda standing before him, holding a cup of tea.

'Drink this,' she said, adding darkly, 'it may well be the nicest thing of the day!'

They were in the suite which had once belonged to Avril's only daughter, one of the star designers in the famous old dress house of Papendeik. Much of the original furnishing remained and Campion sat up now in a gay four-poster, slenderly elegant and hung with demurely patterned grey and white linen. Amanda was elegant herself in a formal housecoat tailored in billiard-table cloth, and she sat down on the end of the bed, grinning at him.

'Did they wake you?'

'Who?' It was particularly good tea and he marvelled afresh at her effortless efficiency. 'Nothing woke me but the desire to see you again.'

'Martin and Helena quarrelling.' Her triangular smile had appeared for a moment but her eyes were anxious. 'They forgot how thin these old floors are. I wondered if I ought to whistle or let them have it out.'

'Of course, they're upstairs, aren't they? He probably feels lousy but I thought last night how fond she was of him.'

'She is. This isn't a fight to the death, little more than an Oh-my-God-and-bang-the-door, but they keep mentioning us and they're probably coming down, so I thought you'd better be prepared to meet the impact.'

'How wise I was to let you marry me! I'm not too bright this morning. I've been thinking about Edward's little contribution to world knowledge all night. Where is he?'

'Having breakfast with poor Uncle Hubert.'

'Oh dear. What a "do" that was. What possessed the old boy?'

She leaned forward and spoke earnestly.

'You think Martin is working with somebody on the side and they've tried those devices out on the children because the boys are so good at it?'

He avoided her eyes. 'I feel Mayo could be hell to work with,' he murmured. 'Obstinate and in some ways utterly thick-headed. The professor is probably the key. He's a great brain and they are capable of anything.'

Amanda lay back against the bedpost in a graceful emerald festoon. 'Mrs Mayo told me that her husband didn't trust his own team,' she admitted. 'But then she told me rather a lot. I feel Martin is utterly loyal; he's that kind of boy. He doesn't notice that Mayo is jealous of him even; the idea would strike him as absurd. I'm sure he isn't behind this.'

'I'd like to agree with you, my love.' Mr Campion was sincere. 'But I don't see anybody else, do you?'

'We'll tackle Martin,' she declared and added, as a knock sounded on the sitting-room door, 'instantly, I'm afraid.'

Martin came in alone. He was unshaven and in a dressing gown but he looked much better. He was a little embarrassed and extremely apologetic.

'I'm so sorry about intruding like this,' he began, 'but I'm half out of my mind with curiosity. Helena tells me that these damn things I missed were strapped on *a pulse*! Is that really true?'

'On a pressure point,' said Amanda. 'This one down here in the neck.'

'Is that honestly true? Did you see it? Are you sure it wasn't a nerve centre? Helena won't let me talk to Sam. She's taken him down to the Talismans.' He saw their astonished expressions and reddened. 'I'd say it's my fault,' he admitted, 'but I'm knocked over by this business. It seems Sam brought home a letter from the headmaster. He didn't give it to her until early this morning and I've not been in a condition even to read it yet! I shall get round to it in a minute or two but first

I've just got to know about these crazy things. I hear Paggen was in the house last night. Did he see them, for God's sake?'

'He tried one and took them both away with him,' Amanda said briskly. 'Look Martin, can you explain a bit, please?'

'Gosh! I wish I could.' There was a flash of his normal charming smile. 'But this puts me back in square one. Strapped over a pulse! It's utterly fantastic but, in my own opinion, just possible. I've been bawled out by Paggen time and again for muttering something not unlike this.'

Mr Campion sat watching him. If this was a histrionic performance it was amazing. On the other hand, if it were not, then he himself was back at square one with a vengeance.

Amanda breathed deeply. 'Albert and I were wondering if you were the explanation,' she remarked. 'We thought you might have given the things to Sam and he had shared them out at school.'

'Helena said that!' Some of his resentment echoed in his voice. 'I find that preposterous. I wouldn't trust a delicate, secret device like that to a little boy, especially if it was anything like as successful as you say. And this idea of me not questioning my own kid strikes me as beyond belief.'

Mr Campion sighed. 'I am no scientist,' he said. 'Anything I'm told about these infernal machines must be in words of one syllable and even then they may trickle off the old drake's back. All I know is that someone appears to have succeeded in mechanising telepathy and so far hasn't done it very well. The point about the pulse escapes me altogether. Why do you find that fantastic?'

'Because it's contrary to the present theory. We have assumed a wave—not a sound wave, of course—carrying an electrical impulse. As you know, the brain generates a certain amount of electricity.'

'Does it? I see. You'd have expected any successful contraption to be applied to the head?'

'Naturally. Paggen's own new device, which I admit is nothing like as advanced as this thing sounds to be, is contained in a great fibre-glass helmet.' The fascination which the subject held for him was smoothing away his hangover and his face was alive and eager. 'I keep being nagged by the idea that the wave hasn't been identified yet. I wonder if there couldn't be some non-electrical method of linking intelligences.'

'Perhaps,' said Amanda, 'the link is not between intelligences, but each intelligence does its own decoding? I mean, suppose an aborigine gets a flash from a sophisticated person who has stumbled on a crashed airplane. Does he get *"Terrible disaster: machine burning"* or *"Exciting: bird on fire"*?'

He shook his head. 'I just wouldn't know. I'm highly conservative. It's only because the phenomenon of thought transference and also of prophecy, which seems to be linked with it, has been recorded ever since writing began that I go on banging my head on the door. I admit I've speculated on the possible role of the nervous system in all this—panic, mass hysteria and that extraordinary phenomenon, infectious euphoria in the young. They're none of them necessarily mental——'

Mr Campion was hugging his knees, trying to drive his mind down the unfamiliar paths presented to him.

'The pulses, the circulation of the blood,' he remarked. 'Consanguinity, love at first sight, heart to heart. *"Trad"*! Martin, my lad, that's where this is taking you. Tell me, what exactly is *"Tr. Amp. N. 400"*?'

Martin stared at him. 'Where did you get that, for Heaven's sake?'

'It was on the receipt which Mayo gave Luke in return for the devices. Transistor and amplifier I can guess but what is N. 400?'

'But that's so like our own! I mean it sounds so like an enormously simplified version of Paggen's device. My God, he must have hit the ceiling! You see, once the existence of E.S.P. was proved ... that was done by work on some twins who were found in the navy ... the difficulty was how to break in. Paggen's first idea was to amplify the signals. The only substance which seems to have any effect at all on the subjects of the various experiments is a carbonised form of the new element Nipponanium. My old chief, Bolitho at Pittsburgh, has been examining this and its effects on degrees of the brain's sensitivity both towards sound and in E.S.P. tests. Professor Tabard is in touch with him but we haven't had a lot of success. Paggen is most anxious not to show anything yet but we have hopes. These devices of yours sound out of this world.'

'Wait a minute.' Mr Campion was making an effort. 'All this is very tough going for me. I know two things only about Nipponanium. It's the last of the new elements discovered since nuclear fission; it was isolated in Japan from a consignment of radio-active carbon imported for eventual medical detective work. Is it the one you use to adulterate aluminium?'

'No. That's Germanium. Otherwise you're not very far out. Campion, I've just got to see these things. You say Paggen has them? I must get down there. I can't telephone because there's no such thing as a reasonably reticent wire to that island, let alone a private one. If we became in the least technical there'd be trouble in no time. I'll have to get hold of a car.'

Mr Campion ventured to intervene. 'Just a moment,' he said again. 'Have you formed any theory about how you got here last night?'

Martin coloured. 'I was wondering what to say about that,' he confessed gloomily. 'Paggen's had enough to put up with lately without me talking about it, but I guess the dark secret of Melisande is not so hush-hush any more?'

'Has she formed some sort of attachment to you?'

'Oh, gosh no! Nothing like that, thank God.' He looked so appalled that they almost laughed at him. 'She's just hysterical. He's been worried about her for some time. She has crazy ideas about him. Doubtless you heard some of them last night?'

'She chattered away,' said Mr Campion lightly. 'Does she do it often?'

'More so lately. I believe it used to be kept for home consumption.'

'I suppose Mr Mayo has been dealing with it by walking out

on her and thinking of something else?' Amanda suggested delicately.

'Well, yes, that's exactly what he did do.' He smiled apologetically. 'He's so busy. He kept it all quiet until she put the bite on him the other day by making an absolutely fantastic allegation about his loyalty—in the canteen of all places! Paggen smoothed it over at the time but he told me about it afterwards. Since then she must have got worse and worse and I'm afraid neither of us realised it.'

'And then came last night?' murmured Mr Campion.

'Aren't you right! Last night I woke up in Arnold's van with Melisande beside me. She told me that Paggen was kidnapping me while he went ... oh well, it doesn't matter. Anyway, she scared me and I realised in dismay that she'd given up talking and started to act! Then I passed out again. Maybe she'd drugged me or maybe I fainted, I was scared enough.'

'Mr Mayo was there, you know,' said Amanda. 'In a car in front.'

'So Helena said.' He was completely puzzled. 'I suppose he found out what Melisande was up to and followed us and decided I was safest here. He took her home, didn't he?'

They nodded but neither seemed satisfied and he tried to give them the story as he saw it. 'Melisande always wants to annoy Paggen and take his mind off his work,' he said. 'She knew he'd set his heart on doing a bit this week-end and had got me to give up my leave to help him. She was removing me so as to hold up the work. It's as simple as that.'

Mr Campion and Amanda wished it were, for his sake. The single-minded approach of the dedicated artist, let alone scientist, was not unknown to them and they hoped profoundly that he would not be too hurt when he found his loyalty in question.

However, the problem was shelved temporarily by an unexpected development. Helena tapped on the door and came sweeping in, looking like some restoration beauty in a tantrum, in her quilted blue silk gown.

'It's true,' she announced without preamble. 'I didn't notice it last night, but now that he's had a whole twelve hours without the beastly thing you can see that everything the man says is true! Oh Martin, what shall we do?'

'Helena, my dear girl, what's the matter?' Martin tried to put an arm round her but she escaped from him and held out a closely typewritten sheet to Amanda. 'You must all read this,' she said. 'This is what the headmaster says. Read it. Then tell me if I can be blamed for refusing to have the child involved for one single second longer.' Amanda took the letter and the others read it over her shoulder. It proved to be a confession from a man who was not used to finding himself at such a loss.

'Dear Mrs Ferris:

'I have been wondering if I should ask you to visit me so that we could talk about Sam. But on second thoughts I postponed tackling the problem until you had him with you once again and could observe for yourselves the new outlook which he has developed so surprisingly.

'When Sam first entered the school I remember thinking that he was one of the most normal youngsters I had ever accepted. At the end of last term, however, and during the whole of this one, the other masters and myself, have all noticed a change in him. It was very slight at first, but is now so marked that I do not feel I should be justified if I failed to call your attention to it.

'To be frank, he has developed a dreamy preoccupation which is affecting his work.

'Dr Page has examined him and assures me he is perfectly fit and his relationship with other boys is normal and friendly. I have interviewed him on three occasions and have talked to him very seriously. Boys do sometimes have the most extraordinary worries but I have never met one before who was both so undisturbed and yet so curiously self-absorbed.

'The masters with whom I have discussed the problem tell me that his work has become peculiarly erratic, varying from
D*   105

brilliance in class to crass stupidity on paper. Mr Short, whom you may remember is our junior man in mathematics, reports that Sam appears to proceed by divination alone, often dropping into absentmindedness but returning suddenly with a correct result which he is then unable to explain.

'I am most anxious not to worry you unduly and I can assure you that children often go through strange phases which clear up as mysteriously as they occur, but all the same, Sam has made me very curious and a little anxious.

'Perhaps you would observe him carefully over the holiday and attempt to discover something about his private world. Later perhaps, we could meet to discuss what is best to be done. I do not know how you would feel about consulting a child psychiatrist? Raymond Goole is an old friend of mine whose help I have enlisted from time to time. If you would like him to have a chat with Sam I will arrange it.

'Please do not be alarmed. I am sure that whatever this trouble proves to be it is not very serious. Sam's health is splendid, his brains are good and he has no discernible vices. This day-dreaming can, I am certain, be cured, but it must not be ignored because valuable time is being lost and Sam must learn to do his work and take his place with others of his age, so that he may hold his own in this strongly competitive world.

'Believe me,

Yours very sincerely,

Robert Sopwith.

Headmaster.'

When at last Mr Campion looked up it was with a very serious expression behind his spectacles but his tone was deliberately light.

Poor Headmaster! He'll be so relieved when he hears about the "iggy-tube". He'll give all concerned six of the best. It's no toy for the growing boy!'

'Children are so wholesale,' Amanda murmured. 'I suppose he just wore it all the time, sleeping and waking, so that it became a built-in aid.'

106

'But it's frightful! Don't you all see how awful it is?' The outburst they were all fearing came from Helena at last. 'It can have ruined Sam's mind and moral fibre and ... and ... everything else. He may be "sub" after this. He may...'

'Nonsense.' Martin slid an arm round her rigid shoulders. 'It's pretty alarming and if I'd guessed what was going on I'd have stopped it. But you and I are not going to panic just because this is something new in the way of hazards. I can't believe that the experience of being shouted down by other people's casual thoughts—because that's what it amounts to— can have done him any permanent harm. I'll talk to him.'

'No. You'll frighten him.'

'I won't. And you'll be there.' He was gentle with her, and the tremendous masculinity of his race was very apparent. She responded to it at once, becoming calmer as he reassured her. He turned to the others and his sincerity was overwhelmingly convincing.

'I hope you'll believe me that I had no idea that these amplifiers were in existence, let alone that the children had gotten hold of them.'

'Could Paggen Mayo have made them without your knowledge?'

'Why no! I told you, Paggen isn't as far ahead as this and the notion that the blood-stream is involved is right against his line of thinking.'

'He did use Sam for an experiment.' Helena turned her head.

'No, Sweetie, he did not. I would never have let him, would I? I took Sam to the workshop one day and we did a few elementary E.S.P. tests with cards and numbers. Sam was pretty good at it. Children often are. After that he stood around while we talked. The Professor came in for ten minutes. That was all.'

'Could Sam have picked up anything while he was there?'

'No. How could he? There was nothing in this class on the island. I must get down to Paggen right away and see what's cooking. It sounds as if we're on the point of breakthrough.'

'Before you go I want to ask you something,' said Amanda. 'When you woke up in the van and saw Mrs Mayo you said you felt a sudden surge of dismay because you thought she'd gone round the bend at last. Did you do anything about it? I mean did you try to tell someone?'

He stared at her. 'No,' he said. 'No, I didn't. But I can guess what you're getting at; I had a small emotional explosion—a sort of spark. Very slight really, but this whole thing seems to run on very low power of whatever kind it is. Why? Did someone here pick it up? On one of the new devices?'

So it was a commonplace already! Mr Campion shivered. Scientists terrified him most by the ease with which they accepted their own wonders once they were in existence. As soon as they were factual they seemed to treat them like old bicycles. The power of the things did not seem to interest them, and they were able to look at truth in the nude, however new and disconcerting, with the dispassionate interest of medicos.

'Uncle Hubert picked up a whatd'yacallit—a signal—from you,' he said. 'He had put on one of the amplifiers, concentrated on his prayers to counteract the mental hullabaloo, exhausted himself and fallen asleep. He awoke with the strong impression that you had been suddenly shocked and dismayed about something. That's all in order, is it?'

'Utterly. It's a typical good result. Tabard will accept the Canon as a witness, too, which is terrific. These things of yours sound better and better the more I hear of them. We'll have to check the times. Don't be astonished if they seem a little haywire. In our experience one often gets a message a few minutes before it's sent.'

'Which shakes me,' said Amanda dryly. 'What's the juice?'

'That's just it. We keep coming back to this spark or overspill. If it's not electrical, what is it?'

Mr Campion hesitated. 'Old Uncle Freud had a rather famous theory when my papa was young about a latent pool of creative energy which got depleted and filled up again. It could, I suppose, slop over,' he remarked. ' "Creative" would seem to be the operative word. I understood it was the kind of life force one needs to lift oneself up by the boot-straps out of some fearful moral abyss, and it seems to be squeezed out of the emotional structure pretty mysteriously. The explanation of the power could be as easy or as difficult as that, I suppose?'

'Oh, that would be outside our orbit,' the young man said somewhat alarmingly. 'You'd have to go to Tabard with that query. He's the great man—human as well. Old Paggen just wants something in a battery and he wants it quick. Gosh! I must get hold of him!'

Another consideration occurred to him and he frowned. 'They've got to have been made by somebody, haven't they? I guess I'd better talk to those brats before I do anything else.'

'Oh, not Sam! Please, not Sam.' Helena was so very frightened. The headmaster's letter crackled in her hand. 'Can't he be left alone? Just for a little while? Just till he settles?'

'Edward is the elder and quite responsible,' Amanda ventured to intervene. 'Let's have him up first, shall we?'

As well as the extensions to the outside line, the Rectory possessed an old-fashioned house telephone with an instrument on the bedroom wall. She turned the handle and was answered by Avril himself who had been walking through the hall downstairs. When she hung up she turned to her husband.

'Edward is next door. He's gone into Miss Warburton's to get some money for Uncle Hubert. He'll send him up the moment he comes in.'

Martin looked at Helena.

'I guess I'll just have to go down and have a word with Sam,' he was beginning when an incoming call on the outside line put every other thought out of their minds.

Mr Campion, who was nearest the instrument, took the message and Luke's vibrating boom was audible to them all.

'Campion? That chap Mayo. . . . Have you got him there?'

'No, of course not. Why? Oh Lord! Well look: he ditched his wife at Robinson's Hotel, Piccadilly, just after they left us.

109

She spent the night there and the car was garaged there. That's checked. This morning she rang me here and asked for me by name. She wanted to know if I could find out what had happened to him "unofficially"! There was none of the hysterical nonsense of last night and I sent a chap round to see her. He says she's frightened and is being most careful not to make any of the wild suggestions we heard before, but he thinks that's what she's afraid of. He didn't pause in the hotel at all last night, just walked straight through it. You know how you can? In at the Roding Street entrance—out at the Winton Street one.'

'I think it's just wife trouble, Charles.' Mr Campion sounded hopeful.

'But that's only half the story.' Luke's effort to speak quietly made him even more distinct to those standing round. 'I've checked the island. He didn't go back. He has two clubs and hasn't been seen in either. He has a sister in Paddington, she hasn't heard of him. He has a girl friend and he wasn't there. I've been as discreet as I can with Mrs Mayo's assistance, but I've had a good look round and in my opinion he's gone. He had those things on him, remember. Anyway, I thought I'd better let you know I'm reporting it to the Special Branch right away. Yes, well, there you are! Better safe than sorry! You'll come down will you? Bring young Ferris.'

11

The Long fox Method

WHEN Amanda came into the church, looking for the Canon, the elegant Georgian interior was misty with London sun. It shone in, high under the pale blue ceiling with the gold stars, and made dusty shafts of yellow light across the dark mahogany arch behind the altar. Saturday morning chores were being done. Miss Warburton, with a black woollen skiing cap perched on her thin hair like a biretta, was making sure that the parishioner who did the flowers had not been a 'silly girl and forgotten the water', while old Talisman fiddled with the cords which controlled the transom over the north door in his weekly attempt to cure its chronic rattle.

Avril was in the vestry, standing before the smallest gas fire in the world, looking thoughtfully at the walls. He was not permitted to help with the church but they liked him to be there on call, and the enforced wait before he did his part and walked round admiring the industry of others was one of his penances.

Amanda stood in the curtained doorway, a worried brown woman in a loose chestnut-coloured coat, and he turned and saw her.

'Is Edward back yet?'

'No, but don't worry. I'm not really alarmed. It's only that it was so unlike him to slide off and not to mention where he was going. There's plenty of time still and, after all, he is on guard after yesterday. They say that sort of attempt couldn't possibly happen again....' The disjointed remarks, each counteracting the last, were very unlike her.

The Canon hunched his shoulders: he was most unhappy.

'When I told him what I'd done he looked at me as if I'd suddenly tripped him up ... amazed,' he observed wretchedly. 'After that he seemed to take it very well. I know he said something about Tuesday. It would all be over by Tuesday anyhow—something like that. He didn't want to discuss it and I was in no position to press him.'

'Did he refuse to tell you anything about it?'

'Not exactly. He said: "You've given them to an expert and he'll be able to explain them to you, won't he?" I'd given him Mayo's card, you see.'

'Could he have decided to go down there?'

'I don't think so.' The old priest was trying to remember, hindered all the time by his sense of guilt and shortcoming. 'My impression was that he thought very little about Mayo, or of him come to that. He talked about other things for a while and I imagined he'd dismissed the whole matter as unfortunate but finished with, when he asked me for money.'

Amanda was surprised. 'I thought he had some money. There was a letter from his mother waiting for him here and she usually encloses something.'

'I did wonder if he was trying to punish me,' Avril said mildly. 'He knows I don't like asking Dot for advances....'

'Oh Canon, how can you?' Miss Warburton herself had appeared in the doorway; bright, kind, and with her nice flat heels firmly on the earth which she seemed so determined that Avril should be meek enough to inherit.

'I gave him the two pounds ten you promised him and I haven't grumbled at you at all, although it is really time you bought some under ... oh well, never mind. Edward has the money he wanted and can go and buy his little friends their presents. He'll be home as soon as the shops shut, which they all do at one o'clock today. He's a sensible boy and older than he looks. *I'm* not worried about him.'

Amanda accepted the reproach. 'It's only that I wish he'd told me he was going out. He's usually so thoughtful. He was buying something for somebody else, was he?'

'Yes, I think he said someone had given him a guinea and he must do some shopping or "they"—I'm sure he said "they" and not "he"—would be disappointed. What does Albert say?'

'I haven't told Albert or Martin yet that Edward isn't still at your cottage. They both wanted to talk to him but they're both fully occupied at the moment. Some excitement has blown up because Paggen Mayo seems to have gone off somewhere last night. Martin has been sent to discover if he can persuade Mrs Mayo not to say anything utterly damaging should the Press try to work up a story, and Albert has had to rush down to see someone called L. C. Corkran, whom he knew in the last war.'

'Edward will be back when the shops shut,' Miss Warburton repeated. 'I'm burning with curiosity. What are the things the Canon has taken from Edward and given to an expert? Are they important?'

'Not very—at the moment,' Amanda spoke hastily but Miss Warburton had heard that tone before.

'Ah, as you're all so scientific and experimental perhaps what I should have asked is what are their potentials?' she enquired archly.

Avril laughed abruptly. 'Potentially they could be Dot's delight. . . . Popular Pocket Omniscience. You'd love them!'

'Oh, what a wicked idea!' She was shocked and huffed. 'You shouldn't say such things; especially in the church, surely?'

'Wicked?' Avril pounced on the word, all his fears returning. 'That dreadful old question. Can Advance be wicked? Oh my dear girls, I do wonder if I have done right or wrong!'

Miss Warburton took his arm. 'You come along and see the flowers,' she said, 'and tell Talisman not to be such a *cackhand* with that transom. He'll take it from you.'

Avril went with her obediently but turned to Amanda as he passed. 'Sam,' he said. 'You go over. I'll follow you.'

Amanda went back to the rectory and, walking round to the eastern side, took the area steps down to the basement. The kitchen door was unlatched and she stepped in to find Sam sitting at the solid centre table with the blue linoleum top. He was wrapped in a blanket as if he were ill, his yellow hair was on end, and his face was red. He was sorting buttons, taking them out of a nine-inch cube biscuit tin and arranging them in little heaps of the same size and pattern. He was concentrating with weary difficulty and a dogged endurance which was almost too good to be true. Helena was sitting opposite him, her face dark and her eyes very grim under straight brows.

'Come along, darling,' she was saying briskly. 'Now the black ones. Keep your mind on it, Sweetie. Don't be silly. Come along.' As Amanda's shadow fell over the threshold she glanced up and met her eyes warningly. 'Not now,' she said. There was no compromise whatsoever, no pleading. The message was curt and unmistakable. Amanda stood her ground and they remained looking at one another.

Amanda said: 'Edward's gone. I've got to hear all Sam knows.'

Helena got up, pushing her chair back with a rattle on the composite floor.

'Not now and not here, darling.' She swept round the table, slid her arm through the newcomer's and took her to the inner door. The force she emitted was enormous. Her entire sum of nervous energy was concentrated in the effort. 'Hurry up, Sam. I shan't be a moment. Just keep your mind on the job. I'll be back in a minute to see what you've done.'

She piloted Amanda through the doorway, up the single flight of stairs and through the old red baize door, which divided the service part of the house from the back hall where Mr Campion and Luke had talked the night before.

'You go in there to Sam over my dead body,' she said.

Amanda stared at her in polite astonishment which turned slowly to consternation.

'What's happened to him?'

'I ... I don't know. I mean I think it's going to be all right. It's only that ... oh God, Amanda, I'm so frightened! He's not thinking properly. He seems to have forgotten how to use his head.'

The older woman put an arm round her and drew her down upon the stairs. 'Sit here a minute. He's missing the iggy-tube, is he?'

Helena dabbed her eyes with a ball of handkerchief. 'He's hopeless without it. I found it out this morning. He came in to the bedroom, gave me the headmaster's letter and went down to find Edward. When I'd read the dreadful thing I went after him and I took him out of the parlour where Edward was and talked to him in the study. He was quite awful ... lost and bored and irritable and sort of blah ... do you know? He wasn't thinking *at all*! I left him with Mary Talisman while I did what I could with Martin who was still pretty ill.'

'Does he know this about Sam?'

'Not entirely.' She was shaking. 'I felt I must see what I could do to jerk the child out of it first before they persuade Martin to let him go to the psychos. Those chaps are out of hand. You've no idea of the dangerous things they can get up to if there isn't a good doctor in charge. I think I can get him right. After all, it's only like a hand which has been in plaster going numb. He'll get well but he must be pulled out of it right away, mustn't he?'

'Of course, my dear. Of course. Who thought of the buttons?'

'Mrs Talisman. She says she's seen something like it before. A little girl she took care of long ago had delirium in a fever which left her mind exhausted and they had to coax it to work again. She wrapped him up like that. She says it'll make him feel it's some sort of illness he's got to get over and he won't be so frightened. He is getting better, quite fast. Let me go back to him. Just let me have a day, for God's sake.'

'Where is Mrs Talisman now?'

'She had to go to the dairy before the shops shut.'

Amanda passed her hand over her hair. 'Edward has gone off somewhere,' she said, trying to sound casual. 'Dot gave him some money. He could have gone quite a way.'

'Look, Amanda.' Helena was trying to control her panic without great success. 'I'm desperate about this ... demoralised if you like. I can't keep any sort of secret. I'm simply thinking of Sam. Let me tell you all I know before you try him.'

It was a diversion. Amanda knew it but she let the husky voice go on.

'When I said there was a flap on at the Island yesterday I

didn't tell all I knew. I couldn't help gathering a good deal more. When Lord Ludor sent for Paggen before the luncheon he told him that there'd been a dangerous leak of information from the island. One day this week, one of the big propaganda papers in the East had actually published the fact that Paggen was working with Nipponanium. But then it went on to say that Martin Ferris (it gave his name and said he was an American "on loan") was experimenting with a device and was using schoolboys as guinea pigs.'

'Martin? Not Mayo?'

'Exactly. That's the trouble. Lord Ludor assumed that this part of the tale was a mistake and the names had got confused. He wanted to know if Paggen had gone mad and *was* experimenting on children! Paggen didn't think there was any mistake. I was with Martin when he told him and I could see he suspected him.'

'What about Martin?'

'He simply howled with laughter. Paggen took his cue from him but he wasn't satisfied.'

'And all that business with the gas and the Micky Finn?'

'That was Paggen. Paggen doesn't want to lose Martin because he's lost without him but he wants to keep him under his thumb. If there's a black mark against Martin he can do that. Unfortunately, Martin likes Paggen and he's too high-minded and loyal to see anything so dirty.... That's what Mayo is doing now, hiding from us until he can cook up some evidence against Martin and associate him with those ghastly things.'

The telephone ringing in the cloakroom next door interrupted the confidence. Amanda flew to answer it and as she took off the receiver she heard the chink at the other end of the wire which indicated a public callbox.

'I want to speak to 'er Ladyship,' a cheerful cockney voice, not too used to telephoning, greeted her. 'That's you yourself, is it madam? Right you are then. Message from Edward Longfox: he says to tell you he's got very important business which is takin' longer than what he thought. He says you are not to worry yourself and to expect him when you see him. O.K.?'

'May I ask your name?' Long experience had taught Amanda much.

'Mr. Henry Caudwell, your Ladyship. Pleased to meet you.'

'And me. Would you be ringing from London?'

'Right in the middle of it. This 'ere box is under Ludgate Hill railway bridge.'

'Is Edward there?'

'Eh ... wait a minute ... no. No, he's just gorn. He'd been waiting to make sure I got you and when he heard me speak he nipped off and on to the top of a bus ...Wanstead one, I think. He's only just this minute gorn. No. Nobody with him. Quite on his own. Perky little party. Well, your mind's at rest, is it? So I'll say good-day. I've got a paper stand here, you see. Goodbye. Cheerio.' He rang off hastily as if exhausted by the experience and she hung up, her tongue dry in her mouth.

'Helena?' she said, but there was no reply. Sam's mother had gone back to the kitchen.

Amanda went after her. She was aware of a crisis the moment she opened the door.

Sam was still sitting at the table in his blanket toga. The heaps of buttons were not complete but he was bright enough and was taking a great interest in the scene before him. Helena, white as paper, was staring at the verger's wife who was stuttering with outrage. The plump old lady was still in her coat and her full basket stood on the table.

'*Inside* the house!' she was saying. 'The man was *inside*. He told me he was checking the meter and he had the cheek to show me the back of an envelope as if he was going to enter the figures on that! Even if you haven't thieved a thing it's an insult, I told him. You think we're subnormally brained, I said. You young educateds think we're deaf, dumb and blind as well as ignorant.'

'He wasn't young he was fifty,' Sam said cheerfully. 'He was as old as Soppy and he's a headmaster.'

'Did he talk to you darling?' The concern in Helena's voice

117

seemed to upset or perhaps to remind the boy. He gave her a frightened look and his face quivered. 'Who?'

'Why, the man, Sam. The man who was here when Mrs Talisman came back. You saw him, didn't you? Well? Didn't you, darling? Answer. You were here.'

Sam turned from her and threw himself down among the buttons in a single furious gesture.

'Was I? I don't know. Perhaps I was. I can't remember.'

'Sam!' It was a cry of horrified protest and old Mrs Talisman came to the rescue.

'Anyway, it doesn't matter,' she said comfortably, 'because I was and I saw him quite plainly and I spoke to him.' She shook her head warningly at Helena and eyed the boy casually. 'You tidy up those buttons, young man. This is the kitchen table. We don't want them turning up in the lunch. Yes, I suppose you're right and this person was about forty. He was tall, quite cool, like a reporter on the telly, but a bit over-gentlemanly, if you know what I mean?'

'Ladylike?' Amanda suggested, inspired.

The old woman nodded. 'Now you've said it. And not even good-looking with it. "I'm just checking the meter" he said, and waved the envelope at me as if I couldn't see what it was, the fool! He hadn't been here long. I don't suppose Sam had even noticed him, walking in like that, straight out of the area as if he had a right.'

'Yes, I did. He asked me if I had my new "toy telephone from school" down here!' The contempt in the young voice was superb.

'Jolly funny! What did you tell him?' For the second time in ten minutes Amanda's heart turned over.

Sam pulled the button tin towards him and spoke absently.

'Oh, I guessed what he meant and so I told him they had been confiscated and I expected my cousin had gone to get some more.'

Amanda's fingers fastened on Helena's shoulder and her cool voice continued to be easy and pleasant.

'Why did you say that?'

'Because it was what he had to do if ever an iggy-tube got lost.' He continued to sort buttons, stepping up the rate of progress considerably.

'Who is Edward's friend?'

'Just his friend,' said Sam, placing a pink pearl button amid a heap of the same kind. 'His special friend.'

'We can guess that.' Mrs Talisman was brusque. 'What is his name, please?'

Sam did not look up. 'Rubari,' he said idly. 'He's a Rumanian living in Paris.'

'Sam! Are you making this up?'

'No, Mom. Rubari is awfully, terribly rich.'

There was a moment of silence in the kitchen while he selected a pink pearl button with great care. When he had got it on the right heap he looked over at the window which gave on to the area. The only light it received came down through the railings from the sunlit square and the scene appeared to remind him.

'The electricity man has a white cat with a brown tail which follows him like a dog,' he said. 'He was telling me I could go up and see it when Mrs Talisman came in and saw him and of course he had to leave '

12

Official View

IN the middle of the afternoon on the same day, Deputy Commander Sydney of the Special Branch sat at his desk, with his signed photograph of H.M. The Queen over it, and concentrated on keeping the interview as smooth as silk.

As a member of the Other Service, as he called Security, he did not expect much trouble from Mr Campion, or help either, if the truth were faced. Mercifully his good lady looked as if she were sensible and well brought up. However, he did feel that Superintendent Charles Luke C.I.D., who had just been wished upon him to help with the enquiry, and who now sat at the second desk looking like some great black Tom jaguar, filled the office to bursting point.

Sydney was as big a man as Luke and his face had some of the quality of polished stone. The C.I.D. man was behaving and trying to remember he was a visitor, but they were both ruthless animals manoeuvring in a restricted space, and it was not a comfortable gathering.

Amanda, still in her chestnut coat, had just told her story and was being taken through it.

'So,' Sydney said, 'as soon as you heard the name Rubari you telephoned the school. You found the Head was on a walking tour and you spoke to his wife. She recognised the name immediately, and she told you that Henri Rubari is a pupil at the school and is somewhere about twelve years old. You then, very sensibly, obtained the number of the school secretary who confirms that the boy *is* Rumanian and *does* live in Paris. The secretary also thinks he should be at home there at this moment. We are enquiring into all those points. The secretary also told you that Rubari's mother is a widow and she gave you the address and telephone number of her Paris apartment. Why didn't you call it?'

As he looked up she met his eyes and noted that he was slightly hostile.

'I thought you might not like me to,' she said, frankly.

'Me?'

'All of you up here. That was why I came instead of trying to report by telephone. If Edward has been getting these things from Rubari I thought you would want to do any questioning there might be to do at that end. My impulse was to telephone Paris to see if they knew anything, of course.'

Luke took the opportunity to interrupt. A uniformed man had brought him a chit just before Sydney had begun to talk and he had been awaiting a pause.

'Caudwell, the newsvendor, is O.K. The man on the beat has known him for years. The old boy repeated the story he told Lady Amanda, word for word. He says the kid was happy and off on an adventure. He thinks he took a Wanstead bus but he can't swear to it.'

'The boy knew where he was going to find his friend, anyway. That's the main thing,' Sydney said. 'I don't think we shall find it was Paris!'

He laughed at the suggestion and was put out to find the husband and wife continuing without him.

'Madame Rubari is in the silk business,' Amanda said to Campion. 'I thought I'd heard the name before in connection with fabric and I called in on Meg on my way here. She says that they're a very successful concern, not very big but extremely high class, dealing with all the great couturiers. Mme Rubari does a lot of her own buying and she is a real widow, not a grass one. She seems to know everybody in Paris who is anybody. That's all the dope I could get you.'

'Good enough! We can do the rest in ten minutes.' Luke pulled a pad towards him. 'It's rather the right sort of set-up, don't you think?' he added to Sydney, who shrugged his shoulders.

'It's a line which will have to be followed.' He spoke as an expert in a very small and very well explored field. 'I shouldn't think it will lead to much. I'm very grateful to you, madam, but I think if you go home now you could quite possibly find the boy waiting for you. When he does come back we'd like to see him.'

Campion touched Amanda's arm.

'Martin, Helena, Sam and Mrs Mayo are all going back to the island,' he murmured. 'It was arranged just before you arrived.'

'They're going in the Mayo car, Martin driving and with a police car escort,' said Luke, who was still slightly shaken by what he considered the high-handedness of Special Branch methods. ' "Go there and stay there". I'd like to see me saying that to a threatened subject.'

'The suggestion came from top level, didn't it, Mr Campion?' Hearing his own words, Sydney suspected that he sounded as if he needed support and reasserted himself promptly. 'I advised it because I felt they should be kept somewhere absolutely safe.'

'Particularly from the Press!' Mr Campion smiled at him. 'Could we drop the formalities, Commander. At the moment the principal concern is that Mayo should be located before there is any breath of public speculation about him. That really is absolutely essential in Security's opinion.'

'His Missus can't give interviews with the Army on the door, anyway,' said Luke cheerfully. 'That's one mercy. Then you're off now, are you Amanda?'

'Please. I'd like to get back in case Edward does come in.' She had risen and was leaning forward to shake Sydney's hand. 'I've told you everything and you're the judge of what is important. I want Edward back safe. I don't think you quite believe in that amplifier, Commander.'

To her surprise he became completely wooden.

'That's one thing I never have to consider,' he said fiercely. 'If I allowed myself to think of the utter uselessness of the secrets which half the villains I deal with pass on to the enemies of the Realm, I'd go mad. All I need to worry about is the man and his evil intent; they're the two things that keep me sane.' He flashed a genuine smile at her to show that he felt the better for the outburst and half-rose politely as she went out.

Mr Campion sat down in the chair and stretched his long legs.

'What about the chap with the cat?'

'The Superintendent's people are checking with the Electricity Board now.'

'I think he called.'

'Of course he did, Mr Campion. Someone came walking in just as the old woman and the little boy said he did. He can have been a sneak thief or a genuine inspector of any one of the dozens of machines people clutter up their homes with nowadays, but in my opinion he wasn't any customer of mine.'

'You know all your customers, do you?' It was a friendly question but the Deputy Commander laughed abruptly and turned colour.

'You are thinking of that new leak of information from that blessed island,' he said. 'Your people aren't satisfied that there isn't a small patch of fungi we've missed up here, which has a contact down there. Perhaps so, but as for an agent calling and asking for information, I just can't see it. I can't see the importance of the cat either. This city is infested with cats!'

'What about the question he put to the kid?' Luke suggested. 'The "toy telephone"?'

'Perhaps he was a post office engineer talking about a real telephone and the child jumped to a guilty conclusion.'

'You almost convince me that any foreign agent to be genuine should have a Special Branch man on his tail, as at Liverpool Street Station yesterday.' Mr Campion continued to look and sound serenely affable.

Sydney took the remark as a compliment.

'I admit we don't get many surprises,' he confessed. 'There's a pattern in these things and once you've seen it you've seen it.'

Mr Campion sighed and became direct.

'Tell me, Commander, what is putting you out so in this particular business? I thought it was the E.S.P. element at first but now I'm wondering if it could be the presence in it of children?'

'Oh, I'm disregarding the children as children,' Sydney exploded. 'A child one knows is so important to one that one doesn't see anything else. I'm merely giving these two young-sters their proper weight. I see that they may have been used in some sort of experiment. Certainly, one minor foreign official I could name thought so, and wanted to have a chat with them, and employed an earnest female member of the submerged army of fellow-travellers to try to pick them up at the station. We know all about him. You can take it from me that he won't interfere again, simply because he won't get a chance. His superiors haven't considered that performance very clever. In fact it was typical of the sort of melodramatic mistake a certain foreign power has to look out for in its people. Imagine anybody taking two British schoolkids in for questioning in this day and age, and expecting nobody to be-lieve them when they got back. That's what he had in mind, you know! You can write him off. He went home this morning on the noon flight.'

'Fair enough.' Luke ducked his chin in a gesture of acceptance. 'So you think young Edward is just out shopping?'

'I didn't say that.'

'Didn't you? Are you changing your ground?'

Sydney hesitated. 'I saw no point in alarming the lady un-necessarily, or arguing with her. Damn it Luke! Surely you see he could be *in* it? He's a person like anybody else. He could have been told some story and offered a chance of a brave new life of scientific adventure in the far romantic East. His father is dead, isn't he?'

Luke's jaw dropped. 'That kid? You're talking like a boys' comic!'

'The world I live in is very *like* a boys' comic,' Sydney said mildly. 'That suggestion isn't off the cards, believe you me.'

Mr Campion stirred uneasily. 'You think that Mayo has de-fected?' he enquired.

'It's the thing that's under my nose. That's the item one

usually misses. Also, I don't want to believe it, naturally. As I've just told you, the island's security has only just had our "full works". It was a top priority job and all personnel were re-screened.'

'Which was followed smartly by this fresh gusher at the beginning of the week?'

'Exactly!' Sydney was nettled and showed it. 'I am staggered by the idea that there could be an *unknown* development on that island. I shouldn't have thought anything unknown to Security could have come out of that damn place for the next twelve months. You're a Security man. You should know what was done.'

'Wait a moment,' Luke put in. 'We don't say the amplifiers came from *Godley's* or that Mayo invented them.'

The deputy Commander smiled his secret smile again but did not comment and Luke's dark face grew a shade darker still.

'You don't know what's coming to you, mate, when that little lot reaches perfection! Mayo didn't make those things. They took him by complete surprise.'

'Possibly.' The Deputy Commander made it clear he did not want to quarrel. 'He certainly came through the probe and so did Mrs Mayo. All her nonsense was explained in lucid medical detail in the report I read.'

Campion gave up fencing.

'My dear chap,' he said, 'you're the real expert. Put us in the picture.'

Sydney relaxed visibly. 'It's not what I *want* to think,' he began. 'But take a look at it like this: we had just closed the files on our investigation into the island personnel when the foreign propaganda press came out with the story you know. I thought the tale about the experiments on kids at school was so ridiculous that I never even had it checked.'

'Understandable,' Luke mumbled.

'It was,' Sydney said defensively. 'Or at least I thought so, considering that we knew that a schoolmaster who was a suspect had put in five weeks at the school last summer and the place had been watched ever since!' He laughed bleakly. 'Now, while I'm still biting my nails, Mayo stages a typical scientist's walk-away. He goes in the accepted manner, whilst out with his wife, but this time Mrs Mayo has been chivvied into repeating her disclosures in front of two witnesses whose very job it is to take any such dangerous talk seriously. Moreover, when he goes, he takes with him secret appliances which have been actually obtained by these same responsible and interested witnesses—I am talking about you two—from two children who have come from the very school mentioned in the propaganda report. Mayo has all night to get out of the country and the next day one of his guinea-pigs wanders off after him. All ports and airfields are being watched *now*, naturally. But we're too late and our precautions mean that sooner or later the tale will break. Believe me, *that is what is intended*. It's all propaganda.'

Luke, who had listened to the recital with mounting dismay, suddenly exploded.

'Too subtle by half!' he protested. 'That's as involved as the old comic story! "You swine, you tell me you are going to Prague to make me think you are going to Warsaw while all the time you are going to Prague!" Who's going to be bothered with that rigmarole?'

'Parliament,' said Sydney placidly. 'Haven't you read of them at it? "Is it true that a senior member of the Criminal Investigation Department of the Metropolitan Police was warned by Mrs Mayo of her husband's intended flight, and did the officer in question stand by while the secret device was handed to Mr Mayo after it was taken from a pupil from *the school mentioned by the Propaganda Press only four days previously?*" A very reasonable question from the right kind of honest mutton-head. That's how I read it.'

Luke was absolutely quiet for a second or so. Mr Campion rose to his feet and wandered down the room to the window and back again. His hands were in his pockets and his chin down.

'I suppose you must be right five times out of nine,' he said at last. 'If you ignore the human factor and most of the details absolutely, you gain a certain advantage, but in a case like this surely the method fails. I've met Mayo and seen him under stress. He's a most familiar type, afraid of the "porpoise close behind him" perhaps, but you couldn't bribe him. If you looked into his soul I should say you'd find that what he really wants from life is a knighthood!'

'This porpoise he's afraid of? Which is that?'

'The one who's treading on his tail. Anybody coming up behind him. The cleverer chap.'

'Oh.' Sydney lowered his ball point. He seemed disappointed. 'If I'm ignoring the human factor,' he said, 'you're overlooking the characteristics of dry rot. One day a floor board looks as solid as ever it was. Then you put your weight on it and suddenly it crumbles like pie-crust. That's what fungus is. I don't accuse Mayo yet, but I say he is behaving in a very characteristic way and according to a pattern we know. Also, and get this right, I think that what he is doing has much more to do with backing up a piece of propaganda than with getting a bit of secret equipment out of the country.'

Campion turned back to the window and Luke took over. He was considerably shaken and it was making him belligerent.

'Talking of significant behaviour, Chum, was there any mention in that security survey of yours of a lad called Fred Arnold?'

'The bartender? He was the natural suspect.'

'I should have thought so. What's he doing down there? A man with his qualifications could earn so much more anywhere else.'

'Exactly what we all thought, Superintendent.' Sydney was pleased. 'Actually there *is* a little mystery concerning him and it took us a long time to tease it out. What do you think it was? He's the Boss's man—Lord Ludor's own personal spy. I can show you his dossier. He led us a dance because he's most discreet and so is Ludor, the old fox. I understand your people are now considering the man themselves.'

127

He broke off. Campion, who had smothered an exclamation, threw up the window and leaned out. They were on the top floor and the wide grey street which ran beside the shining steel of the river was busy and a long way below. It was already misty and the angle of vision was abrupt. Campion drew back and, closing the window turned round, dusting his hands.

'I'm sorry,' he said. 'I appear to have hallucinations. I thought I saw Edward scurrying down to the corner. He was wearing a beret, though, which isn't in the Pontisbright tradition. Those flames of theirs are seldom hidden under any pot! Forgive me, Commander. Luke and I are both ordered down to the Island then?'

'That was what I understood, sir.' Sydney had the grace to look embarrassed. 'Doubtless you'll be informed but I understood that both the Director and the Commander felt that Mayo should be given until the end of the working day to show up or at least to report the devices and, after that, the whole thing should come out into the open—but only as far as the experts down there are concerned. It is felt that the sources of the "secret items" which Mr Mayo has with him must be down there even if they are largely his own, and must be located.'

Mr Campion's pale face was betraying interest. 'Someone has to talk to Professor Tabard?'

'I gathered that was the idea. The minister is being kept in touch and Lord Ludor will be there. You actually tried one of the secret gadgets on, I hear, Superintendent?'

Luke's reply was forestalled by the arrival of a clerk with two messages, one for each of the senior men. Sydney sat looking at his own for some seconds before he cleared his throat and glanced across the room.

'This is the "off the cuff" answer to our Rubari enquiry,' he said shortly. 'The mother is away travelling on business but the boy is at home in the care of an *au pair* girl. Also staying with them in the apartment is the young son of the mother's close friend, Maurice Gregoire Gregoire of Daumier et Cie.'

128

Mr Campion was staring at him.

'Is that the Daumier of the Electronics Group?'

Sydney nodded and decided to look at him. 'I suppose they're Godley's chief competitor in Europe. Gregoire is Mayo's opposite number, isn't he?' He threw the chit down on the desk before him. 'Now I don't know *what* to say!'

'What about this?' Luke passed over his own message. It was on the back of a telegram form as obtained from the public desk in a post office and was neatly written in a precise if youthful hand.

'Dear Mr Luke: Could I trouble you to telephone my Aunt Amanda to tell her not to worry even if I have to *stay away all night*? I have to wait for a friend who may be very late indeed. I shall certainly be back tomorrow. I have had to bother you because I am afraid you may have had the Rectory line tapped to catch me. Telephoning is awkward, because I cannot think how to make it obvious that I am not being *made* to do anything. I will give this note to the man on your door. As he is a Trained Observer he can describe me to you and guarantee that I am not being ordered about. Many thanks in anticipation of your kindness. Sincerely yours. Edward Longfox.
P.S. It is all *most* important or I would never worry you. You will know all about everything on Tuesday.'

As Sydney passed the note to Campion, his comment was unexpectedly human: 'Well, *he* seems to know what he's doing next,' he said. 'It's more than I do!'

13

The End of the World

'I NEVER took to Sydney and his blasted toadstools,' said Luke. 'He was trying to put the wind up me with his propaganda nonsense and he did, which is unforgivable. Wait till I get my iggy-tube. That'll make his outfit look a bit passé!'

He was sitting in the Rectory parlour kicking his heels until Mr Campion, who had been summoned by his own Director from the Deputy Commander's office, should arrive to pick up the car and take them both to the island. Luke had come on ahead to report to Amanda and had found the old house sad with the empty untidiness of a deserted nest now that the Ferrises had gone. He had told her about Edward's visit to the Yard and she had taken it very well.

'He's a funny child,' she said. 'Very like his father. I felt he knew a great deal about the amplifiers that he wasn't telling us simply because he felt we might not be able to follow him.'

Luke grunted. 'They're rum things. Sydney didn't believe in them because he didn't want to and I don't know if I do. Gawd! What aspect of modern life couldn't they alter and upset? What's the odds on the whole idea being suppressed?'

She shook her tawny head. 'Not a hope. Once a key has been found and recognised in science it's like taking the Queen's shilling; the experience is on. This will take a tremendous time, though, and could only make fearful trouble if it gets off on the wrong foot. What about Mayo? Do you agree with the Deputy Commander? Has he defected?'

'God knows!' He was fidgeting, clattering with his foot on the worn carpet. 'If he *isn't* bunking he hasn't been gone very long, has he? That's how these vanishing eggheads always do get away. They just go and no one realises they're not still in the bathroom. What's twenty-four hours' absence, especially after a row with the wife? I can say definitely that he's not in hospital, Turkish bath or hotel under his own name. But we've only been able to establish that much because the Home Office has been after us, bleating like a sheep farm.'

'I think,' said Amanda, 'that he's in a physics lab; that's where I'd be.'

'But he's got one on the island.'

'It's not his. There'll be another irascible genius in charge there who isn't necessarily on his side. They'll be working for the whole station: plenty of other projects are going on down there beside this E.S.P. job.'

'I see,' Luke was very interested. 'So where would he go? He walked out of Robinson's Hotel late last night. He needn't have stayed in London. He could have hopped on a train and gone anywhere.'

'It would have to be somewhere he knew. Where was he before Godley's?'

The Superintendent felt under his chair and came up with a document case containing the notes he had been given by the Deputy Commander, the fruits of the latest probe.

'The Post Office,' he said presently. 'He was with them two and a half years ago. Haven't they got a place in London called Parsley Green? You pass it on the way to the Airport. There's an experimental unit there. I don't know about a laboratory.'

'I imagine they'd have all he'd need. He could do most of the investigation himself better than anybody. It would only be certain analyses he'd have to have help over; those things take an awful long time. There's a famous chap called Fenn at Parsley Green. An electronics wizard. He'd know Mayo.'

'Would he help him?'

'I can't tell you, but he lives in the place so he'd be there at night. There's a flat at the top of the old building. I went there once.'

Luke got up. 'We'll give him a tinkle,' he began, and paused as he saw her expression. 'Perhaps not. They're all very aware of each other, aren't they? A real old band of brothers—like college professors! Never mind. I'll get someone to call round and do it discreetly.' He grinned at her. 'His friend will just think he's wanted for debt!'

He went out to make the call and Amanda remained at the window. The square was empty and the tulip tree in the midst of it was black and forlorn.

On the side table was the collection she had made of Edward's week-end belongings before the latest news had partially reassured her. She had meant to show them to Luke in the hope that his trained eye would pick out some detail to explain the child's behaviour. There was little there apart from pyjamas, slippers and sponge-bag. Experience of the treasure trove which her own son Rupert, now finishing at Harvard, had been in the habit of carrying about with him at that age had taught her to expect something exotic, but here were none of the processed breads and fishpaste laid in against sudden and overwhelming hunger; no device for seeing backwards; no Lion Powder; no hibernating fauna. There was just one small roll of cellulose tape and another of two-inch zinc plaster; a razor blade meticulously packed in a home-made cardboard folder; a box of throat lozenges, sealed; four copies of periodicals (*Punch*, *Make it Yourself*, *Exchange & Mart* and *The Boy's Technician*); a twist of string, and a tube of lanolin. She sighed and turned to the window again. He was a funny little grig, she reflected, with something about him which she felt she ought to recognise and did not; something dangerous and grown-up. Luke had given her the note on the telegram form and she read it for the tenth time.

'Why Tuesday?' she demanded, as the Superintendent came back into the room. 'Why do you think Edward says we shall know on Tuesday?'

'That's when he goes back to school, isn't it? He doesn't want you to worry. It's his main anxiety. I was thinking; have you got a birthday soon? Is he getting you a present? Something difficult?'

Amanda's eyes turned towards the *Exchange & Mart* and widened, but Luke was still talking. 'Speaking of unlikely items, what is this doing here, do you think? It's new since I arrived an hour ago.' He pulled the door wider to show the hall where, leaning against the faded Morris wallpaper, just inside the front door, a sandwich board had appeared. The webbing harness belonging to it lay on the tiles beside it.

On the board was a printed poster with hand-done additions in colour. Its intention was to be sensational.

Repent!   Repent!   Repent!

BABYLON IS FALLEN   Revelations XIV 8.

... and there was

NO MORE SEA!!!!!   Revelations XXI 1.

END OF THE WORLD

The lower third of the sheet contained a drawing of the familiar mushroom cloud, to which a watery flavour had been given by the addition of blue, green and crimson splashes, some of which spelled out the word '*Hydrogen*' in ragged, liquid letters.

'It's old Deeds,' Luke said in surprise. 'Does he often come here?'

'I don't think so. I've never heard of him—unless he's that man who trudges round the West End. All the hydrogen in the oceans to ignite? What a stinker of an idea. Entirely impractical—I hope.'

'That's one of the End of the World Society's posters. They're always dreaming up trouble!' The Superintendent glanced round him. 'There should be a satchel-load of their throwaways somewhere. They're a genuine Society; three old girls and a couple of nutties with an office of a sort in Marylebone Lane.'

'Good Heavens! Who supports them?'

'There's a fund, of course: there always is in these cases. As a rule it's a few pounds bequeathed for a specific purpose under a nineteenth-century will. The money is invested by law, brings in next to nothing and the income is spent strictly as per the Departed's instructions, usually entailing a lot of homework for all concerned!'

'What does this lot do? Publicise the Book of Revelations?'

'That sort of thing.' He was rubbing his blue chin, trying to remember. 'They pay Deeds as much as they've got, I think, but he still goes on staggering round the Town whether he gets any money or not. He doesn't beg but I imagine people give him a little. The Society supplies the posters but he may touch them up himself, I don't know. What would he be doing here?'

'Ah, Charles. I thought I heard your voice.' The words came from behind them as Avril put his head out of the study door. 'Any sign of the boy yet?'

'He is known to be still in London, sir. He was seen and was all right this afternoon, but he's not home yet.'

'I see. We must wait. Could you both come into the study a minute? I have a Mr Deeds with me. Albert appears to have sent him. . . .'

'Campion? But I've only just left him.'

'Yes, I think they met this morning, in the street before Mr Deeds started work. He spoke to Albert about a problem he has and it was suggested, then, that he should drop in to see me on his way home. Unfortunately I don't know if his difficulty is in your province or mine.'

It was an unexpected remark, for the old Canon was usually very sure indeed where his own boundaries lay. However, when they saw his visitor the problem became apparent.

'Good' Deeds was a gaunt man, made to look even taller by the monk's habit and cowl which he wore like a brown duffel-coat over a shabby blue suit. His shirt collar was frayed but formal and his tie, which had once belonged to a member of a long defunct Anglo-Indian yachting club, was a colourful example of a very specialised type of design. He had pushed back his hood, and his head, extremely small for his height, showed grey and closely cropped. He had a pallid face which was made remarkable, firstly by an expression of almost stupefying arrogance, and then by the fact, which did not register upon one immediately but provided a shock after the first few seconds, that his spectacles of black plastic were frames only, and had no glass in them.

He was standing on the rug, tapping his foot with theatrical impatience at the delay caused by their arrival, and reminded everyone irresistably of the strangely self-righteous way in which some people feel they must return an unsatisfactory purchase to a shop.

The old Canon appeared extraordinarily interested. 'It's the Biblical references,' he explained. 'After years of accuracy, Mr Deeds here is beginning to think he is sometimes wrong....'

'That's what *you* say!' said the visitor with vast superiority. He had a harsh, hollow voice, a nondescript accent and nothing but contempt behind his smile, and yet he was piteous rather than absurd.

'No, no. My dear fellow,' Avril was gently firm. 'You and I have just looked it all up and discovered that both the present references on your board out in the hall are quite correct. *Revelations, Chapter fourteen, verse eight* gives us *"Babylon is fallen"* and Chapter *twenty one, verse one* in the same book gives us the poetic prophecy concerning the ending of the seas....'

'I admit that.' The End of the World Man shrugged his shoulders as if he were well aware of some trick which Avril was preparing to play upon him, and Luke, who was jingling the coins in his pockets, decided to interfere. He was tired and preoccupied, and the pattern of mental behaviour presented so vividly was depressingly well-known to him.

'Sometimes the numbers change mysteriously, I suppose?' he began. 'On your board or in the Bible?'

'If you were not one of the Lost, Mr Luke—I know who you are, you see, and I shall write it down—you'd know that nothing ever changes in the Bible. Some of us know why.'

'Blimey! We all know why. Because of the seven vials and the seven plagues and the seven whatnots, as set down on the last half-dozen pages of the Good Book!' The Superinten-

135

dent's psychiatric treatment, if rough and ready, had a salutary effect. Mr Deeds turned away from him and a brief intelligence appeared in his wide blank eyes.

'But surely you can see it's a crime?' he said with exaggerated patience, listening to himself speak. 'I'm being tricked into "Adding unto the Word" so that I may be Flung into the Pit. I'm Labouring to Save and this is my reward—the Sores and the Rivers of Blood.'

'Oh, I see now!' The old Canon seemed relieved that the trouble was no worse. 'It's the curse at the end of the prophecy which is worrying you so?'

'Naturally.' A sad smile of intellectual superiority settled on the tragically stupid face. ' "If any man shall add unto these things, God shall add unto him the Plagues." It's all there. Written down in letters of red and black.'

'Oh, come off it for goodness sake, Deeds!' Luke exploded, suddenly embarrassed. 'This is the man who can put you straight, see? He knows what's the Word and what isn't. That's his job. Those old numbers of chapters and verses, they're not in the Greek, are they, sir? You can set his mind at rest about that, can't you? They're just extras put in by the priests or the printers or someone to make it easy in the translation. That's right, isn't it?'

The End of the World Man perceived the escape route with visible relief. The Canon had no need to speak. A shadow in the blank face cleared at once and immediately he became condescending again, eyeing the proffered easement with capricious suspicion like a spoiled dog sniffing a sweet. Presently he saw another advantage.

'They don't know that, do they?' he enquired almost brightly. 'They're doing their best to destroy me and they fail and they don't know why! It's a crime all the same. If you do your duty you'll march them away.'

'I should say so! Down to the nethermost Hell of Bow Street! No one is altering your board, Deeds. You imagine it.'

The Canon intervened: 'We were discussing that very point

just before you came in, Charles, and it's odd. You told me, didn't you, Mr Deeds, you're convinced that sometimes the reference *"Revelations twenty-one, verse one"* becomes *"Revelations six verses one to seven"*? I must say I found that very extraordinary.'

Luke stared at him. He was not quite so sharply on the ball as usual and turned to Deeds with weary kindliness.

'You shouldn't come and tell me wonders when I'm having a bucket of them from the scientists,' he murmured. 'Do the numbers change before your eyes? No? Well then, who complains?'

'Too many people, Mr Luke,' said the visitor with sudden reasonableness. 'They couldn't all be mistaken, could they? It always happens in the evening, always in the same street. People come and tell me afterwards. "It was wrong again yesterday" they say: or "You changed it. It was different". They tell me together and they've seen it wrong together.'

The hollow voice with its trace of education was eerily convincing and the policeman sighed.

'But they never stop you and tell you *at the time*?'

'No. I wouldn't have it; it's well known. I wouldn't pause once I am on my work. I go straight on, handing out my folders, looking neither to right nor left, nor tarrying in the way. Men must wait until my labour is done and my burden is rested before they speak to me.'

Luke ducked his chin and his white teeth appeared. 'You don't loiter, I'll hand you that. Do you know I thought that was out of deference to our regulations! So people tell you about the alteration afterwards, do they? At the coffee stall? They're ganging up to make a game of you!'

'No. I know when they do that.'

'So? What's the explanation? A sort of barmy miracle?'

'That's not for me to say, nor you neither, Mr Luke.'

The pitying smirk was still on the grey face as Mrs Talisman tapped on the door, opened it and let the white cat into the room.

'Excuse me, sir,' she said to Avril. 'But I thought you'd want

E*   137 to see this. I noticed it from the area. It was sitting on the front step and as soon as I opened the door it came in and went sniffing round those things in the hall. It's the same creature which was about here this morning but it's not the same person with it; not the same at all.'

It was an absurd interruption which took everybody completely by surprise. Luke gaped at the animal and the Canon regarded his housekeeper in bewilderment. Mr Deeds' reaction was more extraordinary. The dark colour rose in his grey face and settled in dull patches on his cheekbones. He grew very still and did not look at anything directly, but his eyes shifted disconcertingly and for the first time it occurred to them all that on occasions he might be actually dangerous.

The cat stalked across the carpet towards him, its distinctive tail with the sandy tip waving purposefully in the air as it began to circle the dusty skirts of the brown habit, purring noisily and rubbing itself against the coarse wool. Deeds ignored it and remained staring at the wall with the same flaring uncertainty about him. Surprisingly, the Superintendent seemed to understand.

'You've been enticing that moggie, Deeds, haven't you? Whose is it? Why do you want it?'

'How dare you! What a filthy suggestion! Take it away! You've enticed it yourself. It's attracted to you, not me. You've got something on your clothes! Take it away, take it away!' Short of confession he could hardly have conveyed guilt more clearly. He was like a stage caricature of a sex-starved Victorian maiden lady accused of thinking about soliciting. Luke began to laugh.

'Keep your hair on, I don't see any crime. It's not a very valuable brute. Why do you want it to follow you if you don't like it?'

'Go away!' Mr Deeds flounced his robes at the animal as if it were the Great Beast of his prophecy and threw himself out of the room with reckless clumsiness. Mrs Talisman squeaked and from the hall came the rattle and clatter of his board as he fought and banged himself out of the house with it. The cat, undismayed and graceful as a swallow, wreathed and circled about him as he strode across the square.

The old Canon was dismayed. 'Poor fellow!' he murmured. 'Did you know how much that would upset him, Charles?'

'Not quite.' Luke was a little taken aback himself. 'He's shocked to find that some little asininity of his which he thought was absolutely secret is perfectly obvious to everybody. He's discovered in a bus without his pants on, that's all.'

'I don't understand it,' said Amanda. 'What was happening to the cat?'

'Oh, he'd made himself interesting to it to get it to follow him as if it loved him.' Luke was a little embarrassed. 'There are various . . . er . . . ungents which will do that; some more salubrious than others. I shouldn't think he was fur-trapping or anything venal. If I know Deeds and his kind he's trying to prove either to himself or some other poor nit that Pussy loves him better than Pussy's own master or missus! That's life—less tragic than ruddy silly, half the time!' He glanced at a shabby knapsack lying in the corner. 'He's left his folders. Never mind, I'll get them dropped back at his room. I'm glad you saw him, Canon. The idea of getting cursed by accident in some way or another is the kind of bogey which seems to ride that sort of bloke. He catches at the idea, colours it, tries it on this way and that to make himself interesting to himself, but it's utterly terrible to him just the same. Nobody knows what those people suffer. If ever this blasted invention of ours gets going we shall all have a few shocks.'

Old Avril shook his head; he was very certain of his ground. 'He will find a way to escape it. That is Pride, the tourniquet round the soul. No little machine is going to cure that, I'm afraid; even the latest.'

' "The Paranoic Sin of Pride!" ' said Luke, unexpectedly in the picture. 'Strewth! What an alternative! Did Campion spot that? Is that why he sent him here?'

'Oh no, I don't think so.' Avril appeared surprised. 'It was the reference he noticed I should say, wouldn't you?'

'Which reference?'

'Why, the second one, Charles. The one Mr Deeds' friends only see him carry sometimes. *"Revelations, Chapter six verses one to seven"*. He told us, don't you remember? He will have told Albert. I looked it up for him but he didn't want to listen. It's that passage with the dramatic repetitions. All the four great Beasts at the four corners of the world sit up and cry the same thing one after the other: "Come and see! Come and see! Come and see! Come and see!" It's a great favourite with the young, or used to be. Albert must have recognised it and thought it was curious. That boy is full of odd information like that.'

' "Come and see!"? What do you know!' Luke was staring. 'That doesn't sound like a street joke. It doesn't sound like a joke at all.'

'A message?' Amanda was startled out of her preoccupation.

'I'm sure of it,' said Luke.

14

The Sound of Drumming

WHEN Mr Campion went upstairs to pack an over-night bag and Luke slipped out to fetch the car, Amanda followed her husband. She closed the door of the bedroom behind her and stood watching him as he hurried.

Ever since he had returned to the house half an hour before, and all through their report on The End of the World Man, there had been something about him which had reminded her of someone she had half forgotten; a pale, blank-faced youngster whose continuous flippancy had masked an acutely sensitive intelligence which as a teenager she had adored.

An explanation occurred to her suddenly.

'Albert, you're frightened,' she said.

He glanced at her, his pale eyes unsmiling.

'Only just off the gibber, Lady,' he said briskly. 'I'm glad you came up. I want to talk to you.'

'About Edward? I was wondering; suppose I got the name of every parent from the school secretary and simply sat at the telephone and made a job of it, telephoning and asking if he's with them? I needn't offer any explanation. How could that start a rumour or put the newspapers on to Mayo's disappearance?'

'So Luke told you about the decision not to put out a general call?'

'He said it was thought to be too early. It is, of course, if you saw him. You did, didn't you?'

'I saw a small boy in a beret from above when I spoke to the man on the door downstairs he convinced me. It was Edward all right, and as far as anyone can tell he was completely alone.' He hesitated, looking at the two utterly dissimilar slippers in his hands as if he were trying to decide if they were a pair. 'That's why I've got the wind up, I think. How well do we know him?' He discarded both shoes as having something unspecified wrong with them, and packed a pair of pumps. 'Do we really know him? Or do we just think that he's another Rupert at that age?'

Amanda considered and he found it like her that she should not commit herself without thinking.

'There's something odd about him,' she admitted. 'It's a sort of austerity. He's very formal and rather boy scout. He's not being disloyal to *us*, to you and me, I mean. I swear that. What's the matter with you, Albert? You're frightening me. Luke's shaken too. He seems to have a vision of a dreadful over-intimate world in which every thought is absolutely communal. Is that what you've been facing?'

'Frankly, no,' said Campion with a sigh. 'In my present state I could almost take that. I've been confronted by something a deal more solid and immediate.'

'What was it?'

'I don't like to think. It had higher-ape blood, I fancy. Amanda, do we know anything about Lord Ludor?'

'Not a lot. It's said that he went to see Tubby Hogan— the blind, bedridden, "Sparks V.C."—not long after the war on some well publicised do-good mission. He appeared in all the pictures, promised a lot of support, and did nothing but bribe the hero's invaluable guide-batman to leave him without notice. Hogan was lying in his room helpless for two days. I heard that in the Alandel Works years ago. Apart from that I know no more than is common knowledge. You've actually seen him, I take it?'

'Only too closely.'

'Does he make faces as they say? It's an extraordinary form of affectation.'

'It is not affectation.' Mr Campion had never looked more serious. 'There's nothing pseudo about him. He's as real and ugly as a busted atom. I've been shut up with him in the Director's office and my impression is that we all aged ten years and the carpet wore out round him while we looked.'

'He got on to the story pretty quickly.'

'Long before anybody else. Hence the truly amazing speed of official reaction. I think Arnold must report to him privately every day on an outside wire, probably in the early morning. By breakfast today he knew everything Arnold knew last night, plus the fact that the Mayos had not returned to the Island as Paggen said they would when they left here. Anyway, Ludor was on the telephone to L.C. Corkran before he arrived at his office and they found Mrs Mayo at Robinson's Hotel for him just after she'd telephoned Luke. Ludor thought the device was Paggen Mayo's own, of course. He still does.'

'That's absurd.' Amanda spoke flatly and his pale eyes flickered towards her.

'He doesn't think so. In fact he has the whole story tied up to his own satisfaction. The instant he heard about Edward's friend Rubari and the link with Daumier's the penny dropped with an audible rattle and he produced a complete and certainly logical explanation. His brain is like a computor. In goes the data and out comes the answer in flat, inhuman terms, absolutely correct if everybody concerned happens to be made to one of the half-dozen patterns which he has found most common. A terrible and terrifying chap, Amanda. Almost certain to be fifty per cent right!' He paused and eyed her. 'His main assumption is that Mayo must have had an unexpected success with his device, realised that under the terms of his contract with Godley's he stood to make less money than he would have done elsewhere, and decided to approach a rival firm.'

'Oh yes?' She sounded amused. 'I shouldn't have said Mayo was that type at all.'

'Nor should I, but Ludor does say so. He has decided that Mayo has been using Sam as a guinea-pig and that Sam has recruited another suitable child at the school—Edward, in fact, who has turned out to be older, more reliable, and has the added advantage of not having parents on hand to get in the way. According to Ludor, Martin is either not in the secret or else he got cold feet at the last moment. Either way, he says,

143

he has been discredited and provided with a bolt-hole by the faked suicide attempt.'

'Good Heavens!'

'You wait, my girl! His Lordship is nothing if not tidy-minded. He believes that the object of this particular week-end's outing is to stage a demonstration for the prospective purchasers. He says Edward and Mayo have taken the day off and are somewhere in London waiting for an appointed hour to effect some sort of trial communication with the opposite lads in Paris.'

Amanda's brown eyes became uneasy. 'He might almost have something there,' she admitted. 'That is how Edward is behaving. It's what I was trying to say about him; he's dedicated. It's peculiar in a child but he's behaving as if he considers he is on a mission.' She stood hesitating, reviewing the position. 'No,' she said at last. 'That story of Ludor's is impossible. We all saw Mayo try the things out last night and the man was staggered. He *couldn't* have been putting on that performance.'

'Ludor says he must have been. He says we were deceived.'

'I don't believe it. Why did Mayo come here anyway? To further the plot to discredit Martin? Or to see if the family had found the things and confiscated them? That's idiotic.'

'Well, is it?' Mr Campion was standing by his open bag, regarding her curiously. 'Ludor says that no inventor would permit his work to go out of his control; he insists that Mayo must have been in touch with the children all the time.'

'—and knew what was happening by Extra Sensory Perception? Whatever next!'

'Lord Ludor believes the thing works,' Mr Campion said drily. 'He admits that communication may not be perfect, but he feels that must come. He says Mayo must have known it the instant that the things passed out of the children's possession, and that he hurried to retrieve them, using Martin as an excuse. He also says that the arrangement for Mayo and Edward to meet today was evidently made beforehand and that the boy has simply carried on, still under the influence of the man.'

'That is utter poppycock!' The engineer in Amanda was thoroughly irritated. 'It's not that sort of device and there is no reason to suppose that it will develop in that way at all. That's roughly the old "electrode implanted in a subject brain" idea—a filthy and completely anti-social concept. This thing of ours is merely an amplifier which increases the strength of certain signals whose existence have hitherto been in doubt. To give it any greater or lesser significance is to make a nonsense of it. This is the beginning. Now we have to locate and simulate the transmitter so that we can control it. No one can know where we go from there.'

'Except Ludor,' persisted Campion. 'Don't forget he was in it from the start. He knows exactly where he intends it to go.'

'But the man can't sit on this, whatever the threat to his business interests! This is a secret which the Earth is giving up. *This is another shot in the locker, Albert!* It'll come bursting out all over the place once it's started. Ludor may possibly delay development for a year or so but ...'

The words died on her lips as she caught his expression.

'My impression is that he only needs a year or so,' he said softly. 'Think about the man for a minute. He's the first of the "power boys" I've ever really seen in the round. One is so apt to see these lads as potential Napoleons or Stalins, straddling vast territories and controlling vast quantities of people. But spend an hour or two with Lord Ludor and you can see that quantity is incidental. He's interested in acquiring complete power over the *individual*—over the rival, the partner, the employee, the secretary, the second-in-command, the wife, the mistress, the friend, the headwaiter, the man in the wig or the coronet or just the innocent ass walking by in the street. He's a great big brutal demigod of whom everybody he comes into contact with very soon becomes openly afraid. He doesn't want to command armies. He wants to command *YOU*. At the moment he's sitting pretty; virtually omnipotent in his own particular empire. Now he's seen a chance, if only for a year or so, of being very nearly omniscient as well. I don't think he can resist it. Upon my soul! After spending a couple of hours' petrified study, trying to understand him, I believe it's as elementary as that!'

Amanda did not speak at once but eventually she said thoughtfully: 'They say that what his boys know about "bugging" offices is nobody's business. Have you heard of that very odd little concern called "Advance Wires Ltd."? That is said to be his. I believe they've got a small experimental outfit tucked away on Godley's Island. But I think you're over-drawing him. You make him sound like an ogre.'

Mr Campion laughed abruptly. 'He's more like an old male gorilla sitting on the top of his own dark tree. He can look out all round him and he can boss everyone under him, but he can't see into every mind in that black labyrinth—not yet. He means to. He's bitten by the idea. Now I must go to that island and get there if I can before he does. Sam and Martin have American citizenship, which is a considerable protection in the circumstances I should say, but even so . . .'

'Edward?'

'I know.' He had taken her hand and stood looking down at it. Presently his fingers closed tightly over her soft forearm. 'Ludor's theory is that Mayo will return to the Island after the test and will send Edward back here with some plausible ex-cuse, trying to keep the whole thing dark until Daumier's interest crystallises in a definite offer. His lordship could be right, so you wait here and the instant Edward appears . . .'

'I'll ring Security.'

'No, my Sweet. I hate to say it but not on your life! Once you get your hands on Edward, *hide him*. Ludor is looking for him and he has highly skilled help and too much influence. He might even find him. My paternal instinct has never been over-developed but I don't feel that chap is any fair match for those of tender years.'

'Really?' She was inclined to be derisive. 'Even an ogre could hardly bite the child with the Director of British Security looking on.'

'Possibly not,' conceded Mr Campion, whose pale face was still obstinate. 'But my serious impression is that the very sight of him may stop growth. And last time I saw the revered Director he was as frightened of the brute as I am.'

Meanwhile, on the other side of the City, a hot and exhausted Edward ceased his steady trotting round the piece of waste land which had seemed so suitable for his purpose, and settled himself to rest against a plane tree. He chose the side of the trunk least visible from the footway and his dark green raincoat faded into the shadows as if it had been designed as camouflage.

He was on a hilly triangle of public land, the last that was left of the once open fields which had given the ancient Borough of Manifold Wick E. its name. The place was remarkably deserted just now, considering it was hemmed in on all sides by new blocks of flats and old mansions freshly converted into dwellings. It was the hour of the evening meal and the children and old people who enjoyed the air space in the normal way were indoors eating. It was cold under the tree and inclined to be misty. The dead leaves were damp and odorous in the sparse grass. The tall streetlamps, glowing yellow, had been lit some time and their deep orange glow took the colour out of the Pontisbright hair as Edward knew they would. He ventured to take off his beret which was abominably tight.

He was in excellent condition but he had been running for a long time and his heart was thumping. He leaned back and closed his eyes and composed himself, trying to forget his anxiety as well as his exasperation. Presently panic seized him and he put his hand up inside his muffler and felt for the patch of bandage beside his thin neck and the small, hard cylinder beneath it.

'Running in' had always taken time, he knew, even in the beginning. He comforted himself with the reflection and thrust the sneaking fear firmly out of his mind that something drastic had gone wrong with this new example. They were

147

going to be furious anyhow, he feared. Front-of-the-house chaps always got furious if something went wrong. He tried not to regret the lost two receivers which had been going so well, but it was difficult; they had been just ripe, just going like dreams. With Sam trained to the *nth* as well. . . . That fourth one had been jolly miraculous. Now, probably, some hamfisted ass was dissecting it. It made one feel sick. His pressure increased on the cylinder and he felt it give, as if he had pressed too hard. He was so frightened by the possibility that he froze like a rabbit and it was then, suddenly, in the moment of blankness, that he got the first burst of signals. There was no sense in them, of course, but they were there, exciting as always. He was still young enough to have no fear at all. No single starling of a feeding flock, receiving an alarm signal from a sentinel, could have been less suspicious of the mechanism by which the warning had been sent. The idea of unspoken communication between members of his own species was no bother to Edward. Many of the other facts of life, as the biology class put it so primly, still appeared to him to be much more outlandish than this simple mind-to-mind or heart-to-heart communion. As Henri had said to him, years before when they had first discussed the newly imparted details of human digestion, 'if you can believe *that* you can believe anything!', and he had agreed wholeheartedly.

Now, curled up under the tree while the yellow lights shone warm and the shadows hung deep, he settled himself to get in the proper mood for good reception. So far, there had been no identifiable personal signal in the general storm. All the usual mysterious 'beefing' was there, incomprehensible adult fears and meaningless moaning about uninteresting emotions, but these he could disregard out of hand. The items he could best distinguish were the yelps about homely things. These were expressions of irritation, mostly. People thinking 'Damn this or that machine', or 'Blast! I've missed it!' or 'Oh! He *knows*!' or 'Look out!'. Sometimes the whole pulsing world seemed to be full of that one intensely human but impersonal command: 'Look out! Look out! Look OUT!' as if it were

the universal message. From the point of view of one trying to
be his own selector it was very exhausting. The boy eased the
bandage off his pulse for a breather. That was the one bad
thing about the iggy-tube. It did stop one thinking clearly. He
had wondered two or three times lately if they were letting
Sam do a bit too much. All the same, it had been useful this
morning to know about 'gen-fatigue'. He had had to warn Sam
about not letting himself be questioned. 'Go wet!' he had
commanded. 'You know how one does when one's iggied up?'
It could all be bad for Sam, he supposed, but then he'd grow
out of it only too soon. He put the worry aside for the time
being and got out his book and pen to make a few notes for
his report.

After a while he got up and brushed himself as well as he
could and resumed the beret, trying to arrange it so that the
tight-head-band did not cut into the seam across his forehead
made by its last application. It had taken him some time to
find the address on his first visit, but he thought he knew his
way back to the house again from here and he set off walking
very fast. He dived down a passage between the older houses,
passed through a small area of seedy shops, found his way to a
main thoroughfare—which he crossed with some difficulty
since the evening traffic was still heavy—and came at last to a
network of neat suburban streets, each lined with a continuous double row of newly prosperous little houses, all enjoying a second youth of brave new paint and nylon curtain-
ing. Edward found Nemesia Road without difficulty and
trotted along it looking for number forty-three. There were
lights at most of the windows, and here and there a touch of
gaiety, such as a bit of wrought iron or a pair of carriage lamps
lit up beside a violently coloured front door.

At exactly a quarter past the hour, he pushed open the
iron gate in the golden hedge which smelled of cats. There
was a light in the front window, he saw with relief, but
no car against the kerb, which was ominous. Hoping for the
best, he hurried down the path and rang the bell.

A girl he had seen before appeared at once, pink and

bothered, and stood looking down at him with good natured if somewhat off-hand compassion.

'Oh dear!' she said. 'It's you. I'm going to make you livid. I'm afraid. I'm so sorry.'

'Isn't he coming?'

'He can't yet. You see he telephoned. . . .' She was not very upset because earlier he had gone out of his way to reassure her, even hinting mendaciously that he was based fairly near.

'Did you tell him I was here?' he enquired.

'No, I didn't. I'm so sorry; I am really.'

She was not thinking of him at all. She was worrying about her clothes. '*New shoes.*' Edward got the flash almost as clearly as Sam would have done. '*Hell! New shoes!*'

'I'll come back,' he said.

'Can you?' He suspected that she was thinking about transport now, *her* transport. It was very difficult to get her, she was so faint. Yet she wasn't unkind. She was friendly to anyone.

'Of course I can,' he said. 'When will you be back? Eleven? Twelve?'

'Oh, eleven. But that's terribly late.' She was late now. Edward couldn't tell if he had heard the clock strike, or if she had suddenly thought it was half-past six and he had received it.

'Don't worry about me,' he said. 'And don't bother him. I'll see him when he comes in. Goodbye. I'm in a hurry, too.' He ran away from her and she closed the door after a moment of indecision. Edward knew exactly what she was thinking.

Presently he returned to the long street and started trudging back to the main road where he had noticed the delicatessen and the cinema.

It was going to be a very close thing. He was short of money and he needed some good greasy filling chips and a phone call, not to Amanda this time. He wondered if he dared reverse the charges and how you did it from a call box. It was quite a problem; the cinema was a must.

15

The Islanders

WHEN at last Martin and Sam walked slowly down the unmade track along the sea-wall to the converted army hut they both felt the afternoon had been too long.

They had lunched on sandwiches in the car coming down and, when the police escort had left them soon afterwards at the military post on the Strada, Martin had dropped off at the main Experimental Block to make a call on Professor Tabard. Melisande had then driven on to her own house and Sam and Helena had continued to the hut on foot.

They had found it in considerable disorder, for nothing had been done to it since Martin had been rescued from the escaping gas by Fred Arnold and Paggen Mayo on the night before. They did their best but there remained the question of food, and as soon as Martin had returned Helena had been forced to send him off again with Sam on a foraging expedition. On her instructions they had been to the canteen and acquired some cold ham and a loaf. Even this had not been as easy as it might have been because the indefatigable Fred Arnold, who could usually find a meal for a friend in an emergency, was not there. He was expected, though. Maureen, the fat assistant, had said so, and she had done what she could for them. She also gave them some lukewarm coffee, but the canteen had been cold and deserted and also a little sticky after the Rectory, whose shabbiness was of a different order, and they had been glad to come away. They chose the sea-wall path home because the tide was in and there was a certain wild freshness about the estuary, with the sky tumbling above it in the failing light like a line full of a giant's khaki washing.

They passed behind Paggen Mayo's prefabricated cedar-wood residence and hurried a little because they did not want to see Melisande again. She had been subdued enough on the way down but there had been real fear behind her eyes and she made a difficult companion. Her daughters would be with her now: solid solemn girls in their teens, who were probably better able to manage her than anybody.

There were a couple of other huts to pass before father and son reached their own; one belonging to the computer's technical expert, who slept whenever he could, and another temporarily empty, so they had no greetings from anybody and no questions, and might have been alone in the world on the grey marsh. Sam had begun to dance as he walked and presently he put his hand in Martin's as he used when much younger.

'It's nice to be home,' he said and the remark cut so reassuringly into the young man's troubled train of thought that he looked down guiltily.

'This is a lousy living space for you and your Mom. I guess I ought to let you two settle on the mainland in a decent house while I fix about staying here when I have to.'

'No. Don't do that. We're all right. We like it here.' Sam was definite. 'We got a bit peeved by Mr Mayo shoving us all around but we don't really care. He's a great man, I know. Why is he so scared of you being clever too?'

'Hey! Don't you go saying crazy things like that!'

'Well, he is.' Sam spoke with the sublime authority of one who has inside information. 'All his thoughts and feels go dithery when he sees you. Like he can't bear to look. There's a master at school who makes it happen to the Head. It's jolly interesting if you notice.'

Martin passed a hand over his face. 'Hell!' he said, adding abruptly, 'so you had one of those devices with you here last holidays?'

'No. They wouldn't agree to it. They didn't think it was safe.' He paused. 'Sometimes I can do it without—almost.'

'What?'

'Only sometimes. It's when I've been wearing my iggy-tube a lot and suddenly leave it off. For a little while it's still almost as if I had it on.'

'Your mind is still in the receiving posture?'

'Something like that.' Sam was not very interested. 'Anyway, Mr Mayo is scared of you and it makes him sickish. He's a bit ashamed of that but not much.'

'How do you know, Sam? Because you feel it too?'

'Well, I feel what he feels but I know it's him and not me. After that I have my own feel, of course, which would be "glad stroke laughing-at" in his case, I expect. Sucks to him!'

'But you also know *why* he feels what he does?'

'Of course. Otherwise I'd just be doing it like animals do, wouldn't I? They react. I think. Well, I do. Don't I?'

Martin said nothing, shutting his mouth deliberately. He had given his word to Helena that he would not discuss the device with Sam without her. It was very difficult to keep the promise.

They were approaching the back of their own dwelling; its creosote-impregnated sides rose dark and forlorn in the disconsolate scene. Martin paused abruptly and stood looking down at a small iron trap-head which stood up an inch or so out of the coarse grass and white sand. It was the main water stop-cock; somewhere near it there would be something of the same sort for the gas supply. He had rejected out of hand the story of Mayo and the fake suicide attempt which Helena had suggested and Melisande's account had confirmed. But he could not forget it. He glanced about him in the grass, feeling guilty. If the gas supply had been interrupted for a moment or so to extinguish his fire on the evening before, there could hardly be any proof of it now, let alone anything to incriminate any one particular person. He found the small iron head presently. It was set in concrete and half hidden by a tarred boundary post. Sam was attracted to it at the same moment and went up and kicked it. As he stumbled he saw something behind the post and whipped it up out of the crevice between it and the white concrete.

'A fab white pencil!' he said. 'Look, not even broken.'

Martin took it from him and stood holding it with the dark colour growing deeper and deeper in his face. It was an ordinary six-sided pencil but the make was unusual and its length had been cut down to three inches. The neatly fluted strokes with which it had been sharpened were as familiar to him as his own fountain pen. It was one of Paggen Mayo's many little personal affectations that he always carried a piece of pencil like this tucked into the bottom of the outside breast-pocket of the suits he changed into once the sun went down. Moreover, when he lost one it was always in the same way, by bending over and permitting it to slip out. This was no sort of proof of his guilt in the present situation, but had he signed the story with his own hand he could hardly have made it more convincing to the hurt and horrified young man who had admired him and been loyal to him.

Helena unlocked the door to them and caught sight of her husband's face as he stepped into the room.

'What's happened?' she demanded anxiously. 'Did you meet him?'

'Who?'

'Vaughan-Jenner. He came looking for you a few minutes ago from Professor Tabard. He thought he might catch you on the road. He said not to worry you but to warn you that the Lord is imminent.'

'Is he? Sorry I missed Drasil. We came along by the sea. Is Paggen back?'

'He said no. I think that was something to do with it. Will you have to go back up there?'

'I don't think so. He'll find me if he wants me. The Professor is frankly excited. I don't think he ever really believed the thing could be translated into electronics or anything else. It's knocked him off Olympus, he's almost human.'

He sat down at the table and Sam joined him and they produced their packages. Helena fed them, and as they all sat eating, the family atmosphere settled and they grew close and content.

Martin looked at Helena. 'Sam says he doesn't need his iggy-tube. He can do it without. What do you know about that?'

'I only said sometimes. Anybody can do it sometimes.'

'I can't and I don't want to,' Helena said firmly but she was relenting. Sam's recovery had been sensational and her fears were subsiding fast. She nodded surreptitiously to Martin, who chose the most important of the questions he had been waiting to ask.

'Sam, when we went over to the lab that day and the Professor came in, did Mr Mayo mention something that had a very long name, something new?'

'Nipponanium? Yes he did.'

'I see. I suppose he called it the "magical element"—he often does?'

Sam nodded.

'And you repeated it to Edward?'

'Not exactly.' The vivid eyes were wide and defensive. 'It was only that whenever I saw it written down in papers and things I put a ring round it with my red biro and cut the bit out, because I wanted to remember how it was spelled.'

'Did you find it in your Japanese paper?' Helena demanded and glanced at Martin. 'It was that sample airmail news service thing. Do you remember? We all fell in love with the beautiful tissue it was printed on.'

'Is that where you saw it, Sam?'

'Not only there. It was in other things too. It was a new discovery. It was in two magazines and *The Evening News* and several other places. I kept them all.'

'Where are they now?'

'I gave Edward one so that he knew I wasn't making it up and the others are in my bag; the one Mummy's lost. Edward said I was to keep them safe and I haven't. Shall I get arrested?'

'You're sure that's all it was? Only the name of the element ringed round?' Helena sounded almost as apprehensive as he was.

'Wait.' Martin was assessing the position. 'Did you ever talk about your bag to anybody outside the island? Anybody at school, except Edward? Any grown-ups at all?'

'Only to one master.' It became evident that he remembered

the incident well, and had suffered pangs of conscience about it. 'He got ill or something and had to leave in the middle of last term. He was a spy, I think.'

'Sam, don't be silly.'

'I'm not. He only spoke to me once. He wasn't teaching my form, you see. Everyone said he was American but I knew he wasn't.'

'That wouldn't make him a spy.'

'No. But when Mr Allenbury confiscated my iggy-tube in class he gave it back at the end of the period, but he asked me about it and I said it was a game. Allenbaggers didn't ask me anything else but he laughed and he must have told some of the others in the common room because next day this Mr Marshall...'

'Who's that? The man everybody said was American and he wasn't?'

'Yes. He came up to me and asked me about it and said could he see it and what game was it. I said my magic bandage had got dirty and I'd thrown it away and it was a silly game about going on a space ship and the magic element was Nipponanium. He was going to ask me some more but the Head came by and of course he hurried off, because masters who teach in the upper forms don't talk to kids in the lower ones.'

'What made you think he was a spy?'

'Well, I had my tube on, see? And as he turned away he thought "Oh blow! I have missed that!" and I picked it up quite clearly. He was afraid because he had missed it and that was how I knew he must be a spy and afraid of getting into a row.'

Martin caught his wife's eye and they both laughed with the same uneasiness.

'You're reducing this to absurdity.'

'I'm not. That's what he did feel. I'm very good on feels. I get them right more often than anybody. I always feel what the sender feels and I know what it is and how much. *You* said so, Mom.'

'I did?'

'I heard you. You said it to the Head's wife when I was taken away from his study into the school the first time. You said "He's a sympathetic child". I asked about the word and it means understanding what other people feel. The dictionary says so.'

'So you decided the master was probably a spy.' Martin retrieved the subject by its tail. 'Did you tell anybody else about your bag and what was in it?'

'The Nipponanium wasn't my only secret,' Sam objected. 'I had my horoscope in it and my marks ever since I went to school, my book of poems I am writing and "How to catch a fairy" ... that's a spell Fred Arnold gave me for my bag out of a very old notebook a man called Hogan lent him.'

'Does it work?'

'I don't know. You have to have some "Venice glass" and the blood of a white hen.'

'That's against it, son. Well, did you tell anybody else about this bag of secrets?'

'Anybody at all?'

'Anybody.'

'I told Norah Mayo once.'

'Did you? I didn't know you talked to her much.'

'I don't. She's *fourteen* although she's the younger, but there isn't anybody else to talk to. Oh, I told Mrs Rogers the char but she's sloped off now.'

'Darling! Mrs Rogers was a cleaning woman and she has left the island.'

'Sorry, Mother. I only said what she said. Anyway she couldn't have taken my bag because she left in the holidays and you both saw it this term. I expect Fred Arnold took it because he's a spy, and spies for the Lord.'

Martin put an arm round his son's neck in a tackler's hold. 'You must say "Lord Ludor" and not "the Lord" and you've got spies on the brain!'

'Norah Mayo thought her father was a spy because her mother said so.' Sam gasped, enjoying the field-day whilst it lasted. 'That was a bit much when she didn't mean it.'

They were still dealing with him and the atmosphere was suddenly united when there was a discreet tap on the outer door. Martin rose to open it.

Drasil Vaughan-Jenner, who stood on the step, was in some ways as unlikely as his name. He was small and dapper and young and his clothes were in the advanced style, very trim and good and outlandish all at the same time. His collarless jacket was a miracle of tailoring and his tight trousers extreme. He had a shrewd, high cheek-boned face and tortoise-shell-coloured eyes, which for all their cleverness were very merry. He came in out of the mist which was rising fast and stood smiling at Helena with polite apology.

'I got sent straight back,' he said. 'Please don't let me disturb you; I don't need to be fed. We lead a harassed life, don't we? All hithering and thithering at the command of Great Brains who are utterly above the common necessities.'

'When did you eat last?' Helena enquired, pushing the remains of the ham towards him. 'You look a bit waif-like or is it merely the Oliver Twist outfit?'

'I had a hurried breakfast yesterday, I think,' he said cheerfully, settling himself before the food and looking about the table with bright, birdlike satisfaction.

'This is very good of you, Mrs Ferris, I shan't forget it when I come to Power! Since breakfast yesterday my Great Man has been all of a twitter and I've not been permitted to sit down, let alone eat! We've been keeping a breathless secret, Martin, both from you and Paggen Mayo, but now, since you've told Sir about your homework, I'm to tell you quicker than soon in case you get offended. Hence the intrusion.'

'You sound light-headed. Try this,' said Martin hospitably as he carved up the half-loaf. 'Is there any news of Paggen down there yet?'

'Not yet. After an hour on the telephone to H.Q. Great Man Tabard now suspects DISLOYALTY. After all, the man Mayo has been unobtainable for a whole half day! Tabard sees no dash to a Foreign Power, you understand, but a sordid commercial default. Mayo is seen in the Lab of Another, in fact. I laughed because it sounded so homey but Big Brain was not amused. He trusts you alone because you came and told him about your mechanical mind-reader and so I'm to confide our little bombshell to you.' He paused, ate gratefully and looked up, his sepia-flecked eyes very shrewd and sincere. 'That thing you mentioned about the possible importance of the blood-stream was the decider,' he said. 'That has delighted him. You'll see why. We are daring to think that we're approaching the transmitter.'

'Really?' Martin caught his breath and the little flush that flickered over his face like a shadow betrayed the jolt his heart had felt. 'Gosh!' It's going to be practical. I've never really dared to hope.'

'Oh, it's major stuff, my boyoh!' The newcomer was eating as though starved. 'It's all in embryo of course and looks it, rather. Both comic and embarrassing, but you'll see it's a real little living cell. I've been working with Len Drummond, you know. George Kestler has done what you might call the biology and I've been slaving away directly under Tabard. We now know everything about poor old Loopy Len except why he was born, poor chap.' He paused and Helena intervened.

'That's the remaining brother! The one who *sent* the commands?'

'That's him. I'm so glad you're in the picture Mrs Ferris. I didn't know how far Mayo stuck to the "no tellee wifee" rule. We had to waive it in our lot. No one would play! Well, after virtually wearing the item poor old Len calls a brain cuddled round my own for months and months, I suddenly discovered that he was one of these "colour-and-week-day" characters. You know them, don't you?'

'People who associate Monday, Tuesday, Wednesday and so on—each with a different definite shade?'

'That's it. No work has ever been done on it as far as I know. It's just a common old "common phenomenon". Some people do and some don't.'

'Monday is pinky-red,' said Sam. 'Tuesday bright pale blue,

159

Wednesday light green, Thursday grey, Friday brown, Saturday white and Sunday yellow.'

'Or gold,' said Drasil Vaughan-Jenner. 'Yes, you're fairly typical of B group. Thursday is neutral—grey or beige, and Saturday is a "no"; that is to say, black or white. The A people are quite different. It's curious, we don't know why. However, Len is B Group and so am I, although we differ as to the depth and type of the various shades. That seems to be the usual modification. There's endless variety there and we wasted a lot of time on it.'

'Wasted?' enquired Martin, who was listening intently.

Drasil grinned. 'We missed the one vital point.'

'Which is?'

'That one's reaction to colour is *emotional*. It's very slight, of course, but everything in this whole business is low-powered. We're dealing in gossamer. Nothing half as vigorous as a cats-whisker this time!'

'What do you know!' Martin spoke softly and then began to laugh. 'It's a genuine transposition,' he said at last.

'Feel into thought—Thought into feel,' said Sam, who was listening with the absorbed attention of one who had, it seemed, already pondered on the problem and discussed it. 'Edward will go crazy about this. It must be reliable too, because you don't change your colours ever, do you? It's a thing you're born with and you keep it all your life. Do you?'

'God knows! That's another great field for homework.' Drasil was talking to Martin. 'We're all kids at this stage, you see. We just don't know. The possibilities stretch out across acres of untrodden country.'

'What about your E.S.P. tests on this to date?'

'That's just it. They're staggering. Something like seventy three per-cent bang on, using all seven days of the week.'

'You use cards?'

'Yes. Len has the colours before him to generate the juice and the Receivers just have the printed names of the days ... if they can read. Illiterates have a duplicate set of colours but they call out the names of the days. Len is in his sound-proofed box.'

'Can you use anybody else but Len?'

The newcomer nodded. He looked positively guilty. 'Forty eight per cent correct with no special training. But they all have to be "naturals". That is, people who have always made the association of days and colours. With your amplifier, however, we may ring up the Jack Pot. I can't wait to see it in action, nor can Tabard.'

'Seven digits!' said Martin. 'Seven separate days and colours, each capable of being transmitted.'

'Exactly! With a computor and a code one could send out *"War and Peace"*!'

Martin whistled. 'The justification of General Smythe-White, by God!' he said piously. 'What about these transmitting types, Drasil? The Lens of the world? Do they have to be "sub-normal" or of very low I.Q.? That seems sort of horrible to me.'

'Oh, if you think about it it's all pretty alarming!' The young man was grinning. 'It won't appear so in a generation, naturally. Get it in perspective and it's not so depressing. After all, the effect of one night's viewing of a whole programme on Channel Nine on anybody's resuscitated Great Grandpa would present some interesting psychiatric data, I should think, wouldn't you? But actually, that problem you raise may not turn up. Tabard feels that subnormals and ... er ... kids—sorry, Sam—only make such good operatives because their forward minds are not entirely occupied. The amplifier may alter all that. The messages may come smashing through into anybody's intelligence.'

'But it's so dangerous!' Helena's cry was silenced by the young man's curious expression as he glanced at her.

'That's eternal too, ma'am,' he said. 'That's another little item which can't be helped. But cheer up, with the danger comes the courage.'

Helena looked at him curiously. 'That's what my uncle the Canon says.'

F   161

'Is it? It's Professor Tabard's great cry. However, the absolutely fascinating thing at the moment is a little item I've been saving for last. You know I told you George Kestler has been doing the biology? Well, he's come up with some very odd figures. They are so consistent that they can't be discounted. Far and away the best results in our colour-week-day tests are obtained with subjects who have one cracking great item in common: their blood group. That's why your latest contribution has sent Tabard through the roof. He's got poor George with him now. It looks as if they're approaching the heart of the heart of the heart, so to speak! What we all want now is the amplifier, please. If that dreary old mick, Mayo—consider that unsaid Martin—will only return with one of these, all will be forgiven and most things forgotten.'

In the silence which followed, while each member of the family was absorbed by his own particular reaction to the news, the sound of a car door slamming just outside penetrated into the room. An instant later someone tried the handle of the hut door and a familiar voice reached them.

'Albert!' Martin got it open but no one came in. The group round the table heard a brief whispered consultation and Martin went out without a word.

The thin man was alone and his face looked like bone in the uncertain light.

'It's Paggen Mayo I'm afraid, Martin.'

'Oh God ... not doing anything utterly crazy? Not refusing to give the things up?'

'No. Can you come with me? I've got to talk to his wife. He's dead.'

'*No.*' Martin was appalled. 'I don't believe it. How, for Heaven's sake?'

'We don't know quite. His body was found this afternoon in a truck, in a pile up on the Pittingham-Saltbridge motorway up in the Midlands. The driver is in hospital and can't tell us anything at the moment.'

'But how could he get there?'

'That's it. Luke's gone up to see what he can discover. They caught us with a police car just outside London on the way down here and took him off to a railway. I don't know anything else yet except that there seems to be a particularly bright Chief Inspector at Saltbridge Central who recognised the name on a tailor's tab and had the sense to ring the Yard. So it's being kept quiet at the moment. There's no hard information about the cause of death but the same D.C.I. is fairly certain it's an Unarmed Combat job, on which he's an expert. That would make it murder.'

Martin swung round on him. 'What about the amplifiers?'

'Exactly,' said Mr Campion. 'There's no trace of them.'

16

Things you could Tell an Old Friend

T H E sea, rushing in and out at speed, had left bright pools in the clay folds and in the air a coarse pleasant flavour like dried fish.

It was some time since the two had returned from their painful interview with Melisande Mayo and Mr Campion had gone to the mainland to telephone in order to avoid using the closely watched island exchange. Martin was still pacing the rough grass before the hut and when Sam was asleep, and nearly all the lights of the main block lost in the sea-wrack, Helena had come out to join him.

She had brought his coat and wore a shawl herself and for a long time they plodded along together over the turf, she turning when he did and neither saying a word.

Presently he put an arm round her shoulders and her head lay heavy against his collarbone.

'I should think this cleared him, wouldn't you?' he asked suddenly. 'He must have been killed *for* the things, that's certain.'

'I think so.' She dared say no more for fear of trespassing. In the last few hours, while she had got rid of Drasil and stood over Sam until she was sure he slept, she had learned so much about herself and her husband that she was still dizzy and afraid of showing how sickening-sweet was her secret relief at the removal of the menace to their life together. Even now she did not quite understand the details of the danger which had passed so dramatically, and it took her by surprise when Martin put his finger on them out there in the darkness and tore the menace apart and threw it away.

'There was nothing effeminate about the old boy except his devouring quality,' he observed. 'He couldn't help that. He was just Momma and Poppa rolled into one demanding boss.

He needed you to help express himself and so he had to have all of you all the time *and* your wife *and* your child all at his command. Otherwise he didn't feel safe.... Perhaps he wasn't. It was all to do with his creativeness, because he was creative, you know.'

Helena kept quiet. The sensation of an intolerable burden lifted was making her feel lightheaded, and the pleasure of having him back with no other allegiance to come between them was all the more acute because she had not understood the barrier when it had been there. She began to understand that he too was deeply relieved without wanting to know why.

'I'd often heard that the personality crystallises after death but it had never registered on me before,' he went on, very happy to have her to tell it to. 'He certainly was no traitor; that I swear. He'd never have kept it quiet from me for one thing. He'd have shown off about it, you know. Twisted it and looked at it and made it—sort of glamorous. Also, he had absolutely no intention of killing me with all that darn silly gas business last night. He simply wanted to get it into Tabard's head ... he never got the hang of Tabard at all, the man was way above him ... that I was some sort of brilliant nut whom no one but he could handle. That's the truth, the old so-and-so!'

He laughed softly, amazingly without resentment, condoning the outrageous act as if he were speaking of some pet animal whom he had known to be dangerous and who had savaged him because it was its nature.

'He was taking those amplifiers somewhere to get a good look at them and at some point on the way he was murdered and robbed of them. It's a spy-killing,' he announced, arriving at the conclusion by much the same process as Amanda had done some few hours earlier. 'As soon as he saw the things he must have decided that his data had been fed to someone outside and he couldn't discuss it with me because he'd put me out of action.'

He walked on in silence for a while and then his arm tightened about her. 'Do you think he thought I'd done it to him?'

165

She realised what an effort it must have cost him even to consider it. 'He'd be crazy if he did,' she said cautiously. 'You were both at work on the discovery. You both wanted it to be made, whatever it entailed.'

'Of course,' he agreed. 'These darn laws are so *beautiful* when you see them emerging,' he added presently. 'That's what Paggen and I had in common. We both saw it as Tabard sees it and were ravished by it in the same way. Some people only get it with mathematics. It's being able to observe a perfect mechanism emerging and that approximates to utter satisfaction. You either experience it or you don't, but I'd have forgiven Paggen any shortcoming because he could help uncover it and share the thrill.'

Helena remained silent. She had no idea what he was talking about but was sufficiently generous to see that it was important and also something that she never would know. She let him go on talking.

'Almost the first thing I felt when I heard he was dead was regret that he'd never know what Drasil had just told us. That would have given him the kick of all time. He was waiting for the next batch of stuff on Nipponanium with his heart in his mouth. He wasn't so hopeful of Tabard's biology team but he'd got a hunch that the thing was going to break wide open any time now. His bet was on the chemists. Nipponanium is being explored in a really exhaustive way. . . .'

Helena took a deep breath.

'Could it have been Paggen who took Sam's bag?'

'Why should he?' He was sidetracked.

'I was thinking of last night. While you were lying across the table and gas was hissing into the room he came rushing down with Fred Arnold in time to rescue you. How did they get in? They don't appear to have broken a window and we lock up automatically.'

'You've got something there.' He paused and looked at her in the starlight. 'He must have had a key. It's possible. I lent him one last time we went on leave. He felt he might have to get in for some reason—you know he was like that. Always fussing. He returned it but he could have had one cut. Oh, he was a darn silly guy. He had this mania to feel in possession. Is that what you were thinking?'

'No. I only thought he wouldn't risk fooling about with the gas if he wasn't sure he could get you out! Maybe he wasn't as feminine as that. Poor Melisande. How has she taken it?'

'Very well ... once she believed it. Maybe she was a little relieved, too. Campion was very good with her. He's under a considerable strain himself. There's some sort of theory that young Edward might have been involved with Paggen's disappearance.... Hell! I didn't mean to tell you that.'

'Edward!' Her thought turned to Sam at once. 'He's not ...? They haven't found ...?'

'No, no. Nothing like that. Campion is trying to get some more details now. This is him, I'd say.'

The wide beam of headlights had swung across the saltings and instead of turning to the main buildings in the island's centre was already on the circular lane which must lead to where they stood. A ground-mist had risen and the vehicle was proceeding slowly, enveloped up to the windows in curling waves of fine vapour which threatened to make the whole area a single feathery sea. Helena went on speaking of Edward.

'A strange person,' she said. 'So grown-up and yet utterly direct, like someone younger even than Sam.'

'That's the family,' Martin said unexpectedly. 'You never met his father?'

'Amanda did and you did. You told me.'

'Only once, but I never forgot him. He came to John S. Hopkins to give a single lecture when he didn't seem much older than I was. He was extraordinary; descended from Tycho Brahe and probably just like him. To meet him was like being confronted by an advanced model. I don't mean someone just brilliant but someone who was a later type of development. He shook me; he seemed so new; steelclad, streamlined and foolproof!'

The headlights turned and engulfed them, and another pair, moving much more quickly, appeared over the ridge.

The second driver knew the ground and had the first to follow, so that the two cars arrived almost simultaneously. Mr Campion's thin figure emerged first, but he turned back and waited as a toot sounded from the little van behind him and Arnold got out. Helena and Martin walked forward to join them.

The barman was not quite his usual bland self. 'You can say I'm slipping,' he was saying, his waxy face shining baldly in the faint light. 'I got an urgent order direct from Lord Ludor's secretary and it seems to have put everything else clean out of my bonce. I nipped straight out in the van to do what was asked for and it wasn't until now, when I came back across the Strada and they told me at the post they'd had to turn you back, that I remembered I'd got this for you.' He held out a slip of paper. 'Telephone message left "await arrival". It was given me by the switchboard.'

Mr Campion took the slip. It was too dark to read.

'What does it say?'

'The Lady Amanda presents her compliments and does not wish to be disturbed. Is that all right, sir?'

'Perfectly, thank you. When did you say it arrived?'

'Just before I went out. About an hour ago. Were you already here by then, sir? I am sorry. I am really.'

'Think nothing of it.' The light voice was so casual that those who knew it best would have been alarmed. 'Tell me about this flat rule the guard at the post is enforcing. No one at all to be permitted to leave the island tonight. Is it often put on?'

'I've never known it before, sir. It's Lord Ludor's own idea and he'll have had a word with the military commander, no doubt. It must be on account of Mr Mayo.'

'You know he's dead?' The words were very sharp and Arnold turned into the light from the car; he was smiling as if amused by an attempt to startle him.

'I was very sorry to hear it,' he said, glancing towards Martin. 'I made sure he'd be back, full of fire and fancies.' He hesitated and finally ventured a little further. 'He was
168

found in the back of a car, I hear. That's right, is it?'

'How on earth did you get hold of that, Fred?' Helena spoke with innocent astonishment and he shot a thoughtful glance at her.

'Well, you lot are discreet, I know,' he said at last, lowering his voice. 'And I've given myself away, haven't I? Frankly, it was told me in the strictest confidence ... and I've only had one conversation with the outside world which was when the order came through, so it's fairly obvious where it all came from.' He made a depreciating gesture. 'I'm trusted at head office. It doesn't look as if I deserve it, does it?'

He was very smooth. Helena was satisfied and the others did not speak. He was turning away when an idea appeared to strike him. 'If I were you, Mr Campion, I'd see if they could do anything for you on Roker's Tail. Goodnight all.'

He raised his hand in salute and slid into his van again. As it raced off through the mist Martin looked at Campion.

'I wonder when that baby got in last night?'

'Too early,' said Mr Campion. 'I couldn't prevail on the post to let me off the island to a telephone but they were decently embarrassed at having to refuse me and came across with a glimpse at the official time sheets. Arnold got back here, laden with stuff from the market, soon after seven-thirty a.m., so he didn't go far out of his way. What was that parting crack about?'

'Roker's Tail is a spur at the end of the island.' Martin pointed to the northern end of the marsh. 'There's a devastated area up there where some old huts and workrooms are rented by one of Godley's subsidiary concerns.'

'Advance Wires?'

'That's the name. They're an unsavoury gang of Teds or Mods or whatever they're called.'

'Roker is the local name for skate,' Helena said. 'And the boys are Tweeters—electrical bods, so Fred told me. They drive extraordinary old vehicles which change colour every time one sees them. No one trusts them.'

'Ah,' said Mr Campion, regretfully. 'The address would

F*   169

appear to have my name on it! I go on past the big house, do
I, and set my compass by the northern star?'

'You stick to the path at all costs,' said Helena anxiously,
'and whatever you do don't try to swim, or worse still walk
over any mud to the mainland——'

'Because wet clay is often quick!' he murmured. ' "Born and
bred in a brier patch", sister Helena. I will be more than
careful. Expect me later. I appear to be staying the night!'

'I thought Amanda's message had frightened him,' she said
as they watched the car creep off through the mist. 'It has,
hasn't it? What do you think? Edward hasn't come back and
she wants the lines kept clear in case he telephones?'

'It could be that but it sounds to me as if she knows she's
under surveillance.'

'I think so. She's rattled. Mother's a Fitton too and they're a
clan with a house language. When they "come their rank" like
that it usually means "Family will please take notice of the
following because I jolly well mean it". I think she was telling
Albert not to phone for Heaven's sake.'

'Which is fortunate because he can't, except through the
firm's exchange,' Martin said dryly. 'This curfew of Ludor's is
amazingly high-handed. If it's to apply to Campion it must
cover everybody. That won't go down with the Great Men!'

As he crept through the ground-mist Mr Campion was
thinking much the same thing. It was an alarming drive and it
occurred to him that had he been in melodramatic mood he
could well have suspected the whole thing to be a trap. The
spur of marsh sticking out into the estuary grew quickly more
and more narrow until for a quarter of a mile, it became a
track upon the stout sea well. Lying hungry on either side was
the clucking black mud only a few inches beneath the draining water. When at last the spur widened again he found
himself on a little peninsular only some eight or nine acres in
area. Ahead of him on a barren plain amid the usual dykes
and derelict farm gates was a collection of Nissen huts, still
daubed with twenty-five year old camouflage and looking like
a herd of prehistoric monsters sleeping in the dark. There

were several tallish masts about but no lights and he wondered if the settlement was deserted.

He drove to where the road ended in a concrete circle and got out to investigate. The mist had shifted again and his torch-beam showed sea lavender amid the grass and the empty cigarette cartons of civilization. There was still no sign of life and he was wondering whether to shout when he ran into a linen-prop lifting a line slung between two huts. The two pullovers and a shirt which fell clammily about his shoulders were reassuring inasmuch as they were still very wet. He pressed on quietly and found a door and opened it. The brightness of the light within astonished him. It was set over an inner door and was in a modern fixture. Everything was well painted and very clean.

He tried the handle and found himself peering into a fine, well-fitted clubroom, discreetly lit with shaded hanging lamps and a sumptuous if unlikely 'coal-type' fire. At the far end was a full-sized snooker table where a young man was knocking the balls about.

'Hello,' he said. 'Play you a hundred up?'

Mr Campion made his apologies and explained his mission and the youngster, who was of the hairier kind, charming and extremely masculine once one got used to his ringlets, considered the problem without taking his eyes from the ball he was potting.

'A London call without going through the Godley exchange? That's a bit difficult. There's nobody about, see? Everybody's out on rush jobs. There's only me and old Pa K. on the whole blessed station. Sorry, I really am.' He sent down the ball, retrieved it and set it up again. 'Ask Mr K.' he suggested.

'I'd like to.'

'He's there.' He jerked his chin towards the dark corner behind the television set and for the first time the visitor became aware of red-rimmed eyes watching him. As he advanced across the composite flooring there was a flurry in the warm shadows and a wizened little man in an old-fashioned flat cap

171

came out, hand outstretched. It was his sniff, and its apparently prehensile organ of origin, which placed him suddenly in the thin man's startled memory.

The avenue of the years rolled back like a dream sequence from a non-profit-making film and the two stood looking at each other, lost in that incredulous dismay with which old colleagues see each other fifteen years older and far less changed than alarmingly over-emphasised by the interval.

'Bert!' said the old man.

'Thos!' said Mr Campion, 'and don't call me Bert. You know I don't like it. What are you doing here, for Heaven's sake?'

Mr Thos T. Knapp was one of Mr Campion's older acquaintances. He cocked a rheumy eye at his visitor, looking even more like a leery ferret than ever in youth. 'Where else should I be?' he enquired. 'It's a natural, isn't it? This is me Mecca, Bert boy. I've found it. This is Ome and Dry, this is. You want an outside call. It's not allowed. Especially not tonight. It could be impossible.'

'I have to have one. Otherwise I have to get off the island without going past the post on the Strada.'

'That's out!' Mr Knapp put up a thin grey hand. 'Don't try that. This is black-butter country. I tell you what, though. Come and see my office. I'm the Old Wizard himself here. That's what they call me. You hold your row, Feeoh. You go on playin'. Come on Bert. Through here.'

As he led his bewildered friend through an inner doorway a chuckle of pure delight escaped him.

'I'd have chosen this,' he said earnestly. 'If my old Ma had suddenly appeared to me with a fairy wand and three wishes...'

'Heaven forfend!' murmured Mr Campion, who remembered the lady vividly. 'What a nightmare conceit!'

'No. Reely. I'd have chosen this.' Thos was not to be discouraged. 'What a world we're livin' in, eh? Dreams come ruddy true! Sit down a minute, Bert, and I'll make your hair curl. There's things you can tell an old friend....'

17

Sparks and Ashes

AFTER marvelling at his good fortune for two minutes, it took Mr Campion rather less than five to discover that he had dropped into a morass nearly as fatal as the one outside. In youth Mr Knapp had been something of a liability and in middle age a deplorable if useful little crook, but neither of these phases had prepared his friend for the lonely old man of the sea he had become. He appeared desperate to talk: marooned amid a generation who treated him as something between an oracle and a pet owl, he seized upon the visitor as if he carried the elixir of life.

At any other moment Campion might well have considered him Heaven sent, for there was very little in the whole Ludor empire of which he did not possess at least a limited view, and nothing that he would not tell the hero who reminded him of halcyon days. But what Campion needed now most desperately was to know how Amanda fared, if there was news of Edward, and what Dearest could tell him about Luke in Saltbridge.

His host was merciless. It seemed he had some considerable status, and possessed a private office which he delicately proved was his own by displaying an American-type name-plate on the desk, and nothing would stop him giving the history of his firm and explaining how it came to be under the Godley wing. This proved to be much as Campion might have guessed. After the war ended, a demobilised signals sergeant—still referred to as 'the Spark' and clearly something of a bright one —had joined Mr Knapp in a shop selling electrical parts on the surface but concealing a small business 'bugging' other people's telephone wires, undercover. In no time at all the newcomer had put the firm on the map, and the moment they spread to noticeable size they were gobbled up by Godley's, who then failed to digest them but found them instead, a dangerous little virus, very difficult to shake off.

Reading between the lines, Mr Campion gathered that Lord Ludor himself considered the concern both entertaining and useful, and Advance Wires Ltd., Prop T. T. Knapp & Partner, traded on the fact, according him an off-hand respect in return for his patronage. Their position on the island was very much in spirit what it was in fact, an arm's-length encampment of skunks, only tolerated by the other inhabitants because of the difficulty and unpleasantness of any attempt to remove it.

'The Spark don't like me wearin' my old cap,' said Mr Knapp, blotting his dreadful nose. 'But I get my sinus on this marsh and if I don't keep my loaf warm I pay for it. I've got a tweed "Macmillan" for when he's here but he's gorn with the others on this Paris lark tonight. That's what brings you, I shouldn't wonder?'

'I shouldn't wonder, either!' Mr Campion agreed affably. 'Look Thos, first I must speak to London.'

'Must you? Paris is where it's happening. We've all gorn to Paris. That chap Fred Arnold from the canteen—we don't use it because they won't have us—drove the team in relays to the station. The orders were, our vehicles were not to be seen leaving the island. The boys are at Southend Airport by now. We were very nearly full strength at tea-time when the message came froo. Suddenly it was "all aboard!" just like old times. Lumme! Do you remember...?'

'Not just now, old boy. First of all I must make a call to Town....'

Thos did not hear; he still seemed absurdly touched by the reunion. 'You're a sight for sore eyes,' he kept saying and he was certainly in a position to judge. 'You've 'ardly altered, ole man ... a bit of string to look at but a live wire inside. Lord Ludor himself is laying on our little Paris caper. The Spark spoke to him personally. Have you ever seen him? They still grow 'em! More sizey now, like everything else. Gawd! I can't get over you turnin' up! Wanderin' in just like you always did. To tell you the troof I was feeling out of it. There's only me an' Feeoh—that was 'im in there with the billiards. But we're left to take the stuff in when the others get 'old of it, so it's not reely I'm not *wanted*, is it?'

'Thos, if I had a telephone . . .'

'No, lissern! I'll do what I can for you later. I want to tell you first that it's a real treat to see your old face! The Spark has took me orf the roof work, see? And I did used to *like* the roof work. The Paris job is dodgy and we're usin' all the noo gear, the light and radar frequencies beam on the windows. The thin glass vibrates to the speech sounds in the room and also acts as a reflector. It's very tasty, very sweet indeed.'

'So you're "bugging" the Rubari apartment, are you?'

While Mr Campion's forward mind had been concentrating on getting in touch with his base, another part of his brain appeared to have been listening. A piece of the pattern slid into place.

'What about Daumier's?'

'If we have to.' Mr Knapp seemed hurt. 'I'm trying to tell you, aren't I? I can let know all you want without you bothering London.'

'I wish you could, Thos! All I need is an old-fashioned telephone line, with elementary privacy, to an ordinary public exchange.'

The flat cap shook slowly and regretfully from side to side.

'And you'd like an 'andsome cab and a penny cigar too, I suppose? Them days is done, Bert boy. With luck you may get privacy at the next stage of development. Or, on the other hand, you may not. As I see it, the word "private" is going plumb out of date. It's goin' to be an ole-fashioned concep', mark my words. That's a prophecy.' He sat back in his swivel-chair and smiled the "drunken-mouse" smile Mr Campion remembered so vividly. 'We're going to do it "look-no-hands" now,' he said happily. 'That's what this Paris lark is about, as you may or may not know. No wires, no toobs, no frequencies, no beams. Nothing. Just 'ead to ruddy 'ead! You knoo, did you?'

Mr Campion nodded. The extraordinary chance which had produced this old ally did not astonish him. In his experience some things were inevitable, and once one became caught up in such a development any coincidence was likely rather than merely possible. But what to Canon Avril would have been one sort of experience was to him another. As he saw it, it was just "like Life" for him to discover the one man who was able to unravel most of the mystery, dying to talk his head off at the very moment when he himself was forced to spend his energy circumnavigating a high-handed move by a bludgeoning business tycoon.

He and Luke had been sent to the island to discover the true origin of the amplifiers and, incidentally, what was wrong with Godley's security. By a simple, impudent move, using his pull with the Army, Ludor had placed him in the position of having to transmit his reports and receive his instructions through his own monitoring system. It was a manoeuvre typical of Ludor; ruthless, but full of elementary common-sense.

'We're after kids. Did you know? Children,' said Mr Knapp breaking into his friend's thought. 'The Spark didn't believe it at first, but I wasn't surprised. Do you remember what we was like with the old cat'swhisker when Marconi first got goin'? Probably not, I do. Proper little wizards me and my lot was; in fac', we was the only part of the general public who understood it at all. Anybody over thirty was too thick to take it in.'

'Does Lord Ludor think some sort of test is to be conducted from the Rubari apartment?'

'Nobody knows. We're trying the kids first to find out. If it's not to be there, we go where it is. That's another reason for me stayin' here. The Spark and most of his lads is bi-lingual.' He used the word with amused pride as if it meant 'two-headed'.

'Why is Lord Ludor so sure there's to be a test?'

'He knows his man, Mayo . . . a very careful bloke, very high in the perfession.'

'He's dead,' said Mr Campion on impulse.

176

'Ah.' Thos was unmoved. 'I'm not surprised. They're nappy, them Frogs.'

'It may be nothing to do with them.'

'We'll find out.'

'Then what?'

'Then we'll find out who's testing, and relay it here. You ought to see my little theatre. I can show you miracles.'

'But you can't get me a line to Welbeck!'

'Oh Gawd!' said Mr Knapp with sudden exasperation. 'What a persistent beggar you always was! Come on. I'll show yer but not a word to anybody and particularly not to the Spark. This is our racing-wire which me and the staff rigged up to keep ourselves amused. It's a lovely drop of old-style engineering in its way. Seventy feet of one-and-a-half zinc piping over the narrowest part of the channel and close on a mile of ex-army field cable, all concealed and connected to the nearest house on the mainland. The old widder there is a keen type and we make it worth her while. She don't earwig much —isn't interested. We have to keep it dead quiet though.'

He rose from his chair and took an old-fashioned iron key from a hook under a calendar which suggested a homely structure somewhere in the background. To the visitor's amusement the flippant notion turned out to be entirely correct. Behind the Nissen huts there was a line of more rustic little buildings with sloping tin roofs. The torch-beam showed them tarred and blistered, and the one at the far end was not only locked but had the name '*Mr Thos. T. Knapp. Chairman. Keep Out*' painted on it neatly by some youthful joker, no doubt in near-hysterics.

The telephone was kept on the seat under a pile of newspapers and Thos brought it out and hung about as Campion settled on the step and got on to the mainland exchange. However, as soon as Dearest came through and he addressed her by that name, his host stepped back, polite and surprised. 'You was always younger than me,' he said regretfully and faded into the darkness, making the thin man's task considerably easier.

Dearest was almost gay. If she retained her archness, less of the headmistress was showing through. Mr Campion was grateful to her. She was remarkably easy to follow and he did not permit her faint flicker of amusement whenever she referred to their boss as 'Elsie' to irritate him unduly.

'Elsie and I have had quite an evening,' she chattered brightly. 'It's lovely of you to ring up all the way from the seaside, but if you're on a party-line I shall have to keep it clean, shan't I?'

'Well I'm not, as it happens. The man on whose estate I'm staying listens in, so I came outside. In fact you'd never guess where I am now.'

'Ah. Some insular types are so possessive. Is he the big boy you meant to stay with?'

'The young people here call him *Tarzan's Daddy-o,*' he said acidly and heard her giggle. 'How's everyone at home? Not you two girls, but the bunch up there by the Church. Has Auntie got her little pet back yet?'

'No, she hasn't. Everybody's looking for it. Elsie and I did wonder if it could have come in and she wasn't letting on, but no. All the people from the big electrical shop are helping. They won't leave her alone.'

'I suppose not,' he said bleakly. 'Has she been out looking for it herself?'

'No. She hasn't stirred and she hasn't let anyone in except the old girl from next door, Miss Whatsit. *She's* been in and out of the house ministering as usual, of course.'

'Of course,' he echoed and hurried on lest she should detect the faint sense of relief which her news was bringing him. If Amanda was staying put and lying low the chances were that Amanda knew what she was doing. The Fittons were always a resourceful family.

'I had to part with Charley on the way down,' he continued smoothly. 'I expect you heard, he got a call from his firm to go up to the Midlands. If you see him before I do, give him a message for me, will you?'

'Of course. Or I could always tell Syd if it's important.'

'May as well. It's only about that sack of waste they found in the back of the truck. Tell him I think there's been a shuffle and it started out in the back of a car from central London after midnight last night. Car, not truck, see? And was probably in the same state in which it arrived in Saltbridge.'

'How you run on!' she said, which was a warning that he was being unnecessarily obvious. 'Don't worry. I'll tell him. Anything else while I'm about it? The last time I heard from them, they were getting on very well. They found a mate up there who knew all the answers.'

'Oh, the Army instructor?'

'No.' She seemed at sea. 'That doesn't ring a bell.'

'I thought he was some sort of gym-sergeant expert? Unarmed Combat?'

As soon as the words were out of his mouth he regretted them. He had no reason to think that anyone could hear him, or that it would matter if they did, but as the phrase left his lips he had a hunch that it was going to be unlucky, for the phone was crackling badly and he was relieved that she let the indiscretion pass.

'Oh, I see,' she said. 'Yes, you're right. That is it. I heard just now, but we're over the moon at the moment. You know that little packet of children's toys we lost? Well, we've found them! All through you, really. Elsie said I was to send her love if you called. She's ever so grateful.'

The net of nervous pain which caught Mr Campion round the face as the information registered surprised him. He had not realised how much he was emotionally involved in the safety of the invention, quite apart from the fact that the children were concerned with it. To cover himself he began to chatter.

'Tell her to think nothing of it. I aim to please. Which of my brilliant suggestions led to the discovery? The misquotation from the big book?'

'That's right. Elsie liked the idea of the promenading person in the fancy dress. We found out there were two of them, just like you said.'

179

'I knew there were two toys?'

'Yes, but two prophets, too. You know, two men in fancy dress. You told Elsie you thought there might be two and she put the whole shop on the look-out. One of them was caught handing over the toys in an envelope with one of his usual handouts.'

Mr Campion held his breath. He thought he heard a movement from the Nissen hut. At any moment Thos must return, athirst for sentimental reminiscence. He strove to concentrate on the extraordinarily difficult parlour-game he was playing with this highly skilful partner.

He had half forgotten that he had mentioned his encounter with the End of the World Man to Corkran, when he had reached him that morning almost immediately after his meeting with Deeds, whom he knew slightly and who had tackled him in the street. The idea of the false Biblical reference appearing on the placard, apparently by magic, had interested both him and Corkran for each had recognised the true quotation from their school days when it had seemed amusing to impersonate the Four Beasts from the four corners of the chapel, each scrubby little boy intoning his cry under cover of the psalms: *'Come and see! Come and see! Come and see! Come and see!'* Evidently Corkran had acted with his usual promptness and had scored sensationally.

'Dearest,' said Mr Campion. 'I love your voice, I could listen to you all day but I ought to get on. Tell me about this character you caught with the toys. Which was he? Not my old barmy friend, surely?'

'No, Mephy dear, the other one.'

'I thought so. Was he known to Elsie? I mean, could he have been something to do with that little firm you were telling me about last night? The one with the funny name?'

'Fungi? Yes, that's right. It was ever such a surprise. We knew him quite well. He had always seemed such a dear old lady. He had his little teashop and his white cat and he was the secretary of the Prophetic Society. . . .'

'The secretary?'

'Yes. Their office is opposite him and they used to have a bigger staff before the cost of living went up, so he had some spare costumes and boards available. He only had to write his own posters and there he was. I tell you we're delighted; we'd never connected him with Messrs Fungi & Co.'

'Had you tried?'

'Hundreds of times! But there appeared to be no contact at all with anybody. He must have been doing it this way for ages. It's the old clients he really works for, you know. Our regulars.'

'Really? The Main Importers? The people who tried to collect the two little things at the railway station?'

'Yes. Elsie had to laugh, she was so annoyed!'

'You do surprise me. I thought from what Syd told me that they weren't interested any more.'

'If you ask me they're always interested,' Dearest said dryly. 'They're like the poor, always with us. We don't know how the teashop man got the toys yet, but of course Syd is on to it and I expect your friend Charley and his lot will want to know the answer to that one, in view of the ... er ...'

'Trouble with the sack,' he said easily. 'Oh, well then, you girls have had a good day. I hope the toys were intact when you got them?'

'Actually no. Both were damaged or looked like it, but apparently it doesn't matter. It's the idea which is so good.'

'How interesting. Where are they now?'

'Elsie has them but they're to go straight to the manufacturers, our head office says. They want to get some more made quickly because of the expected demand.'

Mr Campion's heart sank. He had known that once the amplifiers reached official government hands they would pass automatically to Godley's and thence to Lord Ludor, but he had no power to prevent it, nor reason why he should attempt to.

'Oh well, if I hang around I may see something of them?' he ventured.

'You could,' she said slowly, 'but we rather hoped you were coming home....'

'Why?' It was difficult to keep his tone casual.

'Actually, Mephy, because of Auntie's pet.' Dearest was a smooth player and her remark was as brittle as if she really were speaking of someone else's lost budgerigar. 'It's the Big Boss of the electrical shop who wants to catch that little bird to hear it sing. He knows he has the smaller of the pair safe in his own aviary but it's still in the nest and he doesn't want to upset the parents. Now that he's lost his own bird man he thinks that Auntie's pet will lead him directly to the real handler. He's finding out by listening in. He's a very domineering man and quite alarmed Elsie, which isn't *like* her, so perhaps, Mephy...'

There was an abrupt noise on the line and then nothing. Mr Campion found himself alone in the darkness with the sound of the sea in his ears. As he rose to his feet from the step Mr Knapp materialised from the black shadows of the other sheds.

'You can shout "Dearest" into that mouthpiece until you're black in the face, my lad,' he said cheerfully. 'She won't hear you. Someone's give the line a yank and broke it I expect. That's nothing new. If it's not a blasted cow grazin', it's a busybody. Come in and sit down by the ole fire and let's have a chin-wag. You can't do nothin' more tonight to please her, 'ooever she is.'

A suspicion assailed Mr Campion.

'Thos,' he said sternly. 'You cut that line.'

'Only in your express interest, Son.' Mr Knapp was unabashed. 'Your conversation didn't mean nothink to me except that I shouldn't 'ave thought you'd waste your time on such a yappy Judy, but someone was listening out on the marsh. I spotted them about 'arf time. There was someone there. I could 'ear the breaving distinctly, as soon as I cut in.'

18

The Spy

IT was dawn before the visitor set off back across the island and by then Mr Knapp, so he said, had had the time of his life. Mr Campion was glad to hear it for he had certainly relived most of the entire saga.

During his recital Thos had cooked tea and bacon and kept an informed eye on Feeoh's work while that amiable youth, for all that he looked like the Woodwose, had shown himself at home with some remarkable machinery.

For a while a trace of reticence remained between the reunited friends, since Mr Knapp had recollected with aston-ishment that he and his dear old mate, Bert, had usually operated on opposite sides of the fence in the rose-hung gardens of the past. However, as the hours rolled by, he let it pass. Mr Campion had noticed before that elderly people sometimes seem almost frantic to get rid of themselves as if they were terrified of Death overtaking them with, so to speak, the goods on them. Thus he sympathised with Thos, who hardly gave himself time to breathe. There was no need to dig for information. All the visitor had to do was to keep awake and sort it.

Before midnight Feeoh received the news that the Advance Wires team was safely installed in its Paris headquarters which were, Mr Campion gathered, a small 'bistro' and garage owned by a relative of the Spark's and situated almost underneath a much more respectable subsidiary of Godley's, who had no idea of their presence.

Thereafter, half-hourly bulletins arrived from them and were relayed to London by Feeoh, who worked alone in a fastness called 'the Doings' which the guest was only permitted to glimpse. In the intervals, both men were anxious to oblige and, while Mr Knapp concentrated on food and anecdote, his assistant sieved the ether for anything of general interest. At first he was not very successful but in the end he produced some very informative blanks.

Mr Campion learned that there was still no general call out for a missing child; that the news of Paggen Mayo's disappearance, let alone his death, had not broken; and that there was no mention on any police radio or press news flash of the arrest of the owner of a teashop off Wigmore Street.

Meanwhile, the Advance Wires team at work emerged to the observer as something between a rush of press photographers hunting a celebrated divorcée and a united family of tree-monkeys. They reported that the Rubari apartment was conveniently situated as to 'rooftop cover' and was a 'cush, window-wise', but that everybody in it was snoring his head off and any real results must wait for the morning.

While it was still dark, Feeoh brought a flash into Thos who read it and looked up, a gleam in his wicked red-rimmed eyes.

'There's some bogies here interested in something what started out from London in a car and finished up in a lorry outside Saltbridge in the Midlands,' he announced. 'I don't know if that interests you, Bert? But it looks as though your lady friend has been workin', bless her little heart! Don't worry old boy, it was me, not Feeoh, who chaperoned your conversation with her. I've only told 'im wot to look out for. Beat it, Feeoh, it's getting near the next bleep from the boys.'

Mr Campion took the slip without a flicker on his pale face.

It was a priority call from the Saltbridge police asking for information from anybody who saw the transfer of a heavy object from a grey-green, old model open sports car, one of whose letters of identification was a 'Y', to an empty Baker-Arnold lorry with a black plastic curtain hanging loose over the open back, Registration GTZ 4678. The change was thought to have occurred outside the Green Man Café, Morton, Middlesex, at approximately six-twenty a.m. the previous morning. Witnesses were asked to call either the north London or Saltbridge police.

Thos was inclined to take a proprietorial pride in the speed of the manoeuvre. 'In the last few years we've took wings!' he said modestly. 'You've only got to think of your own work tonight. You made one of your smarty guesses and passed it on to your secretary bird. I suppose that's what she is?'

He made it a question but did not make an issue of getting an answer, patting himself on the back instead. 'I've grown acute,' he observed and went on with his pronouncement. 'She got on the blower to the rozzers and immediately all the modern equipment come into play. We couldn't have hoped for that when I first met you. Before you've had time to settle your grub, here it is acted upon. What was in this 'ere sack of waste? Don't tell me if it's personal.'

'It depends how personal one can get,' murmured Mr Campion fatuously and the wizened old man sucked a tooth at him.

'A corp, eh?' he said. '*A heavy objec*'! I ask you, isn't that the rozzers all over? 'Oo would tell 'em if they knoo? Well, thank you very much, but I'm not interested! I keep my nose very clean these days.'

Ever a man of taste, Mr Campion forbore to comment and Thos continued unchecked.

'As soon as there's anyone awake in the Rubari flat we're to look out for calls, particularly from the Smoke. The Rubari youngster is expected to get a signal from another kid who'll be working with adults somewhere in London. Any reference to it whatsoever is to be noted and reported forthwith, top priority. It's the same old story. Each noo step forwards has its generation of born technicians delivered with it. Along comes the idea, up comes the personnel, know-how built in. That's Nature. I've seen it time and again. Myself, I'm a Whisker man at heart. The Spark, he's born Toobs. Feeoh is a right Transistor type and we've got a youngster with a hooter for Light. Now something else is coming. We've got no dope on it at all yet and the trouble is that we don't know what to look for. It's not sound, it's not vision, it's not frequency even. There's no juice, or anyway, no batteries.' He lowered his voice. 'By what the Spark picked up from one of the Perfesser's

young men—the centre of this island is stiff with number nine
hats y'know—you get on better if you don't *think* too hard,
either, so I can understand kids being important in it. You
want a very fresh mind to understand a very fresh thing. I
mean to say,' he added reasonably, 'to you and me a caper like
this is liable to look like a pack of damn-all if we're not very
careful. And then where are we? On the "Obsolete" tray!'

Mr Campion rose and sighed. 'At any rate Lord Ludor
doesn't seem to have the boy, yet.'

Thos eyed him thoughtfully. 'That's where you come in, is
it? I was wondering. You're playin' the ole guardian angel. are
you? *And* not for the first time!'

'I'm no angel and I'm not playing,' said Mr. Campion dryly.
'Apart from that you're horribly on target. Now I must go
back to the Ferrises.'

'Not yet! I haven't touched on me war years yet. Did I ever
tell you about Phyl the Looter's band...?'

Mr Campion escaped at last and got out into the unearthly
light of morning.

The narrow road ran along the top of the sea wall like a
strand of seaweed across an immense oyster-shell. The mud
was mother-of-pearl, bare and wet and cream and pink and
grey with dark edges and ridges. The cold air, heady with sea-
smells, forced itself into lungs and eyes. The sky and earth
were too alike to be distinguishable and, in the void, there
were shapes and wings like the beginning of the world.

He drove a little way and stopped to look around him. In
all his life he had never discovered any other sight anywhere
which could give him the same sense of loneliness and un-
hindered clarity. The reek of Thos Knapp's friendly fustiness
of mind slid away from him like the memory of a sleazy couch,
as he climbed out slowly and stood back from the main history
and looked at it.

Two designs were sharply differentiated. First there was the
main sweeping curve of the breakthrough, bursting out and
up in a mighty new shaft of growth. What would happen to
it?

186

If it could be thwarted, suppressed outright for a time, or curbed and cut down to fit small uses, in whose hands would the fresh powers lie? And to what purpose?

Or if it grew too fast, escaped control and shot up, breaking through the smoked-glass dome, letting in the ruthless light where there had always been shadow and secret ways, what would the result be then? Could idle thoughts, blown up like sound, sweep over mankind in a madness until the world died raving? What kind of young mentalities must harness such a force, what sort of new moralists brave it? He turned away from a problem to which he rather fancied old Thos had already given the only answer. Doubtless now, as in the past, the story would be the same. With the equipment would come the personnel. For his part, he sincerely hoped so.

His own preoccupying pattern was more immediate. He knew now who had killed Paggen Mayo, delivering the vicious Unarmed Combat chop to the throat with the side of the hand, a blow with which an expert can split a block of wood. Anyone, he felt, who had followed events as he had done, must know the man's identity and yet, now that he came to it, he found he knew less than nothing, because he did not know the man. It was like the children's game: 'You're It! You're It! *But who are you?*'

He was still a long way from the answer as his car bumped over the uneven road, with the dangerous turf edges where the grey grass grew long, hiding the spot where the path ended and the vertical sides began.

He was thinking of the man, visualising him and trying to understand him when he saw the little green van.

It was so insignificant in the vast silver bowl that he found he had been looking at it for a long time before he recognised what it was. It was parked to one side, two wheels almost over the edge, but there was still no room for the Hawk to pass so that he was forced to stop. As Campion came up slowly he could see Arnold in the driving seat. He was waiting, leaning back in the corner, looking at a newspaper.

As the car came to a halt seven or eight yards from him, the light bathed both vehicles in its curious, obliterating, be-littling way so that the two men's significance to each other was somehow lessened. It was too early for sun but the gold was there in promise.

The man in the van raised his eyes and looked for a moment, then he folded his paper, pulled his coat round him and leant forward and opened the right-hand door. He came out very slowly so that Mr Campion had time to see him afresh.

The traditional upper-servant polish was still upon him; worldliness and casual bonhomie enveloped him like a robe. But for the first time Mr Campion could see past them easily. He saw a man of forty-five, compact and essentially powerful, with the sloping shoulders and short neck of the natural fighter. He seemed in good trim if a little taut with his shiny skin damp along the hairline. His eyes, he noticed, had lost all their idle amusement.

Mr Campion had few illusions about himself. He had never carried much weight physically and was unarmed. He was reasonably skilled in those forms of Judo which the West has adopted but he was not particularly young. He was also tired from his all-night session with Thos and, worst of all, extremely irritated. He felt unlucky and the stab of regret at his own idiocy in coming to the island without a weapon pierced him with a sudden sharp intensity.

He wound down the window and waited. Arnold came over, buttoning his jacket, and bent down, his right hand on the top of the door. The face he thrust in was ingratiating: 'Could you possibly get by, sir? I daren't take her any further over.'

The request was so natural that the thin man, who was expecting almost anything else, was taken off guard for the tenth of a second. He did not make the mistake of glancing at the road but kept his gaze on the powerful and very clean hand on the ledge. Even so, the respite was sufficient. Arnold dropped his left hand over the handle of the rear door and was inside the back of the car before the man in the driving seat could turn. It was a beautiful movement, so swift and

smooth. It displayed his physical and mental dexterity as nothing else could have done.

When the thin man turned towards him he was already
tucked into the left-hand corner of the back seat, smiling
apologetically and making himself small. 'Perishing, isn't it?'
he said conversationally. 'You don't believe how cold it can be
in this country until you get out on these mud flats.' The
remark was not quite as casual as the speaker could have
wished. He heard the tremor of nervousness in his own voice
and was put out by it. He laughed to cover it. 'So you found
the old hot-wire merchants, did you, sir? They're a crummy
covey and no error!'

'They seem to be well equipped.' Mr Campion looked even
more blank than usual. 'I've been hearing news from all over
the world.'

'... *and* sending it!' Arnold was still rattled and the words
came out by pure accident. Immediately, the dusky colour
spread over his waxen face, altering it unbelievably. Having
given himself away he resorted to truculence. 'I had to listen
in to you,' he said abruptly. 'You asked for it. I showed you the
way to get a line and you bit it, so naturally I thought I'd
check. I've had my little extension for some time, as a matter
of fact. Old Knapp comes out of the Ark with his field equipment. His own boys put me on his wire; he doesn't know and
wouldn't care if he did. The whole thing only cost me five
hundred Virginians and those came out of the canteen stock.'

Mr Campion did not smile. He had added a trace of pomposity to his usual character study.

'There was no need to do more than you were asked,' he
said stiffly. 'You had only to present your credentials to me in
the normal way and I should have been glad to pass on anything I felt you should know.' The instant the words were out
of his mouth he realised that he too had made a most unfortunate miscalculation. Arnold had not understood that
they were colleagues. Although he had listened to the conversation with Dearest and appeared to have followed at least
some of it, he had clearly not known until now that it was in

any way an official exchange. He seemed thunderstruck by the discovery. His blush had gone but he was showing the whites of his eyes and was emerging as a most uncertain animal, but a fighter rather than a runner.

'I'm sorry I'm sure, sir,' he said at last. 'I wasn't told who you were, see? In fact there's a lot I wasn't told.' He hesitated and then the grievance which had almost demoralised him came out abruptly. 'The Saltbridge police ... I heard you say Saltbridge, didn't I? ... were very sharp on the cause of old Mayo's death, weren't they?'

'Very. The Inspector up there was once an instructor in Unarmed Combat. It was just very good luck.'

'Perhaps so. But that blow is undetectable, let me tell you. It *can't* be traced. It's the one it's too dangerous to tell the public about.' He was actually arguing and as Campion began to recognise the type became more and more his Smart Alick self. 'It fractures the hyoid bone,' he persisted. 'There's nothing to see on the skin and it's *never* suspected.'

'How right you were! Ten years ago.' Campion lobbed his little bomb in carefully. 'The case of the army sergeant stationed in Germany rather altered all that. Don't you remember?'

'Of course I do. It's the classic instance. He did it from the back of a car and he hanged the body up afterwards and passed it off as suicide.' The hideous tell-tale colour had returned to Arnold's face and he sounded sulky. 'What you seem to be forgetting is that he got away with it. It wasn't spotted, even by the Army who'd trained him! It was only the gossip after he married the dead chap's wife that shopped him.'

'That made the police think of it.' Mr Campion was mild but insistent. 'They've thought of it in every case since, and of course they'd think of it again.'

'How do you mean?'

Mr Campion looked foolish. 'If it should happen here,' he said, adding briefly, 'and now.'

Arnold was silent. He was still alarmingly sure of himself. He was a natural improviser, the thin man suspected, stimulated rather than daunted by an unexpected difficulty. At last he relaxed.

'Mrs Melisande was dead right about Mayo,' he said suddenly. 'You knew that, I suppose? That's where he *was* going. Exactly where she said.'

'I find that very difficult to credit.'

'You're telling me! I couldn't credit it nor pay it neither!' A great change had taken place in his manner and Mr Campion learned a little more about him. Ever since Arnold had realised that they were in the same service he had been behaving as if they were in a war together, moving in the same no-man's-land but not on the same job. Mr Campion had met that attitude of mind before and realised with a jolt that nothing now would prevent the barman from talking with the utmost frankness in front of him, nor from killing him without a thought if it suited his book, just as he must have killed Mayo. His bright familiarity and tendency to sidle up close mentally were recognisable characteristics and the thin man, who had hitherto supposed him to be a much smaller and less venomous example of his species, became very wary.

'Have you any evidence at all of that accusation against Mr Mayo?' he enquired, adopting an old school, senior officer approach which he felt might best keep the man contemptuous and enjoying himself. It was an abominably tricky situation and, as he kept reflecting most uncharacteristically, a damn silly way to die.

'He told me to drive to the airport.' Arnold told the story as if he were chatting behind his bar. 'You remember he left you all and followed me out on to the steps?'

'This was at the Rectory?'

'That's right. He told me then. "I'll meet you at the Donkey and Boot, Covent Garden, in an hour and a half", he said. "Wait for me and for God's sake keep your mouth shut."'

'And you did?'

'Why not? I'd got time. The Market doesn't open until five anyway. He didn't even know that. Only the loaders come in earlier. He was the boss of the trip. I shouldn't have been there at all if it hadn't been for him forcing my hand.'

'I don't see how he did force it.' Deliberately Mr Campion sounded sulky and looked marvellously ineffectual.

'Don't you?' It was Arnold's mouth which fascinated the thin man. Every tooth seemed to show and to be small and to turn inwards; he seemed very pleased with himself. 'You chaps aren't at all what you're cracked up to be,' he went on, his blunt but thrusting mind nuzzling in. 'The whole service is a great surprise to me, let me tell you. It's not in the class you all imagine. I mean to say, fancy trusting *Ludor*? *He* told Mayo you'd recruited me. I couldn't believe it. When Mayo came out with it to back his own authority I nearly fainted. We'd just got young Martin Ferris on the grass outside the hut when he spilt the lot. My God! I thought, what sort of outfit have I got tied up with!'

'Are you saying he threatened to expose you?' Official obtuseness sat oddly on Mr Campion's affable face. 'Who to?'

'Look. You're not "with me".' Arnold said. 'Give it something; use your machine. He'd got me to leave the canteen and go down to the Ferris hut with him because he knew I'd got a key ... I have to most of them. The Boss likes me to be able to nip in anywhere if we need to.'

'How did Mayo know that?'

'Because I told him. He once brought me a key of the Ferris hut which he said he'd borrowed. He wanted me to get him a spare cut. I wasn't wearing that! So I told him there was no need as we kept duplicates in the office for emergencies and I sent him off with a flea in his ear. He reminded me of that on Friday night and asked me to go down to the hut with him. He wanted a witness, of course. Well, we got Ferris out and I was dead innocent over that at first. I believed the silly tick *had* gassed himself. Then I spotted what Mayo was up to, making a show of it to discredit the bloke, and I stuck my toes in. I told him I wasn't playing. "Oh, come on," he said. "I know who you're attached to. You were signed on this morning, weren't you? Lord Ludor told me. He's so dissatisfied with

Security he's making them use his own people. It's your job to help," he said. "You go and fetch the van and I'll sign the ticket." So of course I had no choice.'

'Why?' Mr Campion suppressed the query just in time. In the back of his mind a warning light had come on. *"The most dangerous of them all are not very bright."* That aphorism filtered up out of his war-time past and he wondered if the sweat was showing on his forehead.

'I made the story as clear to you and your friends as I could ... I thought you were police then,' Arnold was saying, his wide mouth putting Mr Campion in mind somehow of a couple of saucers clacking together. 'Then, when he told me to meet him I felt I was covered. If there was trouble you both understood I was just a poor little bloke obeying orders and not too happy about them. So, as I didn't want to upset him, I imagined he was simply going to ditch his missus and let her find her own way home, I picked him up.' He paused and sighed at his own gullibility. 'Then I found myself being told to drive to the airport, or as near as damn it.'

'Did he actually mention the airport?'

'No. He was too clever for that or thought he was. These brilliant scientific types haven't anything real upstairs. No "common". They try things on that a child wouldn't attempt. He told me a long rigmarole about some big institution he'd got to visit out on the Aronbridge Road, I was to drop him outside it and then slip quietly home and not say a word to anyone, no matter what I might hear. I ask you, what could be more naïve? You'd think we were both little girls!'

Mr Campion was frowning. 'There *is* a collection of buildings out there,' he murmured. 'They belong to the Post Office. It's their London experimental headquarters.'

'Is it? Then that was how he was trying to fool me, see? He really thought I could take him there and never think of the airport, so he could be into a plane and out of the country with the gear in his breast pocket before anyone knew.'

The soft voice with the smooth, nondescript accent paused for a moment. 'There you are,' he said at last, as of a job which, although satisfactory, had yet not gone quite as well as it might have done. 'He'd discovered who I was working for and he was going where he *was* going, so I had no choice but to do him in and precious little time.'

'But why?' For the second time Mr Campion checked the word. Even though the man had made the tragic mistake of assuming that Mayo was seeking an airport and not a friend's laboratory, why should he feel that he needed to eliminate the scientist simply because Mayo knew that Arnold was spying for Lord Ludor and, absurdly recently, had been entrusted with a very small job for British Security? The only possible answer hit Mr Campion between the eyes with the force of revelation and a large section of the puzzle slid into place.

If Arnold's main allegiance was to yet a third party, a larger and even more jealous Authority, then his attitude took on an utterly different colour altogether.

Meanwhile the man was talking again.

'That telephone chat you had just now ought to have told me you weren't just a common dick. I heard you give that bird, on the line a message to pass on. You told her to tell someone that the "sack", as you called the body, had left London in the back of a car and not a truck. How did you know that?'

'You told me so when you came up with the message from my wife. What sort of car did you leave in? Something parked?'

'It must have been, mustn't it? I thought it was laid up!' He laughed at his own mistake. 'It was standing out in a line of stuff in a dark, tree-lined street somewhere round there beyond Earl's Court. People keep their vehicles in front of their houses for the whole winter in those areas. I chose one with one of these ex-army silver painted dust-sheet jobs over it. I could see by the shape that it was an open sports and I guessed it was old. I just pulled up beside it and nipped round between the two vehicles. I didn't disturb the sheet. I lifted the side, opened the rear door and shoved him from one bus to the other. He wasn't a heavy man. I thought he'd be there till Christmas at least. I'd only just got back in my seat when a couple of blue-bottles came round the corner, laughing their heads off ... some private joke, I suppose.'

'It was a risk,' said the thin man, adding a touch of admira tion to keep him talking.

'Not really,' Arnold spoke happily. 'The dodgy moment was getting him done. It was late but I was right in London, don't forget. A van isn't like a car either. I was driving and he was in a hurry and kept fidgetting. There's a lot of light about in the old S.W. district even after midnight. I took a side turn at last into an alley near Harrods, pretending it was a shoit cut. When I found I couldn't get through I switched off my lights by-mistake-on-purpose while I was swearing and trying to re-verse. He started to try to see where we were, as if he was in a car, and as his head went back I got him. I only took one cut. I've never needed more since the first time. After that, of course, I couldn't lose him soon enough.'

It was a certain type of recital, part boast, part a need to share the terrible act, and part a genuine interest in the re-capitulation of the technical details which Mr Campion had heard before in a dustier land on a noisier occasion. He had not enjoyed it then.

'The owner of the car must have found him in the early morning and switched him into a truck with a curtained back,' the thin man said quickly. 'That's where he was found. In a pile-up on the motorway outside Saltbridge.'

'That's right,' Arnold agreed. 'I got that bit from Lord Ludor's secretary but she left out the kind of vehicle and of course I didn't ask her, knowing already, as I thought. You can see how dodgy this sort of thing is in this closed set-up and peace time! I don't often make mistakes.' His eyes rested on the man in the front seat. 'It's too bad when I do.' His laugh was almost friendly but he made no attempt to disguise the position. 'I'm talking so long because I want a little something from you,' he said.

'Really?' Once again Mr Campion was surprised by him. To save his life he could not resist a flippancy. 'Will you take a cheque?'

'You're a lad! No, I don't mean anything like that and you may be difficult about it, but when I was listening to you I thought to myself: "He knows where that Auntie's pet is. Or thinks he does". You know where the boy is, don't you?'

'I assure you you're wrong. Why do you want to know?'

'Be your age! I need to keep Ludor sweet, don't I?'

At first the suggestion seemed a non-sequitor but a fresh possibility occurred to Mr Campion, who was aware of becoming dangerously stiff, cramped and twisted as he was, looking over the back of the driving seat. Until that moment he had assumed that Thos Knapp had cut off the conversation with Dearest as soon as he suspected that someone else was listening. However, in view of the considerable amount of it which he later admitted to have overheard, it now seemed that the sequence of events might well have been rather different.

Thos, he knew, was hardly a man to put up with real nonsense from his staff such as an unknown tap on his own private wire; in other words there was a double-cross in the story. In which case Arnold's five hundred cigarettes had been shared by the Chairman of Advance Wires, who would certainly reserve the means to cut the barman out at any time when his own business required privacy. As soon as the idea entered Mr Campion's mind he remembered the violent crackle he had noticed on the line when Dearest had protested that he was 'running on'. If Thos had taken action as soon as he heard this phrase which, with his long experience, might well be known to him, Arnold would not be aware that the devices had been recovered.

Mr Campion did not rush the fence. His instinct was to keep the man talking as long as he could in the hope of his concentration wavering.

'I thought Lord Ludor assumed that Mr Mayo was the inventor of the devices and ... er ... Auntie's pet was with him?' he ventured.

'I think you know better than that, Mr Campion.' The expression on the shiny face was reproachful and there was no smile in the flat eyes. In many ways it was a terrible countenance but a remarkably sane one. 'Mayo knew he was on to something. It was written all over him.'

'The amplifiers will be sent down here. Security will hand them over.'

'When they get them.'

'They have them now.' Mr Campion had the uncomfortable impression that he was waving a scarf in front of the poised head. 'The Special Branch have picked up the End of the World Man.'

'Who?' His frank astonishment took them both off watch for a second. Mr Campion recovered first and cursed himself. Of course, it was more than possible the barman would not know that contact.

'I've never heard him called that.' Arnold was very inquisitive and there was a flicker of disquiet about him.

'It was a disguise he adopted sometimes.' Campion was too experienced to make any corrections. In this sort of interview one went straight on or not at all. 'He was the secretary of a Judgment Day Society. He put on one of the monk's robes their employees tout about in, and he was handing the things over to a well-known agent together with one of the Society's pamphlets when they caught him. *I'm talking about the man with the white cat.*'

He felt he was prodding the brute with a stick now and braced himself, but to his astonishment Arnold relaxed and laughed.

'God! How like them,' he said, with professional amusement. 'Can you beat it? Disguise! Fancy dress! You can't cure them of it you know. It's built in. Before the Revolution someone did some first-class translations of a writer called E. Phillips Oppenheim and that's their view of England. Have you ever read Conrad? You should. There's a book of his that's their other Bible on the British. Sooner or later they'll catch up with the modern stuff! Then there'll be some birds in it! Too late for you and me.' He noticed the shadow pass over the pale face before him and shrugged. 'I don't say you are a two-facer, like me,' he said frankly. 'All I meant was that whatever they get up to, so will the British—in their own good time! The British even caught up with *me* in the end, only they didn't know it. You must admit it's a laugh!'

Now that all the cards were on the table and the conversation could have but one end, Mr Campion was almost relieved.

'You put a touching faith in the teashop-keeper's reticence,' he remarked, stretching a cramped leg recklessly.

'Me? Trust the old queer with the cat? Don't be wet! He doesn't know me. I've seen him and I've heard a bit about him but he's never seen me.' He was amused by Mr Campion's reaction and took pity on his ignorance. 'I used the milk bottle routine. It's neat if you don't know it. I can't tell you if it was their idea or his, or if the perishing cat put it up to him!' He was laying himself out to entertain, as he did for any customer in the bar. 'Cribb Street and Dortmunda Street run back to back behind Wigmore,' he continued. 'And between them there's a narrow alley which separates the two lines of backyards. High brick walls with doors in them on both sides; you know the kind of place? It's only wide enough for the dustman, the coppers having a drag, and the milk. My old queer from the teashop used to plonk a crate of empty milk bottles out in the alley whenever he was told to; never at any set time. As soon as he'd gone back in and closed his yard door, acting on orders I'd slide out of the backyard of a house in Dortmunda Street where a couple of old dears I go to see have the top flat and use of a yard. If there was no one around I'd put a half-pint bottle down among the others. It looked as if it was full because the inside of the glass was painted cream and it had a metal cap. As soon as I'd gone by, the old teashop queer would step out for it as if he'd forgotten and put it out with the empties by mistake.'

'Not bad,' said Campion with professional condescension. 'Except that presumably you have to carry a half-pint milk bottle about with you, which seems unchic.'

'I care for that!' The barman sounded sincere. 'Actually

two bottles were kept in the old girls' shed. All above board—
they'd merely been used for paint and allowed to dry; all I
had to supply was the metal caps. I didn't have to do any more
myself. I just obeyed orders and used the equipment provided.
That's their method. The other night, after I'd parked Mayo, I
only had to 'phone my Number One and report I'd picked up
something on the list of wanted items.'

'Did you know what the things were?'

'No, but I knew they'd belonged to the children. There's
been urgent enquiries about a device of some sort those kids
were thought to have got hold of, for months now. From what
I heard Mrs Ferris trying to tell her husband, Mayo had
snaffled them from the old parson at the Rectory so I felt
pretty safe in going after them myself. I knew he must have
them on him. I took a chance, see? I was telling you: as soon
as I reported I'd got something, I was told to leave the milk in
the usual place, right away. Sure enough, by the time I got
there, the crate of empties was already outside with a painted
half-pint bottle amongst them waiting for me. I shoved what I
had inside it and before I'd reached my van I heard the queer's
door open behind me. I did my shopping and I was home here
in under the two hours. There was no traffic—I had a straight
run.'

'This teashop-man was in St Peter's Gate Square that night,
or his cat was,' Mr Campion murmured.

Arnold blinked. 'D'you know, I thought that,' he said. 'I
saw something and wondered.'

'What was he doing? Watching for the children? There was
an unsuccessful attempt to pick them up earlier in the day.'

'At Liverpool Street? So that was it. I had orders to prevent
Mrs Ferris getting transport from here in the morning to catch
a train to London. I thought it might be difficult to stop her,
but Mayo appeared to be backing me up. Actually that was
one of the little items which made me spot that he was with
the old Odsbods—I call my best customers that—and making
for the airport when the time came. Everything began to fit in,
see?'

'Would the teashop-keeper come out to St Peter's Gate Square and hang around after the children himself?'

'If there had been a failure and one of his contacts had fallen down on the job of picking them up? Possibly. No way of telling.' He was disinterested. 'In that service anybody can get orders to do anything; I thought perhaps he was just fetching the cat home. He runs a chronic barney with some other barmy old chap who tries to entice it away to annoy him and they go chasing all over the shop after it. It's a real old "queen's quadrille" by all accounts. I hear this from the old girls in Cribb Street. A neighbourhood like that is as gossipy as a village and he was one of the sights. Now he's gone and let himself be taken! That'll annoy the Odsbods. They've used his "post office" for years. He was there when I came in.'

'Your employers, the ... er ... Odsbods got the flat for your lady friends?'

'Have a heart! One of those old dears went to school with my Mum. She's the tailoress. The other is the milliner. They're nice old ducks, very correct and patriotic. They don't know anything about all this, naturally. I was given the chance of getting the lease for them and they pay the expenses and a bit over because they're so grateful. It's gone on for several years now. It began when I left Lord Ludor's private service and came down here. That's about when it started. It doesn't bring in a fortune, you know, but it's just worth having.'

'How old were you when you went to Lord Ludor?'

It was an unexpected question and Arnold sat quiet, as if he did not want to remember. For the first time in the entire interview he betrayed a normal human reaction instead of the cold, close to the ground, self-seeking which appeared to demand only shallow applause for small boasts and could sell its own country or any other for something 'not a fortune but just worth having'.

'An eater of dust'. The superstitious thought shook Mr Campion deep inside himself. He nearly shuddered. The effort to control it produced a memory of something Amanda had told him just before he came out. It seemed relevant.

But, before he could speak Arnold, who had been watching him, wriggled in his seat and laughed. With his great pink hands, wide mouth and waxen skin he was really disgusting.

'You're something right out of the past, aren't you?' he gasped. 'I like it. You give me a real giggle. You're my senior officer and yet you give me a look which is so naïve that you take my breath away. You don't understand me, do you? And yet I'm dead sensible. I'll put it in baby talk. I'm an employee, aren't I? So I please my bosses and I make a living. I aim to please. All the time.'

'Every separate boss?'

'Well, of course. That's the art of it. That's why the pay is enough. It's all chickenfeed, but it mounts up. Listen. If your trade is secrets and you're a good tradesman you can work for the lot if you're nippy and so have a reasonable turnover. That's the crux of it. Don't tell me it's never occurred to you! *Of course* I had to get cracking as soon as I realised Mayo was making for the airport. That was a risk but it's one you've always got to be prepared to take: physical action when necessary is an essential. I didn't want him turning up at the Viennese H.Q., or wherever, with the items I'd been forwarding the dope about for over a year, did I? Especially if he was going to tell them I'd been signed on by British Security before I could report it myself.'

'Would you have reported it?' Mr Campion sounded surprised.

'Of course I would and so would you if you were in my place. Keep the Odsbods informed and you're taken care of.'

'Don't and presumably the same applies?'

'That's rather good. I shall use that. My Number One could just about follow that. It's true too. You'd never save yourself. One day you'd forget and step in a cab, or accept a lift, or pause in the wrong doorway and that would be that. I've been at the right end of one of those capers in my time and I learned my lesson then.' His smile became depreciating. 'I don't want to hurt your feelings but your set-up ... ours, I beg

G*

your pardon ... is childish by comparison. Well, it's just another Government department, isn't it? Fancy taking me on to pacify Ludor! Oh, I know I'm eighteenth grade or whatever and I must work my way up but I shall. You'll see—or you would have done. I shall get there. Which reminds me, what about this kid? Has your lady got him or hasn't she? It sounded to me as if you thought she had. Come along, be a good man.'

'Why do you think it would keep Lord Ludor "sweet" to have him? Godley's have the invention already, or will at any moment now.'

'That's nothing to do with me.' Arnold was hissing at his obtuseness. 'Clear your mind! So there's been a slip-up. So the Odsbods lose the jackpot. So they get livid. *But not with me.* I'm all right, I did my bit. Old Fancywork and his white cat carry that can. The same with Ludor. All told—the canteen job as well—he's worth more to me than anybody. He gets the invention but he loses his man. I don't appear. Quite likely he gets savage with me because I didn't have second sight and step in and save his prize boffin. I counter them by coming forward with the older kid who can lead him to the men behind it all. Sam's too young. They haven't trusted Sam.'

'You really don't care who gets the invention?'

'Care? What are you? The Boy's Book of Heroes? I don't care any more than the poor old pearl-diver cares which tart is going to wear the necklace. Why should I?'

'Who is behind the invention?'

'Some Japanese.'

'What?'

'What I say. Some Japanese. A little while ago I was looking through a bag of young Sam's, acting on instructions. It seemed to me that was the way the wind blew. I sent it all in except his toy bird. There was no point in taking that, the kid hasn't got much of his own. I noticed it when I got outside and shoved it in a ventilator. Everybody knew it too well for me to take it up to the club. There was nothing very interesting there, nothing definite, but the flavour was Japanese.' A sour smile passed over his thin mouth. 'There's one thing you can bet on and that's that the job won't turn out to be the riot they seem to expect. For each swan produced in a place like this there's enough geese to start a Michaelmas fair. Do you know anything about the invention?'

'Yes,' said Mr Campion unexpectedly. 'When it becomes universal it will be the death of you.'

'Me in particular?' He was interested.

'You in general. They ought to call it the "Saint Patrick".'

He had spoken lightly. He was growing desperately tired of the concentration but was yet very much aware of the disadvantage of making the first move. He did not dream that his reference might be recognised, let alone taken up. To his amazement an expression of intense resentment appeared on Arnold's shining face. It made him look more human but, if anything, more mean.

'Saying I'm a snake?' he demanded belligerently. 'That's what you mean, isn't it? "One of the snakes cast out by St Patrick from every holy hill and plain of blessed Oirland!"'

The quotation and the faint lilt in it brought Mr Campion's earlier recollection to the front of his mind once more.

'Tubby Hogan, the V.C.,' he said suddenly. 'You left him helpless, without warning, for Lord Ludor and a little more money. Not a lot of money. You simply went where money was. I suppose the blind man cursed you. Was that it? From his bed?'

Campion was actually getting the door open. He had turned completely round in the car and with his left elbow he could feel the lever as he strained his right side forward over the back of the seat.

'He used the old curse, I suppose?' he persisted. *"On your belly shall you go and dust shall you eat".*'

The dull colour returned to Arnold's face. 'Old Tub said "mud",' he murmured and turned his head away as Mr Campion threw his weight backwards, the door burst open and the thin man pitched out on to the track.

19

Snake Bite

WITH dull conviction Mr Campion realised that there was no escape. Aware that he was scarcely more visible than a reed in the wide expanse of marsh and sky, he limped to his feet and backed towards the green van.

The barman got out of the Hawk without bothering to hurry, his hand in his coat pocket. He was in perfect condition and his movements were wonderfully smooth. Meanwhile, his quarry remained standing with his back against the van, his hands resting on the bonnet. He looked a civilised and essentially harmless person, his pale horn spectacles, larger in the lens than is usual, making him appear owlish and rather helpless. On both sides lay the treacherous mud, and the narrow track was deserted. Mr Campion regretted that it was out of the question to make a dash for it. The van's position— half over the edge and hemmed in by the Hawk—made escape that way impossible and, in falling, he had wrenched the tendon of his right foot which had given trouble ever since he had broken it some years before. The wind on his face was cold, and the forlorn emptiness all round him overwhelming.

'Up the well known creek'. A favourite comment of Magersfontein Lugg's, his oldest and least presentable friend, slid into his mind and made him laugh. It was one of those irrepressible snorts of pure amusement which are unmistakable and Arnold paused.

'Hysterical? Or something entertain you?'

'Both,' murmured Mr Campion, absently. 'Honesty being the best policy.'

The barman smiled faintly.

'You really are crackers, aren't you?' He came on steadily and the other man delayed as long as he dared before he remarked quietly:

'I've signed your van,' and stepped sideways.

It was successful. The unexpected information was just sufficiently outrageous to break through Arnold's immediate concentration. His right hand remained in his coat pocket but he altered his weight. The scrawled letters A.C. on the paint-work were remarkably legible considering that they had been made with a nail file by a man whose hand had been behind him. The cuts were deep and it would take professional atten-tion to get them out.

There was one instant just then when Mr Campion might have struck but his single step had warned him that his foot was not to be trusted.

Arnold kept at arm's length but glanced briefly at the damage to the paintwork.

'You stupid clot! Why the hell did you do that?' He was quite as scandalised as if the occasion had been normal. 'You think you're clever, don't you?'

'It's the one way of leaving a message.'

'I know. I understand. I'm not so dumb as you think and you're not so damn clever either!'

Mr Campion found him terrifying because he was not pre-tending and the precise frame of mind in which he ap-proached the act he was preparing so obviously was limpidly clear. He was proceeding exactly like a professional killer of any other kind; like an executioner, a butcher, a mercenary, or a vermin exterminator. He took the operation with enormous seriousness aware of all it's difficulties but with no super-stition whatsoever. The annoyance of the scratched paint had got under his skin and he was giving himself time to settle again to avoid being clumsy.

He stood by the nose of the van, facing his victim, and rubbed the marks with an aggrieved thumb but without taking his eyes from Campion.

'How could the busies make anything of that?' he de-manded. 'So they do find it and try to cook up some sort of tale, what do you think *I'm* going to be saying? I can explain a scratch or so on my own van, can't I? You haven't *signed* it.

It's not a cheque for handwriting experts to examine!' He glanced at it briefly. 'Wanton destruction!' he said without noticing the absurdity.

Mr Campion said nothing, and after a while the barman turned back to the business in hand.

'I can see I've got to pass up the old U.C. "oncer" if they're on to it, but that's not the only way of doing the job,' he remarked and slid his hand into his pocket again.

Mr Campion did not know what to expect. A gun was impractical if murder was not to be suspected and he thought that objection probably covered a knife as well. His own bet was a short cosh, one of the thin rubber, professional jobs, expertly leaded, to be aimed at some vulnerable point; behind the ear, under the jaw, or high up on the occiput. When it came, therefore, he was surprised. Arnold withdrew his hand gently and the weapon appeared, a short fine spike in a stubby holder. It was almost as thin as a knitting needle and a little longer than a dart and Campion realised that any puncture made with it by an expert would take a lot of finding on a P.M. table. In a body in bad condition, say one that had been retrieved from a car wreck in the mud, such a wound must be almost untraceable—always supposing there was only one. That was the important proviso, he realised, and he began to weave like a shadow-boxer. If there could be but one strike only, its position must be absolutely exact to ensure death. This would be difficult with a moving target but possible in time if Arnold kept his head, and it looked as though he would.

In the beginning, the exchange was very slow. They moved like wrestlers, looking for a hold. The barman's concentration was worthy of his animal counterpart and his shining skin and unwinking eyes quite as ugly. He feinted twice at the throat and Campion, who was being forced back to the edge of the wall, began to suspect that the real objective was some other point. He was finding himself horribly ill-informed. A pierce-wound in the kidney or the lungs could either of them kill him, he thought, but not immediately.

Meanwhile, the temptation to rush the man and risk it was

becoming unbearable and that, he guessed, was one of the mistakes which this preliminary fencing was aimed to provoke. The discovery that he was utterly out of his depth amazed as well as frightened him. He felt like a hunter confronted by a new creature whose methods had not been studied and whose courage and intelligence were at least as great as his own.

He was almost exhausted when he realised that the feinting was part of the attack. The intention, he saw abruptly, was to tire him until he became slow enough for that thrust into the vital spot to be delivered without danger of failure. Despite the chill morning, both men were sweating and the contest was resolving into a battle without blows, a cold war in which, as usual, all the advantage lay with the attacker.

Mr Campion hung on grimly; every sense strained, every muscle tensed, struggling to match the superior strength of his opponent. Disaster overtook him suddenly and completely. His treacherous right foot turned on a tussock of slippery grey grass and pained him savagely. His eyes flickered and the barman struck, not with the spike but with his unwatched left hand.

The thin man was only just fast enough to turn, so that the infamous Japanese flip which can put a man out for minutes missed the nerve centre beside his ear. All the same he fell flat on his back, his head lolling over the wall, spreadeagled and wide open to the slender shaft.

The blood was boiling in his head and his heart was beating so loudly that he did not hear the distant shout from down the track.

All he knew was that his life appeared to be about to end in a useless and ignoble fashion in conditions of acute discomfort, while the chances of the murderer getting clean away with it were odds-on. His wits had not saved him; he had found a wilier enemy at last.

In his anger he kicked out blindly and caught Arnold, who had turned towards the shouting, on the kneecap and sent him crashing down on his face, his right hand under him.

'Say you fellows, what are you up to?' Martin came tearing up the track on one of those extraordinary old bicycles which appear to exist in communally owned pools wherever academic brains foregather. It made no sound on the smooth track and accounted for him being able to get so close without disturbing them. He threw it aside and went to help Campion, who was getting up. It was obvious that he had been roused from bed, for his slacks and sweater had been pulled over pyjamas and his hair was still rumpled. He was excited and highly curious and also breathless from a hard ride.

'When I first caught sight of you I thought you were arguing.' he panted. 'Then I saw him slam you and I shouted. You went down and kicked out. What happened?' He turned and looked at the motionless figure lying in the track. 'Is he all right?'

'Don't touch him.' Mr Campion spoke warningly as Arnold suddenly raised himself and scrambled to his feet. He stood for a moment and then, without glancing at either of them, he scuttled into his van and slammed the door. It was a retreat. He appeared to take very small quick steps, his head held rigid and his eyes fixed in front of him.

'He threw something down.' Martin glanced at Campion. 'Did you see? It went into the grass. What was it? A gun?'

He was about to walk forward to look for it when the other man caught his shoulder. Arnold had started the van's engine. It looked as if he must go back to avoid going over the wall, but, if he did make a dash for it, they were between him and the car.

They were looking at him when he bent forward, apparently to put the van into reverse. The light was less dazzling and they could both see him quite clearly through the windscreen. His eyes were downcast and his face looked shinier than ever. He was completely expressionless, engrossed in the manoeuvre. And then while they were actually staring at him, ready to leap if they had to, his mouth fell wide open.

It was an astonishing sight. Awful in its absolute wrongness. Presently his head toppled forward as if it had lost its balance and he lay across the steering wheel. The engine stalled abruptly and was silent.

'I don't think we'll disturb that, you know.' Mr Campion spoke very softly.

'But I think he's dead. Did you see him?' Martin was
208

appalled. 'I think he suddenly died, right there in front of us. Don't you?'

'Yes.'

'Hell! But I mean we must find out. We can't just leave him.'

'I rather think we must.' Mr Campion pulled him back. He sounded apologetic. 'It's a very delicate situation. Where did you see him throw something?'

'Over here somewhere. Are you...? Oh I see, you've hurt your foot. Wait a minute. I'll find it. You hang on to the Humber.'

'Don't pick it up.' Mr Campion spoke just in time. Martin straightened his back.

'It's here,' he said, pointing with his foot. 'It was his cork-screw; the safety cap is off.'

Mr Campion's chin jerked upwards. 'One of those com-pressed air contraptions?'

'Yes, a special one. He was crazy about it. It's a pirated Czech model; Lord Ludor gave it to him. It's the same prin-ciple as the normal Sparklet but heavier. You push the hollow spike through the cork, pinch the lever in the handle and send a charge of air into the bottle's neck. When the pressure is suffici-ent, out blows the bung. My God! Could he have fallen on it?'

Mr Campion remained silent for some moments before he said slowly: 'I don't suppose even *he* knew that. He wouldn't have felt anything at all. As he got up he may have suspected it, and torn the thing out and flung it away—in the hope it wasn't true, poor beast.'

Martin glanced at the van in horror. 'Where did it go in, for Heaven's sake? To kill him stone-dead like that?'

'I'm afraid that's a job for the P.M....'

'But to kill him outright! I suppose he *is* dead?'

'Oh yes, he's dead.' Mr Campion opened the door of his own car. He felt suddenly inexpressibly weary. The lungs? The pleura? Between the ribs to the heart itself? The epigastrium? Almost any of the big veins? The list grew longer and longer as he considered it. Almost anywhere in that fine square torso the deep injection of a few centimetres of compressed air, what an amazing amount of damage it could do; what astonishingly little trace it would leave

Meanwhile, Martin had recovered from his initial bewilderment and was becoming practical.

'I'll mark this and leave it, then,' he said. 'I see what you mean. We shall have a bit to report to the police.' He dropped a handkerchief into the grass and set a stone on it. 'He was so popular,' he went on, glancing towards the van. 'I couldn't take him but a lot of people found him invaluable.'

Mr Campion said nothing. He felt that the less told about the barman the better until he could contact Dearest and Elsie. The stroke of fortune which was going to permit him to get the full story back to headquarters still amazed him, for in these matters the full facts seldom get into the records. He had no illusions whatsoever about his own good luck; it had been a very close call.

'I'm remarkably glad you turned up,' he said frankly as he climbed into the Humber and the younger man walked over. 'Why did you come?'

'Sam.' Martin was excited and trying to repress it. 'He came in and woke us. We thought he'd had a nightmare. He said you were "beefing" because you hadn't got a gun. I didn't take it too seriously but Helena did.' He hesitated.' I suppose you were thinking along those lines?'

Mr Campion stared at him.

'I felt something of the sort very acutely ... oh, about twenty-five minutes ago.'

'Don't worry about the time. That whole aspect seems completely hay-wire. There's no indication of the degree of urgency either, as far as one can see at the moment. Frankly, I don't think I'd have bothered to get out and come along if it hadn't been for the other half....'

'What was that?'

'That Edward was worth more than you. And it was a "swiz", as he calls it, to get the wrong one.'

'I didn't think that!'

'Of course you didn't.' A faint grin appeared on the intelligent face. 'That was Fred Arnold's contribution. I didn't like the guy's manner this evening and when Sam reported that item as coming from him, I thought I'd better come out and see what was going on. Sam liked him, you know. He says he saved his cockyolly bird.'

Mr Campion blinked: 'Sam picked up a signal from Arnold as well as from me? Is that what you're saying?'

'Well, naturally he would.' Martin was a kindly expert. 'These flashes appear to bombard us all, all the time, or that's the theory. With the new device people appear to become aware of too many of them while certain sensitives, Sam for example, seem to be able to distinguish and isolate those which come from people they like or at least know well. But we know practically nothing at all about any laws which govern any of this yet.'

Mr Campion passed a hand over his hair.

'Has Sam got hold of another of these devices?'

'No. He says he sometimes gets a flash without one, especially if he's been living with an "iggy-tube" for days beforehand. That suggests a "technique of reception" to me. I don't think it's unreasonable if the devices really are only amplifiers, as we're beginning to suspect. I tell you, Campion, the whole thing is becoming a reality.'

The thin man touched his ear which was still singing from Arnold's left hand.

'I concur,' he murmured, grinning. Martin did not notice the smile. He was thinking, his eyes screwed up against the light which was beginning to stream in golden from the east.

'The potentialities are vast but they're not out of this world,' he said at last. 'I mean it's only another *thing*; like learning to fly or to isolate a virus. It's a genuine breakthrough but it doesn't alter any of the essentials.'

Mr Campion sighed. 'Quite,' he said dryly. 'The snakes and the angels remain but it is another skin off the onion. I'll leave you here on guard and I'll reverse back to the outfit on Roker's Tail. The sooner we get all this reported the better. We're in for a very busy time my lad, one way and another.'

20

Behind the Scenes in an Old Curiosity Shop

'RIGHTIE ho. If you say so. Any friend of yours is a friend of mine but that's stretching it.' Mr Knapp drew Mr Campion into a corner and threw a Gorgon's scalp of curling cables out of the way to permit him to sit down on a metal bench which looked as if it might be live.

It was mid-afternoon on the Monday following the Sunday morning when Fred Arnold had died. They were in a seldom used projection room, now serving as the Chairman's private observation cabin, slung under the roof at one end of Messrs Advance Wires' main salesroom and monitoring theatre.

A cluttered expanse spread out below them and whereas they could see most of it themselves, they were almost invisible from below.

As for the rest of the building, it was sound-proofed in that oppressive way which seems to smother the very pores of the skin and, to the non-technical mind, to produce a strange sense of foreboding.

Thos was tremendously at home in the hide-out. It was also his top secret stores department and possessed an element of 'housemaster's desk' in its suggestion of contraband.

'You can't argue that he's not a "busy",' he added after a pause.

Mr Campion knew that he was not unreasonable but the position was delicate. 'Luke is top-brass when he's at home and he's all right,' he insisted. 'He's also just outside the door, old boy....'

'O.K., O.K.' Thos was stowing various cartons into a locker which ran round the wall. 'I'll just get these out of sight in case. Have him in but remember we're only a cog in a ruddy great machine persided over by a tyke-coon. We're nothing but pore perishers, earning our grub and not knowing quite what we're up to except that we understand we're working for the Government.'

Mr Campion smiled wryly. 'That should cover it,' he agreed and let himself out of the small back door which gave directly on to an iron balcony and staircase leading down on to the marsh below.

The interval, since his last visit, had been filled with County Police, Special Branch and Security activity, none of it made any easier by Lord Ludor's bland determination to keep tabs on every part of the enquiry.

As an object-lesson in getting what one wants by merely stamping towards it through the undergrowth, his had been an impressive performance, and by the time Luke had arrived about four in the afternoon on Sunday the military ban on leaving the island was still in force.

However, the Superintendent had had wartime service with the Military Police which had left him with the two essentials, know-how and friends, and finally, as the result of his efforts, Mr Campion had found himself driven past the post on the Strada by Redcaps late on Sunday. He had been rushed through the town and delivered on the roadside, much to his astonishment, to Elsie himself, who had taken the unprecedented step of driving out from London to hear the story at first hand.

As they had motored round the lanes together Mr Campion made his report and thus another patch of fungus in the oaken timbers of the old British warship was successfully sealed off for treatment.

The Director had appeared very happy but he had been able to offer very little comfort concerning Edward. There was still no sign of the child and both Amanda and the Canon were extraordinarily silent and withdrawn. The Rectory, L.C. Corkran said, was being watched by at least three different interests, one of them Security itself, who was certain that no messages were passing. His personal opinion was that the boy must be already hidden in the house but he had to admit that

Lord Ludor, who had his own methods of investigation, was convinced that Edward was still away.

No attempt could be made to search the old house because no complaint had been lodged. Indeed, what with red tape and the perverse circumstances, a complete impasse appeared to have been reached.

Late on Sunday night Mr Campion had been driven back to the island and today Luke had come over from local police headquarters and had arrived at the Ferrises' hut demanding to see Advance Wires from the inside.

'It's such a damn silly name,' he said, as he and Campion drove across the sea wall track together. 'What does it mean?'

'They're so advanced there aren't any.' Mr Campion waved a hand in airy explanation. 'That's the Thos pattern of thought. He's very modern, always was. It's something to do with this half-century's great discovery: if you run past yourself there isn't anything there.'

Luke laughed. 'You'll do,' he said, but he looked a little uncomfortable and after a while observed cautiously, 'I suppose you're talking about the moon?'

Mr Campion did not hear him for they had already arrived.

Now that his preliminary interview with Chairman Knapp was over he looked down the iron staircase at the Superintendent whom he had left stamping about in the grass.

'It's all right,' he said. 'I've vouched for you. Come on up.'

'I heard what you said,' Thos grumbled as they crowded into the tiny space and Mr Campion made the introduction. 'It wasn't very clever, Bert, not now. When we was young we could afford our sentimental beliefs in the brotherhood of man, uniform or not, but now it's "*of course* we're very happy to see any gentleman from the police". They don't have to be vouched for. We've got nothing to hide.'

'There's no need to be touchy, Mr Knapp,' Luke was at his heartiest.

'Well then, why bring it up?' The deplorable nose was twitching. 'You sit here, Super. Then you'll have a nice clear view and won't be so ruddy noticeable.'

The scene below had much of the bewildering inconse-
quence of a television studio coupled with the gift section of a
department store. Since much of the firm's business lay with
clients who required hidden microphones in other people's
premises, there was a fine florid collection of gifts; chandeliers,
ashtrays on stalks, baroque table-lamps, ormulu clocks and
bedside cabinets, as well as toys in quantity and what are
known darkly in the trade as "small antiques". The fact that
they all contained hidden ears comforted Mr Campion since
he felt it provided a sane if not very pleasant reason for their
existence at all, and he looked at the scene below with growing interest.

An oasis in the midst of the trailing wires, small screens and
loudspeakers consisted of a carpet on which there was an
arrangement of upholstered seats. Each of these could be
combined with one or all of the others to make something else.
They were being arranged now, by Feeoh and a long thin girl,
for some purpose which looked as if it might be an animal
turn and was in fact the imminent arrival of Lord Ludor
himself and party, or so Thos said.

'That's why I'm a bit edgy,' he confided with engaging
frankness. 'We've been bugging your London hideout by the
way, Bert. We had to get our Slough staff out. His Lordship
wants to hear the tape if there's time. We've told him there's
nothing going on there.'

'The Rectory?' said Luke, a muscle on his dark face
twitching.

'That's right. Got the order early yesterday. The old man—
his Lordship—is looking for a child. You know that, do you?'

'That's the youngster we all hope to locate over here as he
contacts a certain apartment in Paris.' Luke was attempting to
combine Police omniscience with a genuine if over-played
effort to be pleasant. 'Yes, thank you Mr Knapp. I think you'll
find we're fully in the picture.'

'Do you? Well then, I can't help you, can I?' The pink rat's
nose was quivering and Mr Campion intervened at once.

'And how are they all at home?' he enquired fatuously.

'Ruddy quiet.' Thos shot a beady glance at him from under sparse white lashes. 'I never listened in to such a family. They've all got a fit of the sulks or sore throats. We can't get anything out of them except the Third Programme. Either that or they're calling the dog.'

As both heads turned sharply towards him he shuffled.

'Well then, pussycat,' he said. 'Name of Cavey. Cavey, Cavey all the time from her ladyship; she doesn't seem to say anything else.'

Luke forgot twenty years of discipline and began to laugh aloud, turned it into a cough without success, and coloured.

'So it's a parrot, is it?' said Thos, irritably. 'Nice to meet a busy who can still do that, mister. Don't mind me. Let it fly or you'll do yourself an injury. Look Bert, I'm going down now to see what's laid on for the Lord Boss. See this?' He indicated a panel of switches on the wall. 'I'm going to leave it that you can hear what's going on down there but you can't be heard yourselves. Touch this, however, and WOT OH FRIDAY! you've joined the party, see?'

It was quite obvious what he meant from the effect of the sudden bellow upon the furniture-movers below and Mr Campion nodded intelligently as he altered the switch once more and the sounds from the theatre faded slowly up until their dead tones were just comfortably audible.

'...only some insanitary, archaic joke,' Feeoh was saying to the long thin girl. 'A little to the left, dear. Heave. Thank you.'

As the door to the staircase closed behind their host, Luke's teeth flashed in the gloom. 'You certainly do find them ...' he was beginning when the thin man raised a warning finger and went round the room looking for something. He found what he wanted in a pewter tankard of old brier pipes and fished it out and disconnected it.

'The mike for the tape,' he said apologetically. 'I knew it must be here and hidden in something vaguely connected with tobacco. Wired, too, which is old fashioned. Modern but conventional, Thos is, and he hasn't noticed that the weed isn't quite the commonplace it was. It's extraordinary how one's old chums never change.'

'Is that the only one?' Luke was scandalised and began to look about him.

'Almost certainly.' Mr Campion was following the slender cable to its source. 'I shouldn't think he ever left anyone alone in this treasure chest in the normal way and if he had stayed here he wouldn't need more than just the one for the record. There it is. No second lead. I think we're all right. Now then, while we have a moment, what about the post mortem?'

Luke seemed surprised at the urgency of his interest. 'The D.I. up in Saltbridge was right in the first place,' he said with authority. 'Paggen Mayo died as he thought he had. Both horns of the hyoid bone were fractured. There was only one blow. No question about it. Straight across the adam's apple. Arnold was an expert. Yes, I had my briefing from the Director before he went back. I expect I've been told all that's good for me.'

Mr Campion seemed relieved but before he could speak the Superintendent went on again.

'To my mind the really fascinating part of that story was the way the body got from the car to the truck,' he said. 'That was straight police stuff and just as barmy as only life can be.'

'The parked sports car at Earls Court belonged to a youngster, I suppose?' Mr Campion enquired.

'You spotted that, did you?' Luke was interested. 'They brought the young man in just before I had to leave. As soon as I saw him I wasn't surprised. They reappear every generation, scatty as cats in the wind! He must be all of eighteen and the car is his life. That morning he got up in the dark to go and meet his gang at the Speedway track, fifteen miles beyond Morton. He threw on his clothes, tore down to the street, lugged the plastic cover off his old wagon, dropped it into his Mum's area for her to put away for him and beetled off for a day's outing without observing a little item like a corpse lying on the floor in front of the back seat! As he came through Morton it was getting light and just outside the town he saw an open transport café with an old truck waiting in the pull-in outside. He stopped, rushed out again and was just hopping back into the driving seat when he happened to look in the back!' He laughed. 'Even then he didn't hesitate,' he went on. 'If he had, it would have been all up with his day's outing. So he was as foolhardy as one only is at that age. He's a very strong lad and he simply picked up the body, heaved it into the back of the truck whose curtains were swinging, and shoved a few sacks lying there over it. Then he drove away and spent the day happily watching other young idiots trying to break their necks. He said he never thought another word about it until he heard the police call in an all-night road club with the rest of the kids on Sunday morning. We believed him; you couldn't be off it. He was quite open.'

Mr Campion's pale face wore that curiously pained expression which is halfway to laughter. 'Didn't the truck-driver spot anything either?'

'Both the truck-driver and his mate were very tired men,' Luke explained. 'They belonged to Saltbridge and they'd been South with a load of furniture for a friend who was moving. It was a quick, cheap, Friday-after-work-to-Saturday-morning job. They had delivered and were coming back and stopped at the café for breakfast. They saw the youngster come in and buy the cigarettes and the proprietor actually saw the car. Its bonnet was almost in front of his counter window but he was cooking breakfasts and didn't watch it leave. After they'd eaten, the truck-driver and his elderly mate drove on, sitting together, until they reached the motorway, by which time they were both dropping with sleep. They pulled into a lay-by and dozed for a bit in the cab and then the driver suggested that the mate lay down on the packing material inside while he himself pulled a finger out and got them home. The old boy was delighted and slid round the back while the driver pulled out into the stream. Just about the time they settled in their lane the mate threw himself down on the heap of sacks and let out a yell like the end of the world. The driver heard him and must have lost his head, poor beast. He stood on the brakes. It was the father and mother of a pile up. Three killed. Seventeen vehicles involved.'

Mr Campion said nothing for a long time. Finally he looked up. 'You were all amazingly quick. I heard the police call as soon as it went out—from here, as a matter of fact. Who answered? The boy?'

'Immediately. He telephoned Saltbridge direct; he isn't a fool, merely preoccupied.' A sudden grin appeared on Charley Luke's vivid face. 'I remember being like that. I was just too busy being alive to get involved with anything not my business. I suppose you were really asking about Arnold's death just now? I still don't know how much we common policemen are supposed to know about all that?'

The thin man eyed him thoughtfully but did not commit himself.

'Did they find a wound?' he enquired.

'Only just.' He was feeling in his pocket for the untidy little bundle of scrap-paper which he used as a notebook. 'The homework wasn't complete until this morning so there was only the preliminary 'phone message by the time I came out. Here you are:— *"Small puncture wound one and a half inches beneath the left nipple and three-quarters of an inch to the inner side. On dissection it was found that the wound had entered the intercostal muscles between the fifth and sixth ribs and the pericardal sac. The left ventrical did not appear to have received injury but there was considerable disturbance* (whatever that may mean) *and the left pleural cavity contained fluid blood."* ' He looked up. 'He fell on the thing. Mr Ferris said that in his deposition. As far as he could see the man was running towards you—doubtless to help you up— when he slipped and fell on the grass which is polished like horsehair, I understand?'

Mr Campion nodded. Luke waited a little longer and tried again.

'The local C.I.D. Super is a splendid, sensible old chap,' he murmured as quietly as his powerful voice would permit. 'One of the old school and bright as they come. He told me that in

219

his opinion any kind of accident can happen to the personnel of this sort of set-up. He told me nothing would surprise him.'

Mr Campion's wide mouth grew wider. 'That's a help.'

'I can tell you he *is* helpful.' Luke persisted. 'The only thing he found a little difficult to swallow was why the man should have parked on a lonely track at first light and sat there holding a patent corkscrew, so that he had it in his hand when he went to the rescue of the driver of an oncoming vehicle, who had tripped on getting out to speak to him! However, finally he found a little something to explain even that.'

'Really?' Mr Campion did his best not to sound astonished.

'Some recent accidental scratches on the bonnet of the van,' Luke said calmly. 'Nothing much, but quite enough to get Arnold in dutch with the firm when he had to put in for a repaint. The local Super thinks he was "improving" them well out of sight or witnesses, so that he could say the damage had been done maliciously whilst the vehicle was standing parked somewhere on the mainland at night; possibly in Covent Garden market.'

Mr Campion's incredulous smile grew into a laugh.

'Who by, for Heaven's sake?' he demanded.

'Boys.' Luke was firm and straightforward. 'Hooligans; the Usual. It's all tied up and the coroner will get it in a parcel. You're a very lucky bloke,' he added seriously. 'That chap was a killer in a thousand. I saw Mayo's body. Neat as a whistle!'

The thin man was saved from the need to comment by a tap on the door behind them and Martin, looking shaken, put his head in.

'So there you are,' he said with relief. 'What do you know about the latest?'

'How come?' Luke stared at him.

'I'm sorry. I felt sure you'd heard.' He came in, closed the door behind him and glanced about him dubiously.

'It's quite safe, I think,' Mr Campion said placidly. 'My old chum has been prevented from making the latest unforgivable social error. It's all turned off. Now what?'

'It's that cablegram.' Martin was still almost speechless.

'From Professor Bolitho to Professor Tabard. Ludor was informed, not unnaturally, and he's hit the ceiling. He was supposed to be out here now, listening to a test which is to take place in Paris—in fact they both were—but instead he's up at the Great Man's house raising Cain. Tabard won't stand for that. He may look like a mole but he's a pretty fierce baby when aroused.'

'Which cable was this?' Luke was being patient and Martin blinked at him.

'It's so crazy I can hardly bring myself to say it,' he admitted. 'It's a message of congratulation on the success of the device and an offer of Bolitho's own notes which could effect the whole breakthrough and help to make it practical.'

The two older men, who were very conscious of the complexity of the country in which they were adventuring, exchanged glances and Mr Campion put a cautious query.

'Is that the Professor Bolitho in Pittsburgh who is doing the new work on the more obscure aspects of the electrical impulses generated by the brain?'

'It is.' Martin seemed amazed that anyone should have to ask. 'D. S. Bolitho: quite the greatest man in his field. He's a friend of Tabard's; they've been corresponding. This afternoon I was with the old man when his cable came in and he was wild with excitement, because since Bolitho has been probing into all possible sources of human energy....'

'I don't understand that.'

'I don't suppose you do or that you will for a bit....' The scientist was diffident. 'But you see, at the moment we've got no way of being sure which message we're projecting. I mean we've got no control over the power used. We don't even know what the power *is*. However, that's all rather beside the point. The thing that matters, and which Tabard hardly noticed, was the item in the cable which made the censorship people on the switchboard send it straight in to Ludor. It said: *"Congratulations on your team's achievement. I salute Long-fox's I.G."*'

'What?'

'I saw it. I read it.'

'But . . .' Luke was frowning. 'I don't get that. I thought . . .?'

'I know.' Martin met his eyes. 'The device is not made by Tabard's team, is it? Who does it belong to? Who has leaked even its name to Bolitho, working on something rather different, miles away back home in the U.S.? Where is Edward and who is behind him?'

'Now you're talking!' Luke leant towards him. 'That's what I've been asking myself. It's taking me to the fair because although I don't understand the technicalities of this business I do usually understand men.' He paused, his face very solemn. 'I don't see *any* man,' he said. 'Usually in a witch hunt like this there are either too many suspects or just one so-and-so you can't pin down, but as I see the picture at the moment there is nobody over here. What about you, Campion? Do you see anyone?'

The thin man was staring through one of the spyholes at the cluttered scene below.

'I almost think I do, Charles,' he said at last. 'The idea came from Thos. I'll tell you one thing; if the answer is what I think it is, any attempt of Lord Ludor's to control this thing is pathetic.'

'What about Edward?' Martin demanded. 'Who is behind him?'

'Now *that*,' Mr Campion was very serious, 'That's another matter entirely. As I see it, Lord Ludor simply must not be allowed to get hold of Edward.'

21

Take-Over

A LITTLE over an hour later Mr Campion was still
sitting in the projection room; he was reflecting that any
device to detect the presence of a personality like Lord Ludor's
would be redundant. Now that the man had arrived the impression of acute nervous tension in the sound-proofed building
was almost suffocating.

Martin was already downstairs. The thin man could see him
standing on one side of the room with Helena and Sam, who
had been summoned to attend. The family unit looked subdued and a trifle pathetic, like an item in a political cartoon, a
symbol of the Norm amid the machinations of Progress. As a
concept this was so foreign to Mr Campion's own nature that
he was taken aback by it until he realised that it was merely
an offshoot of the impact Lord Ludor himself made upon him.
The Baron, splendid in Italian ginger tweed, was something
to have seen. His back, under the wool, was powerful and
aggressive, and his short neck looked full of strength in his fine
shirt collar. He was seated on the middle unit of the assort-
ment on the carpet with a secretary beside him. She was a pale
blonde, remarkably like Merle Rawlins even down to the
scotch-and-soda hair, except that she was twenty-five years
younger and did not yet look spent.

The third person in this central group, bending forward in
an attitude of deference which did not suit him, was a heavy
newcomer, whom Mr Campion assumed was the other partner
in Advance Wires; the Spark himself, newly returned from a
dash to France. He was a very familiar type, as ruthless in his
own way as Ludor, but not of the same calibre. This man was
Regimental Sergeant Major size, by no means negligible. At
the moment he was very nervous and, through the spyhole, Mr
Campion could see the sweat on his pink forehead under the

sparse yellow hairline, and his husky voice, lowered just out of earshot, squeaked from time to time as he talked earnestly. No one else was visible apart from Thos, who hovered in the doorway of a lighted annexe from which ropes of cable sprouted like diabolic vines, yet the impression of activity and nervous strain just behind the scenes was tremendous.

Some of this feeling was contributed directly by Drasil Vaughan-Jenner, who had taken Martin's seat between Luke and Campion and was muttering to the Superintendent as though he believed himself in church. His appearance was still jaunty but there was anxiety in his bright Welsh eyes and his voice was hard put to it to keep its natural laughter.

'My Great Man has thrown Lord Ludor out of his house, locked the front door, pulled down all the blinds and sent me to be eaten instead,' he was saying. 'The position seems to be that either the devices which your people have collected are not the ones which Paggen Mayo took from the children, or else they have been so damaged in the interim as to be almost past reconstruction.'

'I'm sorry to hear that, sir.' Luke's cageyness had turned his voice into a growl. 'I called in at headquarters on my way down from Saltbridge and I saw them and identified them. They looked in no worse condition than when I first saw them. They were very dirty but they always were.'

'That's what we heard.' The young man was eyeing him anxiously. 'But when they were cleaned and freed from dust and adhesive they appeared ... Superintendent, the experts wondered if you could have been mistaken. You were absolutely sure, were you?'

'As sure as anybody can be without having marked them. I didn't try one on again.'

'Ah.' Drasil hesitated and decided on complete confidence. 'What has happened is this; first of all Lord Ludor seems to have had difficulty in getting the authorities to realise that the things were not merely pieces of evidence against some foreign agent they happened to have picked up. In fact I believe the police wouldn't part with them at all, at first. To get round

224

that difficulty Lord Ludor had them examined by experts in London, and it's the preliminary report from these people which has just come through by telephone. They say, quite frankly, that they think somebody has been pulling somebody else's leg.' He laughed uncomfortably. 'Our information is that you tried one and so did Mayo and got, or thought you got, some reaction, but that the only others to use them were the children who, of course, are not reliable.'

Luke's black eyes were fierce under their triangular brows. 'Canon Avril tried one.'

'Ah yes, but he's very old and he was asleep or dreaming, wasn't he? We got that from the original report made, I suppose, by you?'

Mr Campion was listening to him chattering and was thinking that he was not being offensive so much as pleading for a break. Down in the theatre he could see the great tweed-covered back and thought he detected an element of relaxation in it.

'Is it Lord Ludor's idea that the whole thing is a hoax?' Luke demanded, and despite the one-way-round arrangement Drasil peered through his peephole anxiously.

'I'm not doubting you, Superintendent,' he said wearily. 'And Professor Tabard is absolutely certain that you experienced just exactly the sensations you describe. They're entirely what he would expect, he says. But the idea of a swindle or a leg-pull has gone through Lord Ludor's mind. If that proved to be the answer he would be disappointed but he'd overlook the inconvenience.'

'I see, sir.'

'You don't, Super!' Drasil spoke from the heart. 'To speak utterly off the record, at this moment the poor nits in Town are trying to repair one of the things and to analyse the other, with the police interfering at every stage. And all they've got hold of, as far as they can see, are a pair of ordinary inexpensive amplifiers out of a small foreign transistor set.'

'There was no mistake about the thing I tried.'

'I know. I know.' Drasil's muttering was a soothing dapple

of sound. 'Mayo was taken in, certainly, and lost his life because of it, poor chap. We are only wondering if, as you're not experienced in these things, something else, say a small battery, could have been incorporated without....'

Mr Campion ceased to listen and turned up the sound from the auditorium below.

The Spark was still keeping his voice down to the passionate murmuring which Lord Ludor appeared to invoke.

'On my affidavit,' he was repeating, using the old-fashioned term as if it were sacred. 'There's no adult in that flat except the English girl. Mrs Rubari left before we got there and the first thing we picked up yesterday morning was the kid, Henri they call him, talking about her. She's due back on Wednesday. I know we haven't got every word that's passed, sir, but we've got a very great deal. We've kept continuous coverage and transcripts have been kept of everything that could be thought at all relevant....'

'By whom?' Mr Campion almost jumped. He had forgotten Lord Ludor's voice in that mood.

'By me, sir.' The solid west country tone was as uncompromising as his own.

Lord Ludor laughed. He seemed pleased. 'There are no adults there except the English teacher, governess or whatever she is, and only the two boys? But that second boy is the son of Gregoire of Daumier's. Every word uttered in that apartment may be going straight to them, you know that?'

'I know it isn't, sir.'

'How?'

'I've put a Groten-Forbes Two-way on it. If there was anything at all going out from there I should know.'

'They could be doing it openly. With direct lines.'

'Not without me detecting something.'

'You seem very sure of yourself.'

'I ruddy ... I am, sir.'

'Huh.' Ludor stirred himself and nudged the girl at his side. 'How much of the recordings he brought back have you checked?'

'I've glanced through these I've got here.' Her voice was soothing like Merle's. 'There doesn't seem to be much of interest except this test at five o'clock. They keep mentioning that.'

'Have both boys got one of these damn things?' He was still suspicious, prowling round the idea and loathe to leave it.

'It seems so. They don't talk about them in front of the English girl, and they may be purely imaginary; you know how children play at make-believe. She seems to be an employee of Gregoire's. She is merely visiting with the younger boy and minding the flat and young Rubari while his mother and her maid are away.'

'How old is this Gregoire child?'

'A little over ten, I think. Henri Rubari is twelve.'

Lord Ludor's laugh was secretive and snorting in the quiet. 'You think it's all a damn silly goose-chase, don't you? So do I! Silly little beggars!'

The girl hesitated and then, leaning towards him, murmured something. He bent an ear to her and glanced towards Sam. The older Ferrises did not notice. They were talking and it was evident to Mr Campion, looking down on them, that listeners up in the projection room, served as they were by many microphones, could hear much more than individual groups in the auditorium.

'No,' muttered Ludor, watching to see if they heard him. 'The mother is playing up a bit. I want him here in case he can help us locate the elder boy from any evidence that comes in.'

'He's too young,' she said.

'No one is too young if he's useful, but he's gone a bit potty or so the mother says. Pretty girl, don't you think?'

The blonde glanced at Helena and shrugged her shoulders and coloured but it was a reaction which escaped Mr Campion, for at that moment he noticed something much more significant.

For some time Sam, who was sitting on a stool, had been staring in front of him with the curiously blank expression of

227

one who is not thinking at all. Now, exactly as if someone had commanded it, he woke up, smiled serenely and intelligently and then put a finger through his hair and made his eyes cross into an expression of idiocy as naughty little children sometimes do. Finally, he turned his back ostentatiously on Ludor and began exploring the canvas roll which ran round the angle where the floor met the wall, kicking it idly until his mother stopped him.

'It's just on five, sir.' The Spark returned to Lord Ludor from a conference with Thos, who was still in the doorway. 'It's coming through very clear just now. We've got it spot-on; would you like it in here, live?'

'I think so.' Lord Ludor was at his most affable. Having spent his rage at the American cable on Professor Tabard himself, the bad news from the London experts appeared to have soothed him. There was still a strong aura of uncertainty about him and no one else in the room had relaxed, but he himself was at ease, disporting himself with his minions. 'The Father Ape Figure', thought Mr Campion and was rather pleased with himself.

'What are they doing now?' Ludor enquired of the room at large.

'It's that woman again,' Thos so far forgot himself as to speak direct. 'Keeps nagging them.'

'Young Rubari has hurt his hand; he shut it in a drawer.' The Spark intervened hastily. 'The governess says he can't manage a horse with it all tied up and she's trying to get the name of the livery stable out of him so that she can telephone and cancel his riding lesson for tomorrow morning. He's an obstinate little devil. There's been a lot of argy-bargy all day.'

'I thought you said she wasn't his governess?'

'She's not. She's come with the Daumier kid as a sort of minder. She's not much like any governess I ever saw.'

'Have you much experience?'

The Spark hesitated and Mr Campion, who was looking down directly at him, caught a glimpse of the flicker between

the thick bald folds of his lids. However, he avoided temptation and spoke evenly. 'I think she's "au pair", really,' he said.
'One of our boys saw her nip out to post a letter. He says she's
very young and got spectacles. Her job is keeping the boys
talking English and answering the 'phone.'

'Also bossing young Rubari who wants to ride. What business is it of hers?' Ludor sounded as if he might resent it
personally. 'Well, come on. Let's hear something.'

The Spark nodded to Thos who nodded to someone in the
inner room, and immediately a very definite London suburban voice spoke from a bronze grill in the wall:

'Ay think you should, actually Henri. It's getting late. The
place may shut, and if you can't ride tomorrow you'll have
wasted your money. Believe me I do know about riding. All
my people...'

'It's five o'clock,' a crisp, polite young voice interrupted.
'Pliz mademoiselle, you promised....'

'All right, Gregoire, but why can't I stay?'

'Because your glasses will get in the way.' A third voice,
laughing and slightly cruel, burst into the room and turned
into wheezes and chuckles and the chimes of the hour from a
drawing room clock. Sam tugged Helena's arm.

'That's old Rubari....'

'Quiet, dear.'

'Ay shall go and ring all the livery stables in Paris....'

'You can't because the telephone is in here....'

'Then you'll have to play in the other room....'

'I shall take your glasses; then you can't read the telephone
book....'

'Henri! Go away! Henri! ....'

'Oh pliz, mademoiselle. You gave your word....' The
younger voice was frantic.

'Do go away yourself, dear.' Rubari sounded smothered.
'And keep your glasses *off*, you look much better without
them.'

'Henri! You'll break them. Henri!'

'Oh pliz! Longfox will be waiting. Oh pliz.'

'Henri, don't kiss me. It's not nice, you're too young.... Very well, since you're so beastly I'll give you ten minutes here, by yourselves.'

A burst of interference, several ominous clicks and screeches and the sound of a slamming door held up the sound and Ludor began to laugh.

'What is all this costing your firm, Knapp?'

Thos shot a baleful glance at his partner who waved him silent, and presently the loudspeaker became dominant once more.

'... hurry.' Gregoire's clear tones were tense with anxiety. 'We are late. Henri, have you the message? You have it written down, have you not?'

'I hate that filthy girl. I want to ride tomorrow.'

'Why?'

'Oh hell! Because I want to.'

'All right. Don't be so passionate. Let us do this first. It is nearly seven minutes past the hour. Now. We will both think suddenly together: *"A clown bursting through a paper hoop holding a bottle"*. Can you see it in your mind? In colour, pliz.'

'Yes, of course I can. I can see it with my eyes, out there on the hoarding.'

'That is not the same. It must be in our minds, I think. Shut your eyes. Now then. We will both think quickly together; *"a clown jumping through a hoop holding a bottle and the word is..."* '

'That's not fair. One never gets words. Longfox says...'

'Never mind. We will try. Now: We are trying to tell you, Longfox: *A clown jumping through a hoop holding a bottle and the word is "Prosit"*!'

In its own limited way the performance was impressive. The experimenters were absorbed and Lord Ludor sat with his big head slightly on one side and his deep round eyes turned darkly upon the grille.

'Now.' Gregoire was still in command. 'We must write down the time by my watch. Put it there. Oh come, Henri! You are

only thinking of that ride. It is not even your horse. Stop it!
What is the use of hitting...'

'Very well.' Rubari was attempting to be civil. 'Five-
thirteen. Get it right. Now what do we do?'

'Now we put on our own iggies and we wait for Edward
Longfox....'

'I don't want to, very much. I hate the iggies; they hurt like
the birdhouse in the zoo.'

'That is only because you are getting so old so quickly. But
you must try, because although I am so good at it, don't forget
I do not know this Longfox yet, and I have to pick him out.
Have you got that stuck? Is it warm?'

There was a pause followed by an explosive giggle. 'If she
sees all this muck on me she'll want to wash me, I bet you!'

'Oh, do not play the fool, Henri! I see Longfox must let you
in because of the money but you are not the right tempera-
ment. This is the crown-of-the-venture. Come. For two minutes
we will wait. Relaxed, not strained. Don't forget. Relaxed.
Idle. It is five-seventeen coming up. *Now....*'

'He doesn't only let me in because of the money! That's a
foul thing to say! If you knew Longfox...'

'Oh pliz! Shut up. Keep your mind open. Wait.'

Lord Ludor leant back in his seat and grunted. 'What was
that?' he demanded of the Spark, who had muttered something.

'I said it's quite clear they think they're alone.'

'You told me you *knew* they were.'

'I do. No one's listening to them except us, but they've not
detected us with their gadgets.'

'Neither of them know us. They have to recognise one signal
among the rest. Isn't that so?' He looked across at Sam enquir-
ingly. It was a sly, oddly lowered glance under the heavy
brows. The child met his eyes blankly and looked away. Ludor
smiled ruefully and returned to the man. 'They're not playing,' he said. 'They've been taught. There's an adult in it
somewhere.'

'Yes, sir. I don't think he's over there, though.'

'Perhaps not. But Gregoire Gregoire, the second boy's father, is a remarkable chap. I wish we had him. What do we do now? Wait and see what one of these little brutes thinks he's received? Where is that 'phone bell ringing?'

'That's on their mike, sir. The 'phone is in Paris, in the room with them.'

The secretary said something and Ludor turned to her.

'It's not a waste of *my* time. Go away if you like. Now they're going to be interrupted. Yes, here she is....'

'Ay say, Henri!' The poor girl had a most unfortunately affected accent which the microphone exaggerated. 'Let me in at once. Ay have to answer the telephone.'

'It's all right....'

'It's not all right! How dare you lock this door. Let me in....!'

'Oh pliz!' Gregoire's small voice agonised. 'Listen. Do let me hear. It is Longfox....'

'Edward? It can't be!'

'Let me in at once, Henri. Gregoire....'

'Oh, give it here, I can't hear. Edward? Is that you?'

'Let me in immediately!'

'Oh, for God's sake!' The roar was from Ludor, who was bouncing on his seat. His size and primitive quality had never been more apparent. As if in direct response to his outburst a second loudspeaker sprang to life and the tapped telephone, which after all was Advanced Wires' speciality and the foundation of the firm, gave up its secrets without a hitch.

'Did you get it, Edward?' Rubari's voice seemed less mature in its excitement. 'I say, Edward. It *is* you, isn't it? Where are you?'

'Listen Rubari. This is most important. Have you access to a television set?' The new voice, severe but trembling with excitement, sent a stab of pure relief through Mr Campion's chest.

'Edward! How did you get on to us? Where are you? Listen, we've just sent our test message. Did you get it?'

'Henri Rubari, be quiet and listen! You are to get to a

television set by six or whenever evening transmission starts
over there. It's come off a day early. A day early. Understand?
You'll see all about it, I think. They may be relaying it. Don't
miss it; you'll have to hurry if you haven't got a set there.'

'Where are you?'

'In London, of course. Do pay attention, there's a good chap.
I believe this call is costing the earth.' There was an interruption and a man's laugh floated briefly over the wires, shaking the listeners like the appearance of a ghost, shattering
although more than half expected.

'Oh good!' It was Edward again. 'It's all right, we can say
some more. It doesn't matter about the money. Listen—oh
who is that woman shouting? Can't you stop her? Oh, I see.
Well, it doesn't matter her knowing now because it's nearly
done. I'll tell you everything when I see you but you must look-
in tonight. What?'

'Did you get our transmission?' Rubari was being patient in
a grown-up way. 'Be reasonable, my dear fellow. This is the
real object of the whole exercise. It is why Gregoire and myself
are here at all. Did you...?'

Lord Ludor was nodding approval, Mr Campion noticed
with amusement. He seemed to have recognised a confrere in
Rubari.

'In a moment.' Edward was still obsessed with his own news.
'This really is much more important. You'll never forgive
yourself if you don't find a set. Go to a café, or something, if
you're too snobbish to have one. Oh, very well, Rubari, if you
miss it you miss it.'

'Miss what?'

'*It*. All of it. It's been recorded. Where? Oh here, of course;
it's taken all day. But don't worry. About your test transmission: it was jolly bad. I don't think it was the going over
the water. I never did think that would affect it much. What?'

'What was it, then? What was wrong?'

'Just not sustained. One strong clear iggy only, and then
four subsidiaries very faint. It came through when I was jolly
busy, so some of it may have been me. What?'

'What was the flash, you clot?'

'All right. They say I can go on. It's very expensive so pay attention and do it properly. Right? Have you got your script? Well, get it. Now then...'

'O.K.?'

'O.K. I.G. Testing. Report begins: Time: Four twenty-three. How's that? Early? Yes. I see. Well, it so often is. Time is out, I think, don't you? It's not our fault. There's something fundamentally wrong with the system. Oh yes. Hopelessly inaccurate. Right. Well then: *Iggy Flash: Rubari to Longfox.* Gregoire not recognised. Strong interference. A lot of circus stuff; it could have been someone for me but your message was very sharp. Are you ready for the next bit?'

'Ready. O.K.?'

'O.K.'

'Part one. *Thought*: Quality good. Duration: too short. Double image. Full colour. Recognisable. *Dispatch*: What? Oh, that's just that I knew it was you, you ass. Listen. *Gen. Begins*; One: *The beautiful brown horse with the soft pale pink nose will miss me and forget me.* Two: *The Woman has hurt my hand.* Got that? Rubari!'

'Yes. All right.'

'Well then, buck up. Now. Second Part: *Feel*: One: Intense Sadness. Deep to Poignant. Two: Exasperation and Hate. Mark 5. That's jolly high for hate. Message ends. How was that?'

'Good God!' said Lord Ludor, lumbering to his feet and walking down the room ignoring loose cables, small antiques and anything else in his way. 'Good God!' he said again and added abruptly, 'they've got it. The transmission's no good but the reception is there. What's the matter with you?'

The final question was directed to the secretary, who was sitting up looking at him in a sort of horror.

'But it was his *secret*,' she said. 'Being afraid the horse would forget him. That was the thing he *wasn't* telling...'

'Yes, but that was the message which got over however he sent it. That ... oh, I see what you mean.' He was silent for a moment and then when he spoke could have been addressing the entire island.

'*I want that boy,*' he said and might well have added 'Fee-Fi-Fo-Fum' Mr Campion reflected, stung to laughter. 'And I want him here.'

He was answered by a man's voice relayed from the telephone far away in the Paris flat.

'Henri Rubari.' The speaker carried great authority and was vaguely familiar to several people present. 'I am very glad to meet you and to be able to congratulate you on taking part in the pioneer stages of one of the most remarkable developments in this age of ceaseless wonders....'

The pomposity was more recognisable than the tone and realisation hit Mr Campion like a thump between the shoulder-blades, a split second before the voice continued.

'This is Leonard Rafael, Editor of *The Daily Paper*. I am speaking from my office in Fleet Street and I am instructed by my proprietor, Lord Feste, to welcome....'

22

Breakthrough I

IT occurred to Mr Campion, who with Luke had remained at his point of vantage, that defeat had the interesting effect on Lord Ludor of increasing his humanity whilst reducing his size. The rueful smile and faintly soiled, or at least, homely appearance of the resigned loser had settled over him and the change in the atmosphere was considerable.

Those who had trembled were now aggrieved and on all sides people were unfreezing into recognisable personalities as they took sly digs at him, presumably to make sure he was not dying.

'I hadn't a clue,' he said to the blonde secretary who now looked bigger and as if she could take care of herself. 'And even you have no idea how damn witty that is! Take a note: "Pa" Palling goes in the black book.'

She looked startled. 'Won't that upset...?'

'Of course it will. It'll kick over a dozen apple-carts but it's necessary. I never want to hear his blasted lisp or see his face again. Also the name *"Clew"* is a dirty word in all companies, all departments.'

'Very well, but I did tell you.'

'I shall remember it.' He was almost enjoying himself and had even loosened his tie and let his great neck free; this was the Ludor of twenty years before, when set-backs had been more common. 'Where's Vaughan-Jenner?'

'Here, sir.' Drasil had come down and he alone was more wary than he would have been earlier, recognising the animal as more dangerous than before. The older man cocked an eye at him. In the normal way he might have growled at the elegant but extreme clothes but now he decided against personal comment. Instead he said: 'Go and get it into Pro-

fessor Tabard's head that I apologise. Lay it on as thick as you
like but see he accepts it.'

The young man gaped at him but the quick blood, which
had risen to his face, receded as he laughed.

'I can try.'

Ludor's deep round eyes met his own gloomily.

'Keep at it. Don't give in. Tell him my latest information is
that Lord Feste is in the U.S.A. now. On Sunday he was invested with some sort of honorary degree in the University of
Boomville and must have spoken with Rafael, who is always in
close touch with him, before attending the ceremony. God
knows who he's told, so that explains the cable.'

'I understand.'

'Tell Tabard, Mayo must be replaced instantly and properly paid this time. Contact the Godley London Office direct
about that—Mr McBain. I don't know how much Feste
slipped Mayo.'

'Forgive me!' The blonde was emerging as a power before
their eyes. She murmured her objection but it was evident that
it was a real one.

'I don't know!' He shouted the refutal. 'The cable mentioned Tabard's team specifically. These things that someone
is trying on the children and for which Mayo has already been
killed may not have been actually made by him here, but they
must have been made by somebody from his information.
Vaughan-Jenner?'

'I'm still here.'

'Soothe Tabard. Make him look in. Is there television over
there?'

'The latest; he looks in all the time.'

'Good God! Why?'

'He likes it. He'll probably have heard the announcement.'

'Sit and watch it with him. I want his reaction. The programme will be on QTV, Feste's own company. Seven o'clock.
You'll have to get a move-on.'

From the projection box Mr Campion and Luke watched
the jaunty figure slide under them out of sight, pausing only

to give them a discreet thumbs up sign as he passed. The
Superintendent shook his cropped head.

'I can't see anyone looking forward to it,' he said gloomily.
'To me it's such a ghastly idea; much worse than the end of
the world. In fact, it will *be* the end of my world when it gets
going. Think what it'll mean. New hypocrisies, new manners,
new moralities, new sales methods, new relationships, new...'

'World,' said Mr Campion. 'Let's face it and meanwhile,
using the older methods of detection, Charles, what in the
name of sanity do you imagine has actually happened?'

'Search me,' said the Superintendent and had no time to
amplify the statement. The door to the iron staircase had
opened a few inches and the Chairman of Advance Wires now
eased himself in. He had a small tape-machine with him and
put it on top of the locker.

'Message just come through, Bert,' he said. 'Your missus.
Our chaps had been called off the Rectory and were going to
pack up when they got this on the beam from the sitting-room
window. They thought it might be of interest so they relayed
it direct and Feeoh sends it up to you with his compliments.
She's got a tongue when she's roused, hasn't she?'

He set the little spools in motion and after a moment of
husky anticipation Amanda's beautiful voice cut into the
room, a biting intensity in her diction which was startling
even to her husband. Her communication was made in the
form of a statement delivered without pause or, apparently,
intake of breath: —

*'Lady Amanda Campion presents her compliments to the
army of clumsy invertebrates who have had the impudence to
"bug" her uncle's residence for the past thirty-six hours and
would like to inform them that communications with Edward
Longfox have been always maintained, despite the inconvenience to his friends and family, who have been compelled to
take avoiding action. Now that the necessity for secrecy no
longer exists, she would like to advise the plump youth in the
cloth boots, and those assisting him, to look in at a programme
on QTV at seven o'clock this evening. She mentions this be-*

238

cause she feels that technicians who have managed to overlook the fact that the elderly lady living next door to the Rectory, and visiting it continuously with more clean surplices than any clergyman could possibly use in a month of purification services, is also on the telephone, are quite capable of missing an announcement about the young man they are seeking, made on the public broadcasting service over half an hour ago. Goodnight.'

Thos laughed softly. 'Class,' he said. 'I like to hear it. I thought I'd pass it on to you and not the Company, though. The kid was getting on the blower to the old girl next door all the time, eh? And she was slipping notes in to the others with the washing. Very deceitful people are nowadays, aren't they? You wouldn't have got Church people behaving like that when I was a nipper.'

Luke sighed. 'They know about the programme at the Rectory, anyway,' he remarked. 'They'll all be sitting round the kitchen table looking at the Talismans' set. I wish I was there. I hate this place!'

'It's the muffle,' said Thos with unexpected sympathy. 'It weighs on you if you're not used to it. Why don't you stretch your legs outside for a bit?' He was winking at Mr Campion as he made the suggestion, and as soon as they were left alone together he came closer to him with dreadful confiding.

'What's the form?' he enquired anxiously. 'I've told the Spark you're the only one to trust. You're an ole friend. Right out of the Supperating Past, I said! ... Bert will give us the office of works, I told him. And you will, won't you, mate? How bad is it?'

Mr Campion was perfectly genuine in saying that he did not understand him and Thos sat perched on the locker, his incredible nose actually twitching and his red-rimmed eyes anxious.

'Be a sport,' he said. 'It'll be "curtains", will it?'

It took the thin man some seconds to realise that he was being asked if the Ludor Empire was in danger of foundering. Then the spectacle of the original rat getting ready to 'shoulder its parrot and make for the boats' was too much for him and he began to laugh.

'No,' he said, 'of course not. This thing hasn't begun. I should think you've got another fifty years before your divorce investigation service is even touched.'

Thos took this suggestion with unexpected seriousness. 'My Gawd! It could make a right mess of our Divorce Department,' he said. 'I think you're right. It'll certainly take a bit of time, which is one comfort.' He nodded towards Lord Ludor. 'That old Article might get round to stopping it. What do you think?'

Mr Campion did not want to depress him further and so said nothing and he continued to wheedle: 'I wouldn't blame him and nor would a great many other matchoor people. It's not really a *nice* idea, is it? Private thoughts and all that? I was sorry for that pore little kid who was feeling soft about his horse. Suppose they put it down by law?'

'I feel certain they will.'

'Reely?'

Mr Campion put a hand on the thin shoulder; the man actually *had* mouse bones. 'Be your age, Thos,' he said kindly. 'Good Heavens, is this *it*?'

As Luke came chasing up from the marsh every monitor in the place, including one in the projection room, sprang to life and for a moment or so the tail-end of one of those rather frightening advertisements, which suggest that the entire population has developed a Lady Macbeth psychosis, urged the hardened company to get itself and its linen 'Cleaner Than You Realise'.

Then there was a pause, a moment of shooting lights and finally, to the strains of *Land of Our Fathers*, QTV's nightly programme, with Giles Jury in the Chair, came into view. In the past Mr Campion had often found it difficult to believe his own eyes when watching on television the devitalised ghosts of people he knew, but tonight the medium seemed to have a dreadful intimacy. He was vividly aware, for instance, that Jury, an urbane young man rather larger than life, must have

240

insisted on trying the device himself, probably much earlier in the day. It said a great deal for his technique that the only visible effect upon him was a streak of pathos in his inhuman smile.

On his left sat old 'Peggie' Braithwaite, wonderfully at ease from the crown of his shining head to the middle button of his waistcoat and doubtless below, if one could have seen any more. Leonard Rafael, dark, nervous and not as impressive as he would be the moment he opened his mouth, sat on the other side of Jury with Edward between them. The child was either perched on a pile of books or two feet taller than when last observed and looked tired. No one had told him not to scratch and the heat of the lights was clearly considerable. He seemed determined to see the thing through despite a chronic itch. His flaming hair looked as dark as Rafael's but his eyes remained chill and intelligent.

The fifth member of the group was a complete stranger. He was a bony young man who looked like a worried white bull-terrier and wore 'short back and sides' but a deal of hair on top, which misled one into thinking that the person he reminded one of so vividly was not present. It was only when he was introduced as Mr Reginald P. Yates Braithwaite, editor of *The Daily Paper's* distinguished contemporary weekly journal, *The Boy's Technician* that the penny began to drop at all.

The proceedings opened with a roll on the drums. Giles Jury excelled himself. His authority had never appeared less bombastic or more impressive and his relaxed manner was just sufficiently tensed to let one know that he felt it was a truly great occasion.

'One often hears that history is being made,' he said pleasantly, 'but tonight, you know, I really think it's true. Lord Feste, who is the president of QTV as well as the sole owner of *The Daily Paper*, has decided that we shall have the privilege of bringing this news to you instead of saving it until tomorrow morning, when the newspaper would have had it as an exclusive item. He has done this because he feels—and I think we shall all agree with him when we see the magnitude of the breakthrough—that this is something far above the petty rivalries of news services. This is something which belongs to us all.

'The Subject is Extra Sensory Perception and it is because of something amazing which has just happened in that field that this programme has changed the whole of its schedules, and that later on tonight, after the News, you will be hearing from a number of the leading brains in this country whose names will be announced later. The interest in Extra Sensory Perception has increased enormously in recent years, but from time immemorial men have sought to communicate with each other by the power of thought alone. I shall not attempt to explain any of this but will lose no time in introducing those sitting round this table who have so much to tell you: Mr Leonard Rafael, Editor of *The Daily Paper*; Mr William Pegg Braithwaite, the well-known writer and broadcaster and scientific correspondent of *The Daily Paper*; his late brother's son, Mr Reginald Yates Braithwaite, Editor of *The Boy's Technician*, and Edward Longfox, of whom we shall all be hearing more later on.

'Peggie, can you tell us first, please, exactly what Extra Sensory Perception is and then from your own knowledge what it is that has just so amazingly occurred?'

The old journalist seized the ball with the safe hands of a cricketer and when his familiar voice, husky and squeaky by turns, first sounded that evening in three quarters of the living rooms in the land, the actual moment of breakthrough occurred. The crust cracked and the first shoot of the new seedling, strange, awful but wonderfully exciting, appeared to view.

'Extra Sensory Perception is a thumping bad term,' said Peggie. 'Or I think so. The thing we're talking about tonight is the communication between minds, animal or human, when no known mechanism is employed. We've all heard of it, we've all met it at some time or other—or something suspiciously like it. Some of us don't like the idea and some of us like it too much and let it make monkeys of us. However, today I can tell you that all that uncertainty is a thing of the past. The young man who has had so much to do with this discovery—for that is what it *is*, I can't call it anything else—is here with us now. But first of all I am going to tell you how *I* came into the story.' He cleared his throat and got down to it.

'In the early hours of last Sunday morning I was roused from my bed by two young men. There they are: Edward Longfox, son of that brilliant young scientist so tragically lost to us in the Arctic only a few years ago, and Reggie Braithwaite, son of my elder brother Yates, who edited *The Yorkshire Stagecoach* until his death last year. Reggie has a very fine paper of his own to look after and he knows my interest in it, but I was a little surprised to find him calling on me with one of his contributors at two a.m. on a Sunday morning! "Why boy," I said, "are you out of your mind?" In a moment or so I began to think so, for he told me the most extraordinary story of scientific discovery I had ever heard. While I was still staring at him, wondering if to send for an ambulance, Edward Longfox placed something in my hand: it was this.'

He held out a nest of blunt fingers and the camera rushed up to it so that for a moment the transparent cylinder on a pristine square of adhesive bandage lay glistening, and many times its actual size, in the lights. Old Peggie replaced the exhibit in a splendid snuff box. He was a connoisseur of antique silver and was suspected of never missing a chance of displaying a piece lest it might lead him to another. Watching him, both Mr Campion and Luke were amused.

'I was in pyjamas and my throat was bare,' he continued, setting the box on the table. 'So when they told me to fix this instrument over my jugular I did so, still thinking I was taking part in some sort of hoax. The next moment, my Goodness! I was halfway across the room. "This is true!" I cried. "My God, they have done it!"' He shook his head and the lights winked on its shining dome. 'It was a very frightening experience,' he announced solemnly. 'I knew that all over the world—Bolitho in America, Broberg in Sweden, Fischer in

243

Western Germany, Tsybukin and Dyudya in Soviet Russia, Dutruch in France and our own Professor Tabard on his island on the East Coast, to name but a few, have each been creeping closer and closer to the wonderful door of the mind which this little key has suddenly unlocked.' He paused, and his sharp little eyes peered knowingly at his audience as if he knew each one of them. 'Don't ring us up; the door isn't open yet. These instruments are not available and for the sake of you all I'm glad they are not. To try one in its present stage of development is a mind-shattering experience, which could be very dangerous. Great new discoveries and their techniques are not perfected overnight. This will take time. However, the initial step has been made.' Before Giles Jury could stop him he swung round on the editor of *The Boy's Technician*. 'Reggie, you told me just now that our young friend had an apt simile of his own?'

The sudden catch offered him in the slips almost upset the younger Braithwaite, who fumbled, disclosing a delightful Jacques Tati personality. His mouth split into a huge pup-like smile revealing widely-spaced teeth and a boy's sense of humour. 'He said we'd got the point of the pocket-knife through the top of the condensed milk can,' he gasped. Edward studied his nails but his lip curled faintly and Mr Campion suspected that he had thought it pretty good himself.

After this flagrant piece of unscripted nepotism, Giles Jury intervened, more in sorrow than in anger.

'Then you got on the telephone I believe, Mr *Pegg* Braithwaite?' he prompted firmly.

'Naturally.' Peggie had the grace to look guilty. 'I obeyed my first instinct. I contacted my editor. There he is: Mr Rafael.'

The editor of *The Daily Paper*, who had been sitting like a log, woke up, uncrossed his legs, hitched his chair towards the microphone and went smoothly into action like some great automobile starting up.

He had a very ordinary voice and a very ordinary face but he pulled the whole circle into a bunch, including without

244

effort all those sitting round at home. 'When I heard him on my bedside telephone I thought Peggie was overdoing it,' he said, smiling at everybody confidentially. 'But he convinced me and we all went down to the *Paper* office i Fleet Street where I summoned a staff and we did a few preliminary experiments. As soon as I was convinced that we were indeed faced by a genuine breakthrough and not a mere invention, I contacted Lord Feste who was in America. As you know, their time is some hours behind our own and he was just going to bed, but on hearing my news he too became excited and after a brief conference I found myself fully empowered to embark on the programme we had hammered out.'

He broke off to speak directly to Giles Jury who was fidgeting. 'Oh, I'm leaning right across the table, am I? I'm so sorry. This thing is so exciting I get carried away completely. Well now, I'm sorry for that. The first thing *I* wanted to know was the thing which *you* all want to know now. How in the wide world did this astonishing thing come about? What led up to it? Whose were the brains behind it? The man who could tell me was there, waiting—Mr Reginald Yates Braithwaite.'

He nodded to the young man but did not relinquish the microphone: Reggie Braithwaite was not *his* nephew. 'As you have heard, he is the editor of a successful boys' paper owned by the Thousand and One Nights Press, another company of which Lord Feste is Chairman. Mr Braithwaite is in the habit of publishing letters from correspondents. A bright and popular feature which, in his journal, takes an unusual position on the first inside page. Seven weeks ago he received a letter which so pleased him that he decided to publish it at once, giving it the lead position and a headline. Perhaps not altogether unfortunately, *The Boy's Technician* is six whole weeks in print and that letter will not appear until tomorrow morning. However, I have here an advance copy of the paper and now, with the editor's permission, I propose to read it to you.' He put on a pair of spectacles which were almost horse-blinkers and took up a very slim, very new-looking, paper-covered magazine.

'This is the headline given to the letter by Yates Braith-waite: *Seven Pounds for Your Thoughts but Worth It, says Edward*. And this is the letter. I have seldom read a more meat-filled docun nt and I hope you will give it the attention it deserves. H re it is:

'Sir,

'It n ıy not be generally known that it is now quite possible to pi к up the thoughts of other people in signals which are strong enough for the weakest of intellects to detect.

' I he study of E.S.P. has become respectable now, whereas in the past, when it was called Telepathy, it was not. Yet it is only very recently, and at this school, that the scientific instrument which makes reception absolutely fool-proof—except for those who are too old—has been made to function.

'A group of boys, all connected with Science in some form, have banded together to do this in the following way:

(1) It was discovered by research that the new element Nipponanium was the vital ingredient in any such instrument. Note:—Nipponanium as you are probably aware, was not known before, since there was none on Earth until some was produced and discovered in some radioactive carbon taken out of a Dead Reactor.

(2) The same researcher also discovered that the *Iris Transistor Semi-Silent* which is made by the *No-moto Company of Japan* had already incorporated a minute quantity of this new substance in the amplifying element of their product. It was their belief that the sound volume could be made less penetrating in this way whilst the tone remained true and audible, thereby making the transistor sets suitable for school dormitories, etc. where quiet reception is so important.

(3) From another source (also Japanese) it was learned that the *Iris Semi-Silent* had gone out of production because the sound results were not much good, and difficulties were experienced by the manufacturer since the workpeople handling the Nipponanium showed signs of a mystery neurosis and
246

would not touch it after a bit. (These would all be adults, I expect.)

(4) Realising I would have to act quickly as more Iris Transistors might not come over to England, I approached my friend Henri Rubari, who put up the money (in the end) to buy no less than four of these sets which are only obtainable from Messrs. Blank, Blank & Blank, of Blank in Holborn, who are the sole importers.'

Rafael paused and removed his spectacles: 'The suppression of the name of the firm was made in compliance with a house rule of the Thousand and One Nights Press but *The Daily Paper* ascertained the facts and has taken appropriate action,' he said without a tremor and, resuming his black-sided goggles, went smoothly on.

'These sets cost no less than seven pounds each and so we began with one only, which Henri Rubari donated free because of his faith in the idea which, I would like to say, I appreciate. Armed with it, and with the information which my researcher had given me, I set to work, helped by the rest of my Team.

(5) Since it was realised that the human body itself would naturally have to take the place of the rest of the transistor set, including its battery, my first task was to find the correct point of contact. Really exhaustive experiments were made by us all with at first most disappointingly slight results. However, as I believe is usual in these major discoveries, success occurred by means of a sort of accident. It was found that most people got their best results when an amplifier was stuck across the main artery in their necks and various adhesives were tried. (It was very easy to be silly over this and a lot of time was wasted.) Finally I decided that an ordinary piece of surgical plaster was the most practical as well as being the least noticeable and one day, when our precious amplifier had been returned to me in a slightly damaged condition, I rolled it in the zinc adhesive, really just hoping to keep the thing together. My spirits certainly were at a low ebb. Then, like a thunderbolt! Victory!

(6) 'I could not put it on until the next evening because of

boxing practice so it had some hours to soak. It was also very hot weather which probably helped, but this is still subject to investigation and must be tested again and again.

'At any rate, as soon as I put it in position and settled down in peace to make my mind the necessary blank, I got, among a lot of confusing other material, a definite, recognisable, clear flash from Rubari, who was down in the Day Room. It was about fishing, which I am not interested in. He was tying flies and getting exasperated as people do. I was able to check with him at once and then he checked me. I was annoyed with him for doubting my word and he received what I thought about *that* but not quite the message I sent. After that, work went on with great seriousness and the other transistors were purchased. Unfortunately the shop would not sell the amplifiers separately.

(7) I do not want to make any claim for the zinc until proper chemical and, I hope, radiation tests have been made. Without proper laboratory facilities, which I hope to get in France through a friend of Rubari's whom we have got interested, it is not possible to tell how such a trace of zinc would affect the minute amount of Nipponanium contained in one small amplifier or *how it could get at it*. Query: Is it a question not of chemistry but radiation? When one thinks how a trace of Germanium too small even to be detected chemically can affect the atomic pattern of Aluminium, one cannot but wonder.

(8) I wish to say that I am publishing this interesting news now, before it leaks out any further, for a good reason. In our tests on this instrument we have naturally picked up many outside thoughts, mostly from strangers or people only known slightly. Some of these have been about E.S.P. and even our own part in it and some have been against and even dangerous, and so I have decided not to wait but to take action now. My father, who was a very famous man, told me when I was quite young, that an invention belongs to the country of its inventor but that a breakthrough belongs to the world. Having thought it out very carefully I have decided that this is a breakthrough. So the world must take it and get on with it

as fast as possible, for it is not a thing for one lot of people to know more about than another, if it is not to add to their serious irritations instead of clearing them up. I also feel that it will give men and boys in Science a great deal of work of a useful kind and so lessen their interest in explosions and a blasted world and all that waffle. Once this is in general use no one could even think of pressing a button for a bomb, without those affected being warned. But I must repeat that there is a lot to be done before that happy day. Sending is erratic and receiving is not yet really practical by adults, which is greatly against it at present.

(9) The only thing I would like to ask for myself is that the amplifier, when it is perfected, shall be called Longfox's Instant Gen after my father. Also, my researcher belongs to the famous Blank team and he says, quite rightly, that the credit for the first idea of the Nipponanium being useful must go to them.

I send this to *The Boy's Technician* because I think it is a very good paper which should be in most homes.

Yours very truly,

Edward Longfox.

Aged 12 (nearly).

P.S. I spoke this letter on to tape and Rubari's mother's secretary typed it for us.

23

Breakthrough II

A S Mr Campion and Luke exchanged glances up in their
fastness, Rafael closed the journal and laid his spectacles
down beside it. He was unsmiling.

'That was the letter,' he said. 'Yates Braithwaite felt he
should publish it. I should have felt the same, but with *The
Daily Paper*'s great resources perhaps I should have made a
few investigations first. You didn't even buy a set, did you?' he
added, swinging round on the younger man, whose blush and
shy grin put a nation on his side.

'Seven pounds!' he murmured and his gasping laugh conveyed a journalistic world which Rafael had forgotten.

The senior man laughed briefly. 'Anyway, you didn't take it
seriously and who shall blame you? But you did recognise a
genuine scientific approach and you sent the author a charming letter which he has lent me and which, with your permission, I'm going to read.' He did not wait but shook out a
tattered and creased piece of paper.

'As you see he treasured it,' he said, holding it up and beam-
ing upon them as they exchanged the wistful but on the whole
happy glance of those who note they are to enjoy their
triumphs at second hand. 'Here it is: *Dear Edward, That was
a fine letter and I enjoyed it. It will appear in our issue of the
12th of next month. Mind you look out for it. One of these
days you must show me your Instant Gen Amplifier. Perhaps I
am rather too old for it to be quite the boon to me that it well
might be in my professional life but I should certainly enjoy
having a yarn about it. If you should come to London in the
holidays look in and see me. Give your name to the man on
the door—his own is Mr Cachou—and come on up to the fifth
floor.*

'Your guinea for the letter will be sent to you by our accounts' department, probably in about three weeks.
Your very good friend, believe me,
Reginald Yates Braithwaite,
Editor.

He was folding away the letter when Edward put up his hand for it and stowed it carefully in his notebook. Giles Jury laughed and swung back into his accustomed place in the centre of the screen.

'He's met grown-ups before,' he said easily, and was about to round up his flock for the next phase when Rafael over-rode him blandly and the camera, like a faithless cur, followed the stronger man.

'I wanted to read those letters to you,' he said simply, 'because they explain what happened next. Last Saturday morning Edward, who was on half-term holiday in London, set out to visit his editor. He was worried because his two exhibition amplifiers had been confiscated. A deliberate attempt to take them from him, which he had frustrated, had been made in a London street in the morning. But, in the evening, most fortunately as it has turned out, they were sequestered by an elderly relative and given casually to an interested visitor. But in performing this seemingly high-handed and unsympathetic act, the unintentional benefactor did a service to the community which can hardly be over-estimated, for without his intervention *The Daily Paper* could not have made its present important disclosure. As it was, having lost his two amplifiers, Edward had to borrow the money and *buy another*. I stress this fact because it is vital for all who hear me to realise that this little device, to whose magical properties everybody seated round this table can subscribe, was actually *bought over the counter of a London store last Saturday morning*. The only two things which have been done to it since then are that it has been partially broken and that it has been wrapped in zinc plaster. Nothing else. Therefore, no one can lay any claim to it. *No one can declare that it is an infringement of any*

*secret belonging to the British Defence Services nor to those of
any other country.* It is a foreign commercial device, bought in
the open market this very week, broken and wrapped in
plaster but otherwise untampered with in any way, and each
and every word of this claim can be proved, if necessary in a
court of law.

'Very well, then. To return to Edward last Saturday morning: he made his purchase and he walked on down Fetter
Lane. But the editorial staffs of The Thousand and One
Nights Press do not come in on Saturdays and so, when he
climbed up the marble steps of Scheherazade House, the man
on the door—is his name really Cachou?'

'Yes,' exploded Mr Braithwaite Junior, in a gust of delight.
'Christian name, Hector.'

Rafael, who had taken it for granted that the letter had
been facetious, frowned at him. 'Amazing,' he said coldly.
'Anyhow, he seems an excellent doorman, for when he heard
Edward's story and saw the letter he did not turn the boy
away or tell him to come back on Monday but got on the
telephone to Mr Yates Braithwaite's home. He was out, but
Joan Yates Braithwaite was there and she, splendid press-
man's wife that she is, kindly told him to send the distressed
boy along. Unfortunately, there then began a game of hide-
and-seek. When Edward was there the Braithwaites were not
and so on, back and forth, but finally, quite late at night, they
all met up and Edward produced his purchase. In a very short
time Mr Yates Braithwaite made up his mind what to do.
After getting in touch with a kindly neighbour of Edward's
aunt, who otherwise could have been alarmed by his absence,
he drove his wife and their young visitor to Chiswick where
they awoke perhaps the one man in all England whose
remarkable knowledge of the bye-ways of contemporary World
Science enabled him to make a coherent picture of the evidence they set before him.' He wound up the peroration with
a bow to the delighted Peggie and once again Giles Jury
swanned forward.

'Not yet, I'm afraid, my dear chap.' Rafael was ruthless and some of the actual force of the man showed fleetingly through the woollen shadows of the medium. 'Until now I've been simply telling the story as it was presented to *The Daily Paper*; now I have to tell you what *The Daily Paper* has done about it in your own interests.

'I don't pretend to have Edward's scientific methods but I have listed my moves in the order in which I made them. Firstly, I made certain that I had acquired every Iris Transistor left on sale in this country, and I also bought the very few which had gone to the Duchy of Luxembourg, the only other European country to import them. Secondly, I got in touch with Mr Hyakawa, a senior director of the No-moto Company in Tokyo, and he was very helpful. He confirmed Edward's story about the curious nervous malaise which overcame his work-people when they handled Nipponanium, and agreed that it was one of the reasons why the company had ceased to use it. The story was told in a gossip paragraph in a sample copy of the Nipponese Commercial Bulletin which, in a translated version, was for a time distributed in this country. Mr Hyakawa also told me that the formula for the amplifiers used in the Iris Transistor was not patented. The concept was in the nature of a sales gimmick and was thought to have failed. *The Daily Paper* has a Scientific Correspondent in Japan and Mr Hyakawa has agreed to give him all technical data relevant to the composition and manufacture of the amplifiers. In fact, I believe he has done so already and that important information is being analysed in London now. Unluckily, he tells me, there were no stocks of the discontinued *Iris Semi-Silent* transistors left at the factory. The last small consignments may have been sold to Czechoslovakia, France or China, but this has not yet been confirmed.'

'Really Rafael, I think we ought to hear something about Nipponanium...' Jury got the objection in by inserting it sharply like a spike between bricks, but he had mistaken his man.

'That is in hand,' the Editor of *The Daily Paper* assured the world. 'Tomorrow morning—we shall be on the streets at four a.m. as usual—we are printing an exhaustive account of the Breakthrough in general and Longfox's Amplifier in particular, written by Pegg Braithwaite who has never been more dynamic. You can read everything that is known in the world today about Nipponanium by Professor T. P. Symmington of Cambridge University as well as all about the Iris Transistor, its chemical analysis and its technical composition. There will be photographs, artists' scale-drawings and also a short biography of Edward's famous father, Richard Longfox, by a writer who knew him. Besides these, there will be personal statements from those who have had the privilege of trying the amplifier. I have contributed one myself. It was an eerie experience, one which I never hope to repeat, at least in its present form! There is nothing I should like better than to tell you about it now, but there are two important items which really must come first.

'One is a warning, and I want us all to be desperately serious about this. Don't think Rome has been built in a day. Don't scour the shops for the *Iris Semi-Silent*. Don't ring up *The Daily Paper* or QTV. Above all, *do not be afraid*. Your secrets are safe for a very long time. Experts estimate that it will take decades, perhaps even hundreds of years for the prospect which this development offers to materialise. At this moment no guaranteed accurate message can be sent or received. All we know now is that the time will surely come when both will be possible. There is so much to be done before then, that the mind shrinks from even contemplating the task. Not only must we learn how to transmit and receive our thoughts, but reliable baffles and scrambling devices must be invented. Men and women have a right to privacy and *The Daily Paper* promises that it will never permit this privilege to be violated. So don't let that angle worry you; there is no need for it. Also, should any of you by chance possess an Iris Transistor purchased since last May—it is not very likely because very few have been sold—but if you have, then please don't tear it to pieces in an attempt to find its secret. It may be valuable. First of all make absolutely certain of its name and

make, and then only, get in touch with *The Daily Paper* office
or this Programme at QTV.

'However, there is something else—my second point—which
I do feel you may think as alarming as I do. In the crowded
hours since I first heard this news, information has been reach-
ing me from all over the world, little surprising items which
have added up to nothing less than a conspiracy to corner
Nipponanium! In the last few months, less than half-a-dozen
very rich firms and private persons have been buying up all
the known stocks of this element which until now was thought
to have almost no practical use. Tomorrow morning our
financial correspondent and his colleague K. L. Tabbs, *The
Daily Paper*'s keenest investigator, will probe this mystery
thoroughly and fearlessly and will not rest until Greedy Men
have been ruthlessly exposed. Meanwhile, *The Daily Paper*
understands that there is no great cause to fear a world short-
age. Nipponanium can be isolated from the residue of certain
radio active carbons without great difficulty and...'

Transmission came to an abrupt end. The tingling silence
took the audience at Advance Wires by surprise and it was
only when Lord Ludor appeared in the doorway of the control
room with a terrified Feeoh behind him that the explanation
emerged.

'Drat that Old Article!' said Thos unexpectedly. 'He does
that if he gets bored. Goes in and yanks out the mains. He'll
fuse the whole works and 'lectrocute himself one of these
days! How ostentatious can you get? Eh?'

Luke touched Mr Campion's arm and they peered down at
the scene below for a moment before making for the stairs.
They reached Sam almost before Ludor, who had had to cir-
cumnavigate Helena and Martin. The boy was leaning against
the matchboarding, his hands in his pockets. His cheeks were
pink and his eyes downcast but there was satisfaction in his
stance.

Ludor put a hand on the wall above Sam's head and leaned
on it. They were in a circle made up of Martin and Helena,
Campion and Luke, and his tone was restrained.

'So you did the research. Who told you you were on Professor Tabard's team?'

'He did.' Sam's glance flickered upward. 'Of course. Otherwise I wouldn't have known for certain, would I? When I was helping over at the workshop, the Professor came in and looked at me and said, "Is this one of your wretched twins, Mayo?" and Mr Mayo said, "No, he's normal." And the Professor said, "Oh, I see he's on the team." So that was that.'

'Where did you see that the transistor set contained Nipponanium?'

'In its Free Literature. You send for it if you'd like to have whatever it is and haven't got the money. Then, after you've read it, if you still want it, you save up for it.'

Ludor was interested; it was his great gift. 'You read all that stuff in very fine print? I didn't know anyone did that.'

'Of course. That *is* research.'

'I suppose so. Horrible job. Have you got the brochure here?'

'No, it was lost with my bag. I didn't know how Edward would get on without it but he managed very well. He dribbled the ball right down the field, didn't he? Got it past everybody. And that editor shot it straight in goal, wham!'

'You could have asked for a second copy of the brochure.'

'Could we? They'd already given us one.'

Lord Ludor regarded him with disgust. 'You're too young altogether,' he said and meant it. 'How long before you get your Ph.D.? Ten years?'

'I expect so. Probably more. I'm nearly nine.'

'Get it and come to me and I'll employ you.'

'Thank you.' A faint streak of otherworldliness showed in Sam for a fleeting moment. 'It's very kind of you,' he said seriously. 'But do you think you ought to promise? There's going to be a lot of change in the next ten years. You may not have anything for me to do.'

Lord Ludor turned away from him and went back to the blonde secretary. 'I hate that damn kid,' he said.

THE END